The Mule Spin

CW01099560

The Runaway

Books by G J Griffiths

The Mule Spinners' Daughters
The Quarry Bank Runaways
Mules; Masters & Mud
So What Do I Do?
So What's Next!
So What! Stories or Whatever!
Fallen Hero

For children: Ants In Space
They're Recycling Aliens

Poetry: Dizzyrambic Imaginings

The Mule Spinners' Daughters

The Runaway from the Altar

G J Griffiths

Dedication

This book is dedicated to Walter who provided two ideas: the first about the robbery from Quarry Bank Mill; and the second about John Wroe of the Christian Israelites.

Contents

'There was a time when meadow, grove, and
stream,
The earth, and every common sight,
To me did seem
Apparell'd in celestial light,
The glory and the freshness of a dream.
It is not now as it hath been of yore;-
Turn wheresoe'er I may,
By night or day,
The things which I have seen I now can see no
more.'

Taken from "Ode" by William Wordsworth

Chapter 1
The Mule Spinners: 1842

FAMILY TREES
(When this story begins)

Esther Sefton (of Hackney Workhouse)
(b?) Later housekeeper, farmer
|

Joseph Sefton m **Ellie Brightwell**   **Daniel Sefton**
(b 1790 d 1834)   **(b 1791)**   **(b 1802)**
Mule spinner, |ceramic paintress,   transported,
Farmer |farmer   farmer
                 |

Gabriel   **Sarah (Sally)**   **Wesley**
(b 1815 d 1839)   **(b 1816)**   **(b 1820)**

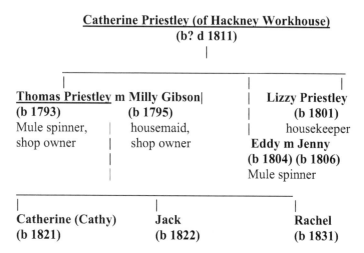

Catherine Priestley (of Hackney Workhouse)
(b? d 1811)

Thomas Priestley m **Milly Gibson**			**Lizzy Priestley**
(b 1793)	**(b 1795)**		**(b 1801)**
Mule spinner,	housemaid,		housekeeper
shop owner	shop owner		**Eddy m Jenny**
			(b 1804) (b 1806)
			Mule spinner

Catherine (Cathy)	**Jack**	**Rachel**
(b 1821)	**(b 1822)**	**(b 1831)**

THOMAS had just finished closing his general store when he turned to his wife, Milly. She could see the tears he was blinking back in the corners of his eyes but said nothing about it. She could also see that he wanted to speak of something, and assumed that the 'something', whatever it was, was causing his tears. Instead of remaining silent she said, "Let's go and sit in the parlour, Tommy, with a nice cup of rosey lee, hey? It's been a busy day."

Instantly Milly regretted using that expression for a cup of tea as it always reminded him of his lost friend, Joseph. Milly suspected that Joe was the reason behind the tears. Thomas nodded and swallowed hard again; he smiled and tried to appear his usual cheerful self. But the memory of his last words to Joseph persisted in his head: *I hope that's what thee is gettin' now, Joe. I don't suppose*

Wesley's ever gunner 'ear that story from thee now, eh? Sleep peacefully, pal.

The story was about an amusing incident when Wesley's father, Joseph, had imitated the actions of a cow - herded by Tommy. Wesley had desperately wished to hear it told from his father's own lips. It was not to be. Tommy had wished his friend an 'everlasting sleep of peace' at his moment of passing into the hereafter, just as the local vicar had expressed it a few days earlier. Today, the painful memory had come back during a conversation with his last customer of the day, someone who had lost her husband during the Peterloo Massacre. Thomas still found it difficult, even after a few very contented years with Milly and his children, to understand why God had spared him, but not his best friend.

In 1806 two boy apprentices, Thomas Priestley and Joseph Sefton, broke their indentures and ran away from Quarry Bank cotton mill in Cheshire, England. They were returned by the authorities, after weeks of travelling to London, and later they qualified as skilled mule spinners of cotton yarn. Towards the end of the 18th century and at the start of the 19th, Samuel Crompton's spinning mule was probably the most significant mechanised invention of the textile trade. Many years later, as adults, Thomas and Joseph decided to leave the cotton industry behind and each took up a different occupation. Thomas became the owner of a general store in Stockport, while Joseph took to farming near Leek in Staffordshire. Both men had suffered various misfortunes along the way: Joseph eventually died through a lung disease, byssinosis, commonly contracted by many mill workers; Thomas lost his left arm through injuries he'd incurred when he had attended the Peterloo Massacre in 1819. However, both men always felt blessed by God in having a loving wife and family of their own.

Joseph Sefton married Ellie Brightwell, a talented paintress of bone china from the Potteries. They had three

11

children: Gabriel, Sally and Wesley, who were all brought up while living on their farm in Cheddleton. Thomas Priestley married Milly Gibson, a lady's maid in a large house in London. They also had three children: Catherine, Jack and Rachel. Thomas' mother, Catherine, had died years before in Hackney workhouse having given birth there to Lizzy and Eddy. At the time of this story Lizzy was in service as a housekeeper in London, whereas Eddy still worked as a mule spinner in Quarry Bank and had his own young family there. The mother of Joseph, Esther Sefton, had eventually moved with her other son, Daniel, to also live on Sefton's farm in Cheddleton. When she was a young mother, well before this time, Esther had moved from the same Hackney workhouse into service. Daniel, also born in the workhouse, was indentured by the parish authorities to work for a harsh chimney sweep but he ran away. He had surprised everyone when he returned from Australia a few years later, to which country he'd been transported for the crime of murder.

Chapter 2
Once Upon a Wedding Day

"**BUT,** Sal, it doesn't seem reet for me to give thee away. What with me being younger than thee by more'n four year. Aye, thou should've asked Uncle Daniel."

"How many times do I have to tell thee, Wes? If I can't have our faither or Gabe take me to the altar then it has to be thee, little brother. I trust thee, and love thee dearly, as much as our dear maither and more'n anyone else in the world."

Wesley was tempted to ask about her trust in Sebastian, the man she was to marry in a few weeks' time. He was a man who Wesley could not 'take to' and felt, deep down inside himself, that Seb was just not worthy of his sister. Sally Sefton still persisted in calling Wesley 'little brother' even though, standing at over six feet tall and weighing five stone more, he towered over her. He had hated her pet name for him for the first sixteen years of his life but now he was very fond of it and it had become one of his unspoken treasures.

When their father had died in 1834 from byssinosis, it was because it had caused serious pulmonary emphysema. The mill workers knew it as cotton lung because the air in the mill was always filled with a haze of cotton fibres. The working conditions in many mills shortened the lives of their workers so much that it was rare for most of them to reach the age of forty. Joseph had been a cotton mule spinner at Quarry Bank mill for many years, having commenced there as a child apprentice taken from Hackney workhouse. He had always reckoned that his few extra years of life were probably earned through his taking up a farming life and breathing fresh country air. Even though it had the taint of animal manure, Joe had preferred that to the pervasive odour of machine oil and sweat in the factory. Marrying Ellie, his heart's desire, had been his greatest motive for hanging on to life. He had been determined to deny the grim reaper for as long as possible in order to be with her and his children.

Sally and Wesley had just finished moving their small flock of sheep to a different field and the subject of Sally's marriage to Sebastian had come up again. This was due mainly to Wesley's misgivings about doing things properly, according to the advice he had received from Ellie, his mother, and Granny Esther, Joseph's now elderly mother.

"But still, I do wish, so much, Gabe was here instead of me, Sal." Wesley's deep voice cracked before he reached the end of his sentence and before the gate had swung to under his angry shove, penning the flock in the field. He quickly wiped his damp cheek with a rough fustian sleeve before turning to face his sister.

"Come here, thou soft lummox," whispered Sally as she hugged him to her and laid her head on his chest, blinking away her own tears. "We could never swap thee for Gabriel. Don't be daft... It'd be so much better if I still had two brothers to look out for me... But Gabe's gone to join Faither and that's that, Wes. And I'll have Seb looking after me in a few weeks' time."

Even as Sally heard herself saying those words she was regretting them. But she let them lie there, hanging in the air, still hurting her ears and her pride. It was better for Wes, and all the other doubters she knew, to think the truth of them - for now at least.

"Aye, well, I suppose so. I suppose you're reet." Wesley sighed. "If only Gabe hadn't gone up to Manchester market, eh? Just when that blasted cholera were spreading all over!"

"None of us knew though, Wes. Manchester news takes ages to get to Cheddleton and Leek. Even news from

14

Hanley and Stoke can take a week, and that's only five or six miles away."

"It doesn't seem reet though, do it? Uncle Daniel gets sent to Australia for killing someone – and, reet enough, he suffers terrible treatment for years - beatings and scurvy and what have thee. And, and, well he's still with us." Wesley shrugged his shoulders and sighed even more loudly. "It makes thee think though… While we've lost our faither and Gabe – both on them good, honest, hard-working blokes… well, I think –"

"Shush, little brother. Please don't say such things, specially when Granny Esther's around. She reckons he's paid for his sins and God's forgiven him. And he has, really, don't you think?"

Wesley pursed his lips as they separated and he briefly took her hand in his. "Aye, well, I reckon thee's reet about that and all. It canner be denied Uncle Dan's a good worker. He still does the work of two men most of the time." Stepping into the lane he glanced at the setting summer sun and then back at Sally. "Come on, our Sal, let's get going I'm reet hungry."

As they walked in silence to the farmhouse Sally's thoughts turned to a consideration of her trousseau and the choice of flowers for her wedding day. But then she felt a growing resentment that anyone who really knew her, including her family, would ever consider Sally Sefton a weak woman who needed a strong man to take care of her. She and her mother had often talked about the men in their lives, Wesley, Gabriel and even their father, Joseph, agreeing what a hopeless state their home and personal comforts would become without the thoughtful and considerate women of the house. But the devotion between each member of the family was never in doubt and Sally was secretly hopeful she could achieve that same state of contentment in her future with Sebastian.

While he became more and more resigned to his fate of giving away his sister in church, Wesley's thoughts turned to the advice from Granny Esther. In her younger days Esther had been the housekeeper to the Critchmoles, a rich gentleman's family in London. She had told him, "Above all the fuss and foll-de-rolls of the day, Wesley, remember what an honour it is for you to be the one that represents your father, a man who was respected and loved so much by his family and friends." His awareness of this thought suddenly gave him pride. The pride he felt grew stronger, puffing out his powerful chest, pushing aside the doubts, and eventually replacing that feeling of resignation. *Aye, I can do it for thee, Faither*, he thought.

***

The wedding was to take place at Saint Andrew's Methodist Church in Cheddleton. Since it was required by the local parish for the ceremony to take place in the morning, Wesley and his Uncle Daniel, had risen from their beds an hour earlier than usual in order to complete all their chores around the farm before getting themselves 'poshed up' for the big day. Their Sunday-best suits had seen much better days and the women of the family had insisted they bought new ones, which Wesley did but Daniel had just replaced his jacket.

Peter Stonier was to be the usher. He was a hired help on the Sefton's farm, having worked there for nearly ten years, like his father before him. Peter's father had been an usher to many weddings and was a popular man and a proud bell-ringer for Saint Andrew's. He had died two years after Joseph and now his son, a loyal worker and trusted friend of the family, had agreed to help the guests to their appropriate place amongst the ancient wooden pews. He was probably as nervous as Wesley on the day and his lips moved silently, but constantly, reminding himself over and over: *Bride's side on the left, groom's side on the right.*

He took great care to leave the front two rows empty for the immediate family when he escorted ladies down the aisle on his right arm. Sally had instructed him, every day for a week, not to walk too quickly as if he was dragging a reluctant cow back to the barn for milking. This applied particularly to three of the more elderly matrons from the local village; the Lewin sisters who would insist to be present despite their arthritis. It gave Peter organisational problems. "But how can I have three of them on me arm at the same time, Sally?"

"Well, thou must take them one at a time, Peter; one at a time. It's obvious."

"Oh, aye, Ah knows that all reet. But which one's first, eh? Tha knowst what they can be like."

Peter had secretly thought that if he had listened more closely to his father's instructions about bell ringing then he could have been performing that task today instead of being an usher. Fortunately, as it turned out on the day, the Lewin sisters solved Peter's escorting problem for him. When the elderly trio arrived at Saint Andrew's, in their mothball-scented finery, Peter stepped forward to help them down from the equally ancient barouche carriage. It was kept and hired out by the inn-keeper in the village for just such occasions as weddings and funerals, and would have been more accurately described as a calash carriage for that was what it had been. The previous enterprising publican of the Three Tuns had acquired it second-hand from a young gambling gentleman down on his luck at the turn of the century. This present, and equally resourceful, publican later had it restored to such an improved state he'd begun to describe it as a barouche, as this made it more attractive to the lesser members of the local middle class gentry.

Amelia, the eldest of the sisters, was to be helped down from the carriage first and she made it clear to the chief, and only, usher. "Well don't just stand there like a tailor's dummy, young Peter. Give me your arm down

17

from this rattly beast of a carriage. My sisters won't be requiring any assistance to their seats after we are all down."

A similarly shaky, highly pitched, treble voice then declared from the calash:

"Oh, no, not at all, Peter. Amelia decided yesterday that Clara and I could provide mutual support for each other down the aisle. But we would ask you to help dear Amelia in a most stately fashion, as befits her station in our community… And then we will follow you accordingly, slowly and steadily, of course."

This last vocal assurance belonged to the second eldest sister, Jane. She was the most ameliorating daughter of the three ladies, and many visitors to their fashionably humble home would remark together, later on leaving, that Jane should perhaps have been christened Amelia. The discussions and disagreements between Amelia and Clara had often resulted in long and embarrassing silences, with or without the presence of guests.

Having alighted from their conveyance, the sisters paused for a few seconds to examine Peter's appearance, him with his unruly mop of hair plastered down with a touch of lard and wearing, surprisingly shiny, black boots. There were muttered comments of approval from Amelia about the white ribbon favours pinned to his shoulders. All four persons then processed in a most seemly way to their seats on *the bride's side* of the church.

The organist's obviously amateur efforts to play the accompaniment to *All Things Bright and Beautiful* were an assault on the ears to most music lovers. Fortunately, there were few present that day apart from two very young lads who had recently taken up the trumpet and pinched each other between their giggles. However, the lack of musicality in the church was not to be the main problem affecting the wedding at all. Something much more serious was still to come!

18

Inside the church the area in front of the pulpit and the altar had been decorated by three lady parishioners with a profusion of summer flowers. They had excitedly consulted with Sally one market day and the selection of honeysuckle, dog rose and ox eye daisies complemented the bouquet she was to carry, although they had added large bunches of lily of the valley and lady's bedstraw to the church display. There was a heady confusion of colours and fragrances to greet the congregation as they entered. As a special surprise for Sally the trio of flower arrangers had gathered baskets of corncockle and cornflower blossoms to scatter down the aisle. Gathered by themselves and their children, the previous day, the carpet of flowers would provide the couple with the traditionally lucky beginning to a happy path through their future life together. Seeing this delicate path of fragrant petals caused Sally to catch her breath as she made her way down the aisle with Wesley. They followed behind Catherine, the first bridesmaid, and Luke, the groomsman.

On reaching the altar the groomsman turned to the right and the first bridesmaid to the left. Close relatives of the bride and groom, who had followed them down the aisle, formed a semi-circle about the couple during the marriage ceremony. They held their breath in anticipation of Sally's expected denial of promising to obey Sebastian. Charlotte and Emma exchanged glances with each other and with many others present for they had started the rumours about the missing promise. Sally Sefton was known by her family and friends to be a very strong-minded woman who would not shrink from telling someone directly her opinion. When before the wedding, one day, this pair of her close friends had heard her say that she was not going to repeat the *obey* part of her wedding promise they'd told her:

"No, Sal, thou must be pulling our legs. We've never heard of such a thing. Sebastian will not be expecting to hear that."

"Oh, but he will. We've talked about it a good few times now and I said that if we were to make a good match together, *then* I expected him to treat me as an equal."

They stared, open-mouthed, at her for almost a full minute, exchanging glances, before Emma asked, "And what did he say? Did he walk away; never to come back to thee?"

"Obviously not, Emma," said Charlotte, scathingly, looking up to the ceiling and with a slow shake of her head. "Because we are invited to Sally and Sebastian's wedding."

Sally grinned and replied, "He said, 'Sal, my dearest darling, Sal. I have wanted thee for my wife ever since I glanced across the auction arena and saw you bid for the dairy heifers. *What a beautiful and spirited girl that is*, I thought. And, my darling, I was hooked, hooked like a speckled trout from yonder Rudyard Lake.'"

Charlotte giggled. "Not the most romantic way of putting things, eh? Heifers – and at a cattle auction – him like a trout – no doubt with his mouth open, gasping for air."

"Well, never you mind all that," said Sally. "He told me he would always treat me like an equal – till death will us part. And I took that as his bond. Tut! Trout indeed! Sebastian brings me little gifts every time he comes to our farm and he always smells so fresh and clean… so different from pigs and sheep."

Her friends giggled again while Sally added, "And he told me his family approve of the match."

The truth of the matter was that Sally had always been a great reader and she had discovered Thomas Paine's book about the 'Rights of Man'. This then led her to read another book about the 'Rights of Woman' and this book had actually been written by a woman. Sally found that she greatly admired the author, Mary Wollstonecraft. Like much of her carefully selected reading material, the contents regularly occupied her thoughts. Many of Sally's thoughts were no longer shared with her acquaintances or close friends, having found them to be less likely to discuss politics or religion. She'd grown tired of being called 'odd'.

Sebastian had not quite got around to telling his family about their engagement to be married until shortly before the wedding day. It was an argument he wished to avoid for as long as possible, but a small untruth, of a very pasty hue, he'd decided would keep Sally content until he did face his parents.

Emma and Charlotte exchanged looks once more and raised their fine eyebrows, pouting doubtfully. They were unsure what to ask next. Then Emma suddenly inquired, "Is Sebastian romantic, when he calls to spoon, and walk out with thee?"

"Oh, his hugs and kisses are romantic enough, thank you. And thou may look thy looks but that is all I am going to say on the matter. We will suit each other well enough, and my heart will be Seb's and his'll be mine, when we are wed."

On the big day Emma and Charlotte watched, fascinated, as Sally and her wedding group made their way to Sebastian standing at the altar. She was frowning very slightly as she took in his movements, which seemed to her to be unsteady. He was swaying very slightly from side to side. His groomsman brother came to stand alongside Sebastian on the right. The pair of young men, each tall and strapping, differed mainly in the colour of their hair; the brooding dark groom contrasting only with his corn-coiffured best man.   Luke had put his left arm around the groom's shoulders and appeared to be holding him up. There were muttered, guttural comments between the two men and when she arrived to take her place next to him, Sally was astonished to see Sebastian's sweating and florid face. He grinned inanely at her and then he sighed, a long and alcoholic exhalation that caused her to blink and look away.

21

"Aha, here she is. My dear one, hic! And only one – my Shally – my Shally Shefton," he declared in a loud voice causing a few smiles and titters in the congregation.

"You're drunk, Seb," she hissed up at him between gritted teeth.

Parson Trunchman held out his two hands and looked resigned to the coming proceedings. He began to address the congregation:

"We are gathered today…"

"No, no, Parshon," interrupted Sebastian. "Let me speak first… Shally…hic! I've changed my mind!"

There was an audible gasp from everyone in the church as they waited for Sebastian's next words.

"Shally Shefton, I love thee very much – and – and I always will, hic! But I've been thinking and thinking… And thou must agree to obey me as my future wife, shee. And that's it, shee! Yes, that's it! Love, cherish and obey, shee."

He giggled and swayed towards Sally, who stepped back, swaying in her turn, but away from the groom's breath. Feeling embarrassed and angry, the bride was determined not to shed a tear. Fearing she was about to swoon Catherine Priestley, dutiful as first bridesmaid, stepped forward to protectively enfold Sally in her arms. Before Cathy had taken two steps, to the astonishment of all those present, but to Sebastian's astonishment in particular, the beautiful bride grasped her beautifully weighty bouquet in both hands to fetch the groom a powerful swipe across his left cheek. This felled him instantly, pulling his groomsman down with him so that they both lay, correctly, on the *right side* of the altar.

Chapter 3
Sebastian Brewer

SEVERAL months after Joseph Sefton had died, the Seftons had met together in order to discuss the many changes that had occurred to the farm and the family. With the help of his old friend, Thomas Priestley, Joseph had left a will that gave joint ownership of the farm to his wife, Ellie, and their three children. At that time his brother, Daniel, and his mother, Esther, had sold an adjacent farm to Joseph for a nominal sum in exchange for their right to live there in perpetuity. Both farms had been combined as one ever since and were jointly known locally as Seftons Farm. There had been an agreement, drawn up by Thomas, which meant that Ellie and her children each owned a quarter of the newly formed, larger, farm; but that had become a third part each when cholera had taken Gabriel from them five years later.

Before losing her older brother and despite the trauma of losing their father, Sally and Gabriel had been running the farm together. They were the eldest and naturally the most experienced of the three children. Their Uncle Daniel and Wesley had continued to work just as diligently as ever but took no part in the running of it, leaving important decisions to Sally and Gabriel. Their mother was perfectly happy to offer occasional pieces of advice when asked for it, taking the same attitude as Daniel and Wesley.

"The way I see things, me dears, is this, thou both know what thee's doing when it comes to the land and the stock, so I'll let thee get on with it."

Brother and sister had many disagreements during the five years of managing the farm together. However, they found a compromise most often, with Ellie or Daniel usually acting as referee before the final settlement. The most common area of strong argument between Gabriel and Sally was about her choice of young men, on the very rare occasions she had 'stepped out' with them around the farm. There was the time Gerald Beeston had also come calling at the farmhouse, just a month after Abel Clayton.

"I don't know what thou found so dreadful about Abel Clayton, Sal." Abel was a farming friend of Gabriel. "The feller knows all about farming and such. But this here Gerald Beeston, he knows nowt but scribbling in his faither's accounts, bowing and scraping ter folks, wi' airy fairy ideas what he reads in books."

Gerald was a young shop assistant she had met at Sunday school. "And thee says you're going to walk around the lanes and the orchard with him, eh?"

"That's right, Gabe. I like his turn of conversation. It makes such a change from cows and mucking out, and the endless chat about bad weather. We talk about some of the books that we read to the children on Sundays, like The Absentee, and… Oh! And Ivanhoe by Sir Walter Scott."

"Oh, aye, and who are they when they're at home?"

"They're just stories, Gabe. Ivanhoe is an exciting knight who is brave and bold, from the past, and The Absentee is about the son of a lord who lives in Ireland."

"So thou don't just teach the kiddies about the scriptures and the Bible then?"

"No, we teach them how to read and then they will get to like some of the books that are coming out all of the time nowadays."

"And what good is that if they can't afford to buy them, eh? It's teaching them to collect clouds in their pockets, if thee asks me."

"It's learning how to read that's the main thing, Gabe. And thee knows only too well now our faither's gone, how important that can be."

"Aye, for bills and contracts and such like. And reading the Good Book of course." He pulled a doubtful face. "Tall seems a mite too fanciful to me, our Sally."

"People can't be working all the time, can they? We want a bit of leisure, like reading novels as well, Gabe."

"Leisure? Leisure! Oh aye, Ah've heard on it, but it's never come my way when Ah've been awake, Sally Sefton."

Wesley, listening to them argue, usually sided with his brother and also could not understand Sally's willingness to accompany these men who made a living using their minds and not by the sweat of their brow. However, he knew better than to get involved, so very sparse were the times when he had won an argument with his assertive sister. But her confidence had already been badly dented by her father's death, and then by her grandmother's passing in nearby Burslem. Sally had a very particular soft spot for Sarah Brightwell, after whom she had been named, and who had always been 'more fun' than her other grandmother. Sally had become her nickname when she was a toddler and it had stuck. Her outward show of aplomb was then to be seriously damaged by the death of Gabriel, rendering Sally's affections and judgement to become secretly vulnerable to the attention of others.

Sebastian Brewer had been attempting to court Sally during the years following Gabriel's funeral. It was only in the two years leading up to the intended wedding that their relationship had resembled anything that could be called a courtship. In the beginning Sebastian had been there at Gabriel's graveside, offering a professionally

25

comforting, black-clothed, arm and a clean white linen handkerchief to Sally.

His father, Jonas Brewer, was the undertaker in the nearby market town of Leek. He had long expected his sons, Sebastian and Luke, his older brother, to assist him with funerals as soon as they had reached the age of ten. Jonas' wife, Martha, felt uncomfortable with the idea when they were very small but grew to accept her husband's wishes once the young boys had been fitted out with the correct sombre clothing and her neighbours had remarked, "Such fine examples of young manhood, Martha. You must be very proud of your sons." Her pride grew with every new compliment about the excellent addition to a family cortege that Brewers Undertakers could make. It had been her task to convince each son, on approaching his tenth birthday, of the pleasure they would feel when acting according to their father's expectations. On Jonas' part it was nothing less than their duty to him to comply. To tell them, "Well done," would have been frivolous and excessive.

However, there were moments in the evenings, when Jonas and Martha were alone, when he took time to remark, "You see how right I was, my dear, to include the boys from a young age. Oh yes, a very good day. I am well pleased with the day." The glowing pride he displayed in the correctness of his decision after each successful funerary occasion filled their sitting room. Martha tried again to encourage her husband to extend a little of the success of the day towards their children. "Perhaps, Jonas, you could share some of your pleasure with Luke and Sebastian."

"And encourage the sin of pride in them? I think not, Martha. My only regret is that of not including them from a younger age, perhaps two or three years earlier."

In fact both sons had originally found the novelty of donning the 'family uniform' and performing the solemnities of 'the day' a source of naïve entertainment.

But when they were regularly denied the responsibility of taking the reins of the horse drawn hearse, and strongly chastised by Jonas if they displayed a hint of a smile or a low titter, the novelty began to wear off. The duties surrounding interment became more acceptable to Luke once he had been informed that he would inherit the family business, when his father would finally need the 'best box' they had. Whereas, in later years, Sebastian had grown more resentful about his own situation as an employee, and in particular he was not eager to work for Luke one day. Sebastian was forever grumbling and threatening to live and work in another town. He had ambitions of his own but not necessarily in the undertaking trade.

Coping with three funerals within just those few years had hit the Seftons very hard. In addition to losing her husband and her mother, losing her eldest son had finally taken a lot of the usual fight out of Ellie. Sally, known for having the strongest constitution of her three children, somehow found the strength to comfort her mother for many months each time. She and her uncle now ran the farm, with input from Wesley from time to time. But on the day of Gabriel's funeral she'd hated every single minute of the expected ceremony.

Before that day and shortly after the two previous funerals, their Uncle Daniel and Granny Esther had insisted upon starting up another pot of the family's savings - for 'burial money'. It had caused an unexpected row between them and Sally, but Esther had won the day when she'd explained that she would soon be the 'next to go', and that it was 'not far off'. Now in her late sixties, the surviving grandmother to Ellie's children was much frailer and she was often heard complaining to God about letting her 'go on too long in this hard life.' Even so, later that same day she would be adamant about doing her usual chores and could be found feeding the chickens and cooking for the family's dinner.

The accumulated burial money eventually turned out to be a fortunate thing. When Mr Brewer, the undertaker, had explained in his funeral parlour the need to ensure eternal rest for their loved ones from grave robbers, Ellie, Esther and Sally discussed it together on their return home. They were worried whether there was enough saved, for it would be done at whatever cost they all agreed. The rumours about a growing problem from grave robbing had only recently reached the Leek and Cheddleton area. Many families who could afford it paid for expensive iron fences to be erected around family burial plots.

Sebastian had visited Seftons Farm the very next day to finalise arrangements and to tactfully remind them about the teaching institutions' unfortunate need for cadavers. He was keen to meet the girl who had returned his smile that day at the auction. He and Luke had accompanied their father to bid for a sweet-natured, black Friesian mare, to later draw their hearse. Although neither Sally nor Sebastian mentioned the smile, she briefly recalled to her mind that she had felt flattered to have attracted the attention of this well-spoken, handsome and tall young man. He did not have the powerful build of the men in her family but seemed to have the deportment of a graceful and sensitive person. To her surprise, Sally found it much to her liking and the feeling grew stronger as he explained the arrangements.

"I fear protecting the plot can only be satisfied by having such a safe-guard to make the grave undisturbed. There is much to be said for paying a little bit extra for the more ornate iron railings, so as to show your respect and true feelings for your loss, for Gabriel and Joseph. It is less, utilitarian, if you understand my gist."

The extra expense was then discussed and during this conversation the shared ownership and value of the farm came out. Sebastian, sensibly, took no part in the discussion but he liked what he'd overheard about the farm. He very much liked what he saw in the figure and face of Sally, and her long auburn hair was an attraction noticed by many young farmers. For Sebastian, indeed, her potential fortune in the future may also have had some influence upon his growing affection for her.

"Aye, it's a very sad time for thee and all your family, Miss Sefton," said Sebastian, as they walked back to the inn for Gabriel's wake.

"Thank thee for the loan of your arm, Sebastian. I felt quite faint for a few moments back there, when the vicar was finishing his words over Gabriel's grave."

"Well, I could see your brother was needed by your mother, and your grandmother sought the comfort of her own son, Daniel. I was glad to be of some help to thee."

"I'll see to it that you get your handkerchief back, and thanks again, Sebastian," replied Sally as she let go of his arm and walked a little faster to catch up with the rest of her family.

"Oh, no, you may keep it, Miss Sefton," he called out, turning away from the path and heading back to his father's shop. But she could no longer hear him; her grief at losing her dear brother suddenly hitting her as soon as she caught up with Wesley, grabbing his right arm, their mother clinging to his left. Wesley was the youngest child, but was now a strapping young man in his twenties, performing what he felt was his new role as the man of the house.

At the inn Sally was very unhappy about the drinking and occasional mirth that was loudly expressed through too much alcohol. On each occasion of all three bereavements her mother and grandmother had felt that it was only right to conform to the various customs expected in a decent household when there had been someone deceased. The older women had wandered about the farmhouse drawing curtains, stopping clocks at the time of dying, placing veils over mirrors. Sally had found the whole thing hard to bear after her father's death, but had somehow discovered the necessary strength for her mother's sake and for appearances. She had sat for a very short while near the head of a short, close family, line, accepting tender embraces and the condolences from friends and acquaintances during Joseph's wake. Now, Sally was unable to repeat the act – not even for her precious brother's wake – certainly not once the drinking began in earnest.

Sitting alone, hiding, in the gloom of a small backroom, quietly provided by the inn-keeper's wife, Sally dabbed her cheeks afresh. When a man's voice gently interrupted her sorrows she started slightly but then relaxed as he became visible. Sebastian offered her another, mercifully dry, clean, white handkerchief.

"I do hope that I'm not disturbing thee too much, Miss Sefton… Only, as I said, I could see that your uncle and brother were very much needed by the other ladies in your family… So I returned and, well, if I can provide thee with some comfort until they... that is… if it's needed."

Sally tried to gather herself together enough to refuse his help, but with the first mumbled word from her mouth came a new torrent of tears. This was his cue to sit beside her, cradle her gently with one arm around her shuddering body, resting her head on his shoulder. For a while she became inconsolable and the publican's wife slipped in and out of the room with glasses of water, wine, ale or port in an effort to make things better. Nothing was consumed save a little watered wine at Sebastian's experienced suggestion.

Much later when the two emerged from the inn, with Sally hiding her grief swollen features beneath the black veil, it was noticed that Sebastian had replaced the appellation of 'Miss Sefton' with 'Sally, my dear'. He was to call on her many more times from that sad day as their relationship grew closer and warmer.

When Sally had emerged from the inn Cathy was waiting for Sebastian to leave her side, only then did she approach her. Gently linking arms with her she spoke softly, attempting to offer some comfort, "Dearest Sally, we are going to miss Gabriel so much. We know how terrible thou and thy family must be feeling today."

There was little obvious response from Sally other than a disconsolate sniff and a close hugging of Cathy's arm to her bosom.

"Perhaps we may talk later when things are quieter. We have some news about our pa's shop which may be of interest to thee and your ma."

"Perhaps later... Aye, Cathy... later."

Ellie and Wesley were approaching them and Cathy made as though to release her arm.

"No, no, stay with me, please, Cathy," murmured Sally clinging even tighter to her arm.

***

Much earlier that day the Priestley family had travelled by coach from Stockport to Leek and, apart from an old gentleman sat in the corner, they occupied all of the seats. Thomas Priestley, his wife, Milly, and their three children, Cathy, Jack and Rachel, were attending Gabriel's funeral. They were warmly considered as near relatives by the Seftons, having been known to Ellie and Esther for very many years. Thomas' general store in Stockport was doing well, and had been steadily expanding its range of goods. It was often frequented by members of the local gentry ever since Thomas and Milly had begun to specialise in the new patterns of coloured dress silks as well as the new drapery and furnishing fabrics. This had been made possible by the introduction of Jacquard looms in some of the mills with which Thomas had long had contact. When setting up his shop, years ago, he had originally collected cotton waste in order to trade it with mills that spun yarn suitable for cheaper bed covers and candle wicks. Thomas had once been a skilled mule spinner for Quarry Bank mill and could easily recognise a yarn's quality, good or bad, when he saw it.

The dramatic changes in the shop's fortunes were exciting for all the Priestley family. Milly and their eldest daughter, Cathy, had to supress their enthusiasm a little under the sad circumstances but felt certain that the Sefton women would be curious to hear about the new brocades and damask fabrics that they now stocked. This was in contrast to the sombre mourning black that Ellie and Esther had been sewing and altering for Gabriel's funeral. Thomas had supplied the original black material for Joseph's funeral at much less than cost in an effort to soften the blow. He had felt so 'useless' at the time and, having been present in the room when his old friend had passed away, it was all he could think of to try and help.

"Can I show Sally my new dress afterwards, Ma?"

"Not straight away, Rachel," replied Milly gently. "Everyone is bound to be feeling very sad and upset."

"But I brought it specially to show her and Aunty Ellie. Thou said I could," she whined.

Before Milly had a chance to speak Jack spoke up, "Don't be such an impatient Poll. Gabriel's died. That's why we're going to see them. Or had thou forgotten so soon? Thou's just a little noddle head!"

The old gentleman cleared his throat and rustled his newspaper, frowning over the top at Rachel, spectacles clinging to the end of his large red nose. The young girl smiled sweetly but had no response from the man other than a loud *Harrumph!* Rachel's lips changed immediately to a downward glum turn with her big blue eyes casting their look to her feet.

"Ma, tell Jack," she grumbled. "He's being so horrible to me."

A very big sigh and a glare from Thomas was the signal to end the arguing between the children. He glanced at Milly opposite him who shook her head at her teenage son and then turned to Rachel again.

"You must be more patient, my dear, and remember this is a very, very sad time for everyone."

"But I hardly knew Gabriel," replied Rachel. "So…"

Cathy took hold of her little sister's hand gently and whispered to her. "But we all did, Rachel, and it is one of the saddest things to ever have happened. As sad as when our pa lost his arm at Peterloo. And as thou knows so well, we were not even born then – none of the three of us. But still we find the thought of that, so, so sad." She touched her eyes with a handkerchief at her own words and Rachel nodded solemnly.

"Sorry, Ma; sorry, Pa," she whispered. At the mention of Peterloo the old man's eyebrows were raised as he glanced at Thomas, and he sank down behind his rustling newspaper once again where he quietly remained for the rest of the journey, apart from intermittent sighs and harrumphs.

Chapter 4
Catherine Priestley

ALTHOUGH she was a few years younger, Catherine Priestley had become very important to Sally over the years following her father's death. Cathy and Jack had once been invited to spend a few days at Sefton's farm during their school holidays and she could not wait to visit the farming family. Jack did not accept but instead preferred to help out in the family's shop in Stockport, which came as a big surprise to Thomas and Milly because he constantly grumbled about working there. Only his sister knew why Jack had declined the farming holiday. Not only was he afraid of most of the animals there, including cows, sheep, pigs and even chickens, Jack hated the smells of the farmyard and was inclined to vomit if he had to muck out a stable or sty. Jack was obsessed with machines and was intent on becoming an engineer one day. He could take machines apart and fix them but he found animals too unpredictable, and suspected that they did not like him.

One day, when Cathy had found her brother in tears in his room, she comforted him and he'd told her about his father's strong words to him over failing to clean out their small stable. The empathy that Cathy had shown her brother was a quality essential on the day she'd discovered a distraught Sally. Her empathetic emotions, her slight stature and her fair hair were inherited from a grandmother whom, sadly, she would never know; the mother who Thomas had lost during his enforced apprenticeship at Quarry Bank mill.

It was on her second day at the farm and during breakfast when Esther had told Cathy that Sally could be found in the barn grooming Boulder, their dray horse. She paused at the barn door when she heard Sally in a conversation with someone, but her words were punctuated with sorrowful sobs.

"Just what is the point, eh? I'm not going to church no more... If God is in there he ain't listening to me no more... Old Parson Trunchman says I must... trust in God because his ways are not always open to his followers... Well, we've lost our faither and Granny Brightwell this last twelve month... So ... God has lost... me."

There was then a lot of wailing and sobbing at which Cathy had to peep around the stall, only to find Sally hugging the horse around his powerful neck. Boulder stood patiently, twitching his ears, waiting.

"Thou'll never desert me; eh... will thee, Boulder... Faithful... always... Thou has never... never... ever let me down, Boulder, mate... But ... God... has, and..."

Sally clung to the horse's neck again and her shaking shoulders drew Cathy from her hiding place.

"Oh, Sally, come here, my dear," said Cathy as she held her friend and drew her towards some boxes in the corner, where they sat. After another hour of tears and stuttered explanation the two young women were closer than ever. It became clear to Cathy that Sally was finding the strain of appearing outwardly strong to her family too much to bear. Sally took after her mother when coping with grief by trying to stay as busy as she could and finding something to do every waking minute of the day.

The death of Joseph left the farming family desperately bereft. Soon after Ellie had lost her husband, her mother, in Burslem, also died and to Sally it meant she should try to take on the duties of both her parents. But Gabriel and Daniel were rejecting her offers around the farm and Granny Esther insisted on taking over the farmhouse and kitchen. Regrettably the pain and personal grief, gnawing inside each of them, had led to frequent loud arguments between them all. Her mother went to stay for a time with her two bachelor brothers in nearby Burslem. She was convinced they wouldn't be able to cope without a woman, without her, or Sarah, their mother, in the cottage. So Ellie had left with Gabriel one morning with a bag packed, muttering about her sons to herself: *Joshua never could learn to cook for hisself... and Abraham'll be in pub every night... Aye, ye can be sure of it... boozing and gambling his wages away...*

Later that same day Cathy and Sally went for a walk to a field of their sheep. It was twilight and she had gently extracted a small promise from Sally while talking in the barn. In return Cathy had promised to tell her something about her pa – something that could possibly help Sally find her faith anew. They approached the kissing gate and Cathy said, "So where are all these baby lambs, Sal? I can't even see the flock of sheep."

She was now standing on one of the gate struts, stretching to look across the field.

"Oh, they must be in the hollow, the other side of the meadow. If we just walk up the rise a little we'll catch sight on them there, Cath."

On the way Cathy had mentioned to Sally snatches about Thomas' loss of his faith and his experiences when he had travelled to Ashton-under-Lyne to hear a lay preacher speak. She continued as they walked to the top of the small hill.

"Aye, Pa says Jack and me can go with him next time. Ma went with Pa last time. Just to accompany him thee might say, 'cause she's never had doubts about loving Jesus and believing in the Lord... but..."

When she had paused, trying to find the right words, Sally turned to face Cathy and said, "Thou doesn't have to tell me if it's too difficult, Cath."

They had reached the top of the rise and the flock of sheep were now visible a hundred yards away. There were still a few fluffy little lambs skipping and gambolling about their mothers in the fading light, drawing some 'oohs!' and 'aahs!' from Cathy's throat. And then that 'adorable' sight had to give way briefly to a magnificent sunset, which both young women stopped to view in silence, just for a few seconds. They were unaware that their fathers had shared a similar dusking experience many years previously and from the same spot. Cathy's arm curled around her friend's waist and the taller girl placed her left arm around Cathy's shoulders. As the two young women shared the moment the redness of Sally's flowing locks contrasted with the tightly gathered golden coil in Catherine's nape, the changing sunlight shifting its glow from one to the other.

"Ee, by gum, Sally - what a sight, eh? It does my heart good to see that instead of all the smoke that seems to fill the skies in many towns these days."

"Aye, Granny Esther calls it the awe and wonder of God. Although she says that for every new born cow, lamb or piglet – or anything else she can come up with, eh!"

They both giggled and then Cathy became suddenly serious, speaking with her finger pointing west towards Stoke-on-Trent. "With all that smoke and the sunset behind, it looks like the entrance to hell over there. Is it the bottle kilns?"

"Some of it, Cathy, and Grandpa Abe called it the new hell when Shelton Bar's steel company started up, when I was a kid it was. The fire thee can see, lighting up the smoke and the sky as well, is from the blast furnaces. When the wind's in the right direction we can smell the smoke from here."

"When our pa lost his faith he reckoned he would go to the old hell… for a time anyway, thou knows."

Sally did not know what to say to this. She had always had such strong affection and respect for 'Uncle Tommy' as they had become used to calling her father's best friend. He had been very important to the Sefton family at various times in the past. His wisdom and tactful approach to things made him a paragon in her eyes. Cathy saw the doubt in Sally's eyes and continued. "Jack and I have been attending Stockport Sunday school for a few years now and we heard about the prophet John Wroe, through one of the teachers there. But Pa has heard him speak."

Sally and Cathy had now forgotten about the sheep and the sunset and, as if by some silent agreement, they both sat down on the mound, gathering their skirts beneath them against the light dew.

"Why should this prophet be of any interest to me, Cathy?"

Sally sounded slightly offended and Cathy explained with as much caution and affection in her voice as the young woman could muster. She loved Sally like a sister and hated to think she might hurt her feelings.

"Apparently, he has the ear of the Lord and he was told by God to create a new church. It is to be called the Christian Israelite Church."

She paused, glanced at Sally, saw from her expression that she was curious, and so carried on.

"They say that after he became ill a few years ago he was blind for a week and during that time he was troubled, by visions."

"Visions?"

"Aye, but he realised that it was God speaking to him through the Holy Spirit. And the message was about the scriptures and what it said in the Bible, in Revelations."

Sally's curiosity was now roused enough to make her head nod towards Cathy as a sign of encouragement to continue further.

"I don't remember the exact verse, but it's something about freeing thousands of people who were the descendants of Israel. He was told to rid himself of all worldly goods and travel, preaching the word of God."

"Oh, I see, thou means like Jesus Christ."

"Mm, yes." Cathy nodded enthusiastically. "That's right, Sal; just like Jesus. He's gathered many followers."

"And are they his disciples? Like the same as Christ's twelve apostles?"

"I don't know about that, because there are many hundreds now – so I'm told."

"But his church is in Ashton-under-Lyne, you said."

"It's still being built, Sally, and will be known as the New Jerusalem, the Christian Israelite Church. They are constructing a wall around the town to contain it, with four gateways, one at each corner of the wall. It will be a very grand affair, I expect."

"And Uncle Tommy has been there when he was low, to hear the prophet preach?"

Cathy nodded. "Pa has had some very troubled times in the past, when Jack and I were much younger, before Rachel was born."

Cathy paused again, to stare into the distance.

"I think it was just after your pa died."

Sally nodded understanding, and the two held hands.

"Pa said that Preacher Wroe's words comforted him greatly and that it gave him new hope. He said that he understands much better now, about Christ's sacrifice for the sins of everyone on Earth. How the power of God can keep our souls alive through eternity, until Jesus returns to Earth."

"All our souls? Even non-believers?"

"Pa said that John Wroe's words led him to accept that the life within each person's body is the soul. And that if we are ever to get immortal life of the body, then God's Laws must be kept."

39

"What? Kept while we still live – on Earth?"

"I suppose so, Sal. I want to hear the prophet speak for myself and I will someday soon."

"Is it far? This Ashton place, where the new church is, where you may hear Preacher Wroe?"

"No, just a few miles north of Stockport. If you come to stay with us soon then we could go together."

Sally smiled and said, "I feel that I might do that if it becomes possible. If thou and Uncle Tommy are so filled with encouragement through the words of the prophet… then… then I would like to see this holy man for myself. Just listening to thee has made my heart lighter already, Cath."

"It would be so good if you can, Sal. As for Jack, well I don't think he'll accompany me – not while his head is so full of oil and machines and cogs and levers! To hear him go on sometimes, about being an engineer, well… Although, if we paid to travel on one of these new steam trains and they have one to run from Stockport to get there, then I have no doubt he would accompany us. He'd travel to Shelton Bar's hell and back if you gave him the chance to do it on a steam train!"

The two girls stood up and continued their walk to the flock of sheep, with poor absent Jack suffering the butt of their mild jokes for a while. Unfortunately, the busy lives that each family, the Seftons and the Priestleys, were leading at that earlier time meant that circumstances would delay their visit to Ashton-under-Lyne.

***

Like her friend, Sally, Cathy also began to teach the younger children in her Sunday school and enjoyed it. The Sunday school movement had grown and caught on tremendously since the days of the philanthropists, Hannah More and Robert Raikes, who were two of the major innovators. In the industrial areas many thousands of working class children attended Sunday schools by 1851, learning 'the 3Rs', the Bible and even more subjects in many schools. Anglicans and Dissenters had co-operated to set them up, though many more were also founded on a sectarian basis.

The combination of Cathy's greater involvement through Stockport Sunday school, and the education taught to her at Mr Macdougal's boarding school in Flixton, meant she became determined to teach others full time. Both she and Jack had been sent to the school for years but, whereas she was an avid student, flourishing in most of her subjects, Jack was inclined to love only the technical subjects, such as science and mathematics. Cathy became a pupil teacher in Mr Macdougal's school during her final year and wanted to specialise in her favourite subjects of history and geography. After a probationary year Cathy was offered a permanent position there, which was a source of enormous pride for Milly, her mother. Thomas had hoped to hand over his business to Cathy, being 'the one with the brains', but he kept his disappointment to himself.

She found both subjects particularly exciting and her enthusiasm in the schoolroom for them was infectious enough to reduce most of the disciplinary problems to a minimum. The classes for many teachers, including Cathy, could number many dozens of pupils and so reprimands and sanctions could be harsh. She worked hard to avoid using the strap and often found it was sufficient to remove a misbehaving pupil from their normal place in the room. They had to sit in a wicker basket and be hoisted up to the ceiling with special work that had to be completed before they were allowed down again. She was so intent on her professional development that it meant there was very little time for 'leisure' for a few years. The attention, and mistaken assistance, she received sometimes, from an older male colleague, did interfere with those efforts, however. They first met one day while supervising the pupils at lunchtime.

"And did you leave Matthew Parfitt in the wicker basket? I can't see him anywhere in the refectory, Miss Priestley."

"Well, yes, yes I did, Mr Longton. I gave him an ultimatum, to finish copying the verses from Psalms before he would be allowed down."

Mr Longton's bushy brown eyebrows were raised slightly, more in admiration than in surprise. He smiled at Cathy, briefly, and then he knitted them once more when he called out to a group of pupils across the hall.

"Charlie, if I see you do that once more then the whole room will stay behind for a fingernails check after last lesson! And it will be your fault, Charlie Pepper! Your fault!"

There was a low communal groan that rumbled across the hall. This was followed by threatening whispers, aimed at the unfortunate Charlie, to desist flicking crumbs at the girls sat at his table. Mr Longton chuckled and said to Cathy, "Your boy Parfitt can hardly write his own name down in a legible manner. He'll be there until Christmas I expect. Good for you, Miss Priestley. What did he do, to deserve such punishment?"

But now Cathy was worried that she had been too harsh and she replied, "Oh, do you really think so? I can't back down now, can I? It would seem like I didn't mean it, to the rest of the class. And they are so difficult sometimes in Bible studies." She paused to think things over for a few seconds then added, "And yet, the class can be wonderful in History… so engaged and involved."

"Which verses from Psalms were they?"

"We had been discussing the birth and crucifixion of Jesus and Matthew kept calling out that his father had told him that Christ had never lived. I was telling them about the prophecy in the Bible, about the coming of Jesus as the Messiah. But Matthew was rude, calling out, not raising his hand when I'd told him several times to do so."

"Which verses?" repeated Mr Longton.

"Psalm 22, verses 1 to 20. You may recall them, regarding the early prophecy about the coming of the Messiah," she repeated, feeling a little irritated.

Mr Longton laughed and said, "Most appropriate. But especially the lines: *My God, my God, why hast thou forsaken me? Why are you so far from saving me, so far from my cries of anguish?*"

Cathy was curious about his reply and regarded him with a quizzical look. He responded with, "Well, Matthew Parfitt is probably feeling 'forsaken' and abandoned by you at this very moment. Do you think he's still hanging there from the ceiling or, more likely, climbed down and escaped - running home as we speak, most likely?"

Cathy had stopped listening to him before he had spoken his final few words. Feeling agitated now she said, "I must return to my schoolroom and check how he's doing. Do you mind supervising on your own for a few minutes, Mr Longton?"

"Not at all, Miss Priestley. Please go ahead."

Standing proud and commanding at the door of the refectory, with an amused expression on his face, he was unable to suppress his chuckles and shaking shoulders. This attracted very many curious looks from the pupils and silence had descended upon the whole refectory. It was broken only by a brave call from Charlie Pepper.

"Are you feeling all right, Mr Longton?"

"Yes, thank you, Charlie. Now get on with your meal – everyone! Time to clear up soon."

Cathy returned with the unfortunate Matthew Parfitt ten minutes later, when the rest of the young diners were returning their eating utensils to the cook's serving counter, prior to being dismissed to the 'quad' for the few

43

minutes of 'free-time' left before the bell for afternoon lessons. The ten year old boy was sat, glumly eating alone, a few yards away from the two teachers while they finished their meal.

"Yes, he was fast asleep in the bottom of the wicker basket. I could hear his snores before I'd entered the schoolroom."

The two smiled at each other in a conspiratorial fashion and Cathy felt her cheeks blush, when she realised that his face had no trace of mockery in it at all, as she had suspected on her way back. James Longton was eager to assist his new colleague in any way he could but found it difficult to concentrate whenever he looked at her lovely features. She took after her mother, who was from London, in her way of speaking but, more significantly as far as James was concerned, she had Milly's pretty face, her winning smile and her brilliant blue eyes. James felt his heart pounding in his chest, his usually logical thoughts dissolving into a scrambled mess, and he was worried about what she might think of him. Had he sounded pompous and a prig when he had recited those lines from Psalm 22?

"And, erm, had he completed the imposition you had set for him?"

"No, you were right about that of course. But I told him that if he promised to complete it later in his own time, then I would allow him to eat his lunch before afternoon bell. He has until tomorrow or face further consequences."

James' first instinct was to say, *Excellent, Miss Priestley. Well done!* But he had second thoughts and felt some tact could be necessary, so instead replied, "That sounds like a good strategy because you haven't backed down and it will trickle out to other pupils. That you mean what you say."

Cathy paused as she gathered her plate, knife and fork together, and stared closely into Mr Longton's deep brown eyes, looking hard for any hint of sarcasm. Unknown to her this intense look became like a drug to him; while he could not get enough of it there was a force from it, overcoming him, invading his very being, a force that could overpower any resolve he might intend. James felt as though his insides were melting.

"Thank you, Mr Longton. I thought about it on the way to my schoolroom and realised that it's important not to impose a sanction that's too hard to complete, or even for me to apply."

James could not think of more to say. He excused himself and left to prepare for his next lesson, his brain in a mess and with the sound of his pulse pumping in his ears. Cathy, confident and determined to become a better teacher without his assistance, had noticed his strong good-looks but found his helpful attitude just a little too much. He did occupy her thoughts, briefly, later that day when she took a prep lesson before returning home to Stockport.

Hm, I wonder, Mr Longton... I know you are older and more experienced - but wiser? What a pity you have too much awareness of your own self-importance. I think I must be careful not to share too much with you in future.

Chapter 5
Aims and Ambitions

THOMAS had returned to Ashton-under-Lyne several times during the intervening years before Sally's wedding, and Cathy had accompanied him twice. This news was much to the annoyance of Sebastian Brewer whose efforts to become Sally's 'intended' had been constantly thwarted, either by her work on the farm or her newly found religion. Sally and Cathy had exchanged letters occasionally from the time of their teenage years often comparing their Sunday school teaching experiences. But since their conversation in the Seftons' barn Cathy's words were mostly about her new job as a professional teacher and her opinions about John Wroe. In her letters to Sally, Cathy would include some of the prophet's statements and her father's version of them, his interpretation. This had resulted in Sally constantly visiting Parson Trunchman for his advice and informed wisdom about John Wroe and the proclamations in Cathy's letters.

The elderly rector scratched his head of white hair and held his chin in one hand while reading to himself: *That all have sinned and come short of the glory of God.* This was followed by: *That God has reconciled the whole world to Himself through the sacrifice of Jesus.*

"You say, Miss Sefton that these are some of the words of the preacher, John Wroe?"

She nodded and Parson Trunchman read them out aloud this time and looked thoughtful.

"Well, I can see nothing which contradicts the teaching of the Anglican Church at all. In fact I recognise them, because I think you'll find the first is from the book of Romans... and... the second of course is from the Gospel of Saint John. We usually say, *For God so loved the world that he gave His one and only Son, that whoever believes in Him shall not perish but have eternal life.*"

"I knew I'd heard that before, Parson Trunchman. We've taught it during Easter in Sunday school."

"I would hope so, my child. It is at the heart of Christian teachings. This man, who you say they call a prophet, does not appear to be a charlatan. He sounds like a good person."

"My friend, Catherine Priestley, has invited me on several occasions these past few years to stay with her, so that we may travel to Ashton to hear him preach together. Sometimes she's joined the crowds with her faither at his meetings... And erm..."

"Let me guess. You wonder, whether I would object?"

"Well, aye, Mr Trunchman. Thou's been so helpful to me and the family over recent years, see. I wouldn't like thee to think I'd stopped listening to thine advice and comforting words."

"Sally, this man, John Wroe, seems to be spreading the good word, God's message, so I see no harm in listening to him."

"What about the new church?"

"I'm not so sure about his Christian Israelite Church. I will write to my bishop and try to find out more. I am very curious to know more myself."

"It was through hearing about his teaching, from Cathy, that made me return to St Andrew's, you see."

"Your absence did cause me some concern, believe me."

"Oh, and then talking to thee when I could... Well, as I say it has been such a comfort, sir. Thank thee. I'll write back to Cathy and see what can be arranged about the farm with Wesley and Uncle Daniel, while I'm away in Stockport."

47

"And you'll let me know how you get on, Sally?"
"Of course, and thank thee again."

***

Sebastian had discovered something that gave him great hope for his future prosperity. His father was reading an article about the new railways and passed the newspaper to Sebastian for his attention.

"Did you not say there was some railway activity going on near to the Seftons' farm the last time thee visited them, Sebastian?"

"Yes, father, it has been going on for a couple of years now. Why, is it in the papers?"

"Well, not specifically about that place. But there's something very interesting about speculation in the whole railway development. Read it for thyself. I wonder we might buy some shares. We'll speak to Luke when he comes back, eh? See what he thinks."

Sebastian read: *More and more money is being poured into the railways as the price of their shares keeps increasing up and up…*

It occurred to him that such an investment could be his pathway into setting up his own business. Jonas had always been loath to spending much money at all, whether on the house where they lived, or in expanding his funeral undertaking business. But the mere mention of investment in railways, by his father, told Sebastian that it must be a good thing. When he had once mentioned buying a suitable property in Cheddleton, that he might manage as a new branch of Brewers Undertakers, his father had mocked him. Luke had silently sided with his father, and it was disappointingly obvious that was the end of the discussion, causing the small rift between them to become a wider fissure.

Jonas had retorted, "I think thy management skills are going to take a lot more years to develop, lad, afore I'm willing to trust thee not to lose us money and clients."

It was back then that Sebastian had decided to look for any opportunity, which might come his way. He had to find something, anything, which could take him far from the suffocating influence of his father. He had a list of ideas in his head: a cotton mill; a flour mill; a department store in Hanley; canal transport; and even mining, coal or iron ore, he was not sure. What he did know was that he was good with his brain and not with his hands. With the right venture and his management then he would become rich and successful – if he could only raise enough funds. Everything he had considered required considerably more money than his salary as an employee in Brewers Undertakers would give him.

After visiting Seftons Farm to discuss Gabriel's funeral arrangements Sebastian had taken it into his head that he could become a 'gentleman farmer', by marrying Sally. As things stood he would then have a third share of the Seftons' farm and by his careful supervision he could expand it even further. He knew that they had acquired more land adjacent to the farm at that time and it was doing well. He could see that Daniel, Sally and Wesley were absolutely expert in farming, but with his business acumen as well they could set about expanding the farm even further, take on new workers if necessary. He'd read about the rapid increase in the population of local towns and they would need food. While the Corn Laws kept the price of grain high and with new developments in agricultural machinery that he'd also read about, then new success in farming was not far away. A little persuasion was all that was needed and as a member of the family he could more easily provide it. Turn more fields over to growing wheat, expand the dairy side of things, all this was so obvious to Sebastian. This plan grew on him more and more each time he received instructions from his father about some task or other in the funeral parlour. He just needed to get his foot into the farmhouse door; but marrying the lovely Sally would be the key, and a beautiful bonus into the bargain!

Now there was a different possibility, with this new railway shares and investment idea that he was reading about in the newspaper giving him second thoughts. This could be something to make them all, but especially Sebastian, much richer, much quicker. He found it exciting to have a new iron in the fire of his ambitions. Maybe it would be better to sell off a lot of the Seftons' farmland to raise the investment money? Whatever was best, he decided, the first and most delicious part of his plan was to marry Sally Sefton.

***

During the months after losing her brother to cholera, Sally and Sebastian 'stepped out' around the farm twice before she consented to go for a ride in his pony and trap. They had chatted outside the church for a few minutes each Sunday before this and it had been noticed by the village gossips. So, well before Sally had agreed to go for a picnic one fine afternoon, Clara and Jane Lewin had agreed that she and Sebastian were a 'couple'. Not that they approved of young people going for walks or rides in the country without a chaperone, as they seemed to 'these days'. But, as they remarked to each other on their journey home, "Young Sally is not getting younger and she is well past her twenty-first birthday."

"Such an attractive young woman, Clara. I'm surprised that no-one has taken her off Ellie Sefton's hands before."

"Sebastian Brewer will be quite a catch. He is a fine man, with an excellent education behind him, so I hear, and his father's business will always be a sound one of course."

They could not wait to share their suspicions with Amelia who had stayed at home that Sunday with a bad cold and more aches and pains in her joints 'than a body can stand'. Amelia's first reaction was to dismiss the idea as too ridiculous. "A man as sophisticated as Sebastian has become, would never take up with a lowly farm wench – pretty or not." Nevertheless, all three sisters had found a new interest and would be eager to pay close attention to how this relationship progressed.

The couple intended to stop on their countryside drive to picnic near a village called Ipstones. The route there had been chosen deliberately by Sebastian so that they would pass by Cheddleton Flint Mill, crossing the River Churnet. There had been much activity in recent months with the new railway line that would run alongside another major development, the Caldon canal. As they crossed the bridge Sebastian slowed the horse down to a gentle walk and drew Sally's attention to the progress below.

"Big changes for Leek and Cheddleton coming in fast, eh, Sally? Improvements for everyone."

"I suppose so, Seb. But I'm not so sure it's a good thing sometimes. Granny Esther thinks things are moving too fast."

"There's going to be more jobs for folks around here. And fortunes to be made, according to my father – if you've got the capital to invest. The railways are the thing of course; I've been reading it up in the papers."

"Oh, I see," replied Sally. She shifted her attention towards the Staffordshire moorland ahead of them. "It's such a lovely day, Sebastian. Let's find that beautiful spot thou were telling me about, and enjoy more of it, while we've got a day off."

"Right, Sally, thy wish is my command." He gave the horse a slight flick with his whip and added a click of his tongue to encourage a trot. *No matter*, Sebastian thought. *The seed is sown, for now*.

The view towards the Peak District from Ipstones Edge was one of gentle rolling hills and the sparkling of the river below, gently rushing south, added to the romance of the day. They ate silently for a while taking in the tranquillity of the beauty spot. Sebastian had bought Sally a slim book of poetry and she was reading it while he leaned against a tree, her back against his chest. She paused to take in the view, sighing happily.

"This is a lovely place, Seb. How did thee find it? Which girls did you bring here?" Sally was intent on letting him know that she was not as naïve as he may believe.

"What a thing to say, Sally. I may have been here before but not with another girl. Read me one of the poems. That would be perfect."

"Well, my dear, I might ask thee again about that - one day soon. But for now this poem is one I like. It's called, *The World*."

Sally paused, awaiting Sebastian's response. There was none. She took in a deep breath and commenced, *"The world is too much with us; late and soon, Getting and spending, we lay waste our powers: Little we see in Nature that is ours; We have given our hearts away, a sordid boon!"*

Sally paused once more, thinking about the land that had been retched up for railways and canals. She waited yet again for his remark about those lines. Sitting on a blanket together they were unable to make eye contact, she with the back of her head on his chest, and he with his back resting on the bark of the large upland oak that still clung to the limestone below their resting place. Sally felt his breathing chest, rhythmically, pushing at her hair and found it somehow comforting, but there was still no comment from him.

"This sea that bares her bosom to the moon;" Her pause this time was because some of the young farmers she knew would have made a ribald reply to that phrase,

whereas either of her brothers would have tutted and said something very disapproving while in her presence. But still from Sebastian there was nothing. *How curious?* she thought.

"*The winds that will be howling at all hours, And are up-gather'd now like sleeping flowers…*"

It was this line that caused Sally to look around the heathland at the struggling foxgloves beneath the brimstone blooms of gorse nearby. There were patches of brilliant white cotton grass and golden spires of bog asphodel in the peaty hollows further down the slope they had climbed. She listened to a distant song thrush in a hedge, only to have its singing accompanied by a low continuous humming. It seemed to come from behind her and it was getting louder every second.

"Sebastian Brewer, how unromantic of thee! Snoring thy head off while I read thee a poem of love and nature. Well, I never…"

She jumped up and stood a yard or two from him with her hands on her hips. Sebastian spluttered his apologies in an incoherent fashion and stared up at Sally, blinking and squinting in the sunlight that dazzled him, coming from the sky behind her.

"No, no, Sally, my dearest. Please believe me when I say it was not the sound of thy beautiful, dulcet tones… It, er… it was…"

She cocked her head to one side and said, "Oh, aye. What was it, then?"

"I was doing a bit of book work, for my faither till late, see. And I didn't get enough sleep, Pet."

He had taken to using some of the local parlance lately whenever he was trying to get back on better terms with Sally or attempting to get around her. She had noticed and was not in the least fooled by his wheedling ways. Sally disliked it as it lowered her respect for him. The truth was that Sebastian had finished his bookwork much earlier so that he could join his friends in the Three

Tuns Inn. Their drinking session had gone on well past midnight and he was still recovering from a severe headache when he had called for Sally that morning. Sally was not fooled.

"I suspect thou had just a drop too much of the falling-down water as Granny Esther calls it. Just like Gabriel did from time to time."

Sebastian just groaned. His thoughts turned, for a few guilty moments, to the events that had occurred in the Three Tuns before he had crawled home. There had been an argument about settling his gambling debts, earlier at cards, and then during a game of skittles. When his brother, Luke, had arrived later Sebastian immediately asked him to settle the amount, promising Luke that it could come out of his next week's wages. This had happened before, on more than one occasion, and when Luke refused this time, Sebastian lost his temper. He forgot how often his older brother had rescued him from such awkward situations, in the Three Tuns, but also at home, or in the funeral parlour when Mr Brewer took Sebastian to task about his shoddy work. His father had never let him forget his worst mix-up, at a time when he was much younger.

Sebastian had clothed a deceased colonel, who was the local squire no less, in the clothes of a farmer who was to be buried the next day. Instead of placing the squire's regimental, leather-bound swagger stick complete with its silver plated top, in his hand, Sebastian had inserted a sickle. In the coffin alongside the military man was the farmer's favourite shepherd's crook. The incident had cost Brewers Undertakers more than the fee for the funeral; they lost much of their good reputation locally, both for reliable decorum and their rigorous attention to detail. To this day Mr Brewer still insisted that much of their business had gone to Biggleys in nearby Biddulph, just a few miles away.

With his head in his hands, up on Ipstones Edge, Sebastian groaned repeatedly. He looked so vulnerable and pathetic, so much less than the tall, confident, well-educated man who Sally had become used to seeing call for her, and her heart softened. She smiled to herself and knelt down taking his hand in hers.

"Seb, I know what men can be like sometimes. My faither, uncle and two brothers all like a drop of cider or ale from time to time. Faither used to say it 'took the edge off hard times' occasionally. When the weather was against us or the crop was poor or we'd lost some of the herd."

He looked into her eyes and admitted, "Well, yes, I had a drop too much last night, but…"

"Don't say any more, Seb. Just promise me it's not going to be a problem for us in future."

"I promise." He paused, thinking. "So… we may have a future then? Together."

Sally Sefton felt certain that Sebastian was a man who she could learn to love; a man who was educated and so different to any she'd met in her life thus far; his hands were smooth against her cheek, not rough like the bark of an oak. Her mind told her that they would make a good match, he was clever and she was caring, diligent. Yet Sally's heart told her nothing. She knew that Sebastian wanted her, but he was not going to hear the answer he required until she'd decided he would treat her as an equal. That would take time so, for now, this fish was not quite ready to be reeled in. Sally leaned forward, took his other hand from his face and kissed each of his palms, taking in the scent of his cologne.

Gently cupping his face in her hands she kissed him on the lips and whispered, as though it was a secret to be kept from the world. "If thou's to become the man of my dreams, my dear Seb, then our future together would seem to be very likely. Provided…"

Puzzled, Sebastian said, "But… when… if –"

55

"Provided, we understand a few things, together, agree things between us and –" She stopped speaking suddenly and asked, "Seb, why did thee buy me this book of poetry?"

"Sally, my darling, the more we meet, and talk… about the world and nature, then more and more I see we are kindred spirits. I, too, love that poem that you chose… Please believe me, I do feel bad that I fell asleep as you read it. And it was through drink… So, I… er…"

She placed her forefinger on his lips. "Not now, Seb. I'd like to go home."

"Yes, of course, I just wanted to say there's another poem in the book by Wordsworth that he calls, *Perfect Woman* and as soon as I read it, it reminded me of you. Truly! Have you read it?"

Sally looked hard at him. She was not about to be fooled by his flattery. *Kindred spirits? I wonder?* she thought.

"No, but I will read the poem soon, you devil! I'm eager to see whether I can ever live up to this… this paragon of William Wordsworth's – and yours it seems. For now, I think I am happy to take the reins and prove my skill with horses."

The ride home was in silence for much of the way, until Sally broke it when she pointed out an abandoned cottage on the land near to the Caldon canal.

"That would make a good home one day, for newly-weds. What do you think, my dear?"

Sebastian's jaw dropped open but from it came no sound, other than a perplexing hiss of strangled air. Sally patted his hand, smiled at him, kissed his cheek and then geed-up the horse. Their conversation for the rest of the journey was about whose land it was on and what improvements were needed in Sally's opinion. If a listening passenger had hung on behind them they would have observed Sebastian's enthusiastic agreement to everything that Sally spoke of. When the confused but happy young woman arrived back at her home, much later, she sat alone in her room reading the poem, *Perfect Woman*, over and over. Whilst her happiness increased with every new scan and interpretation, the last four lines also increased her confusion; increased it enough to be replaced by some consternation.

> *"... A perfect Woman, nobly plann'd,*
> *To warn, to comfort, and command;*
> *And yet a Spirit still, and bright*
> *With something of angelic light."*

Chapter 6
Prophets and Preaching

"**WHEN** I stopped the pony on that bridge that overlooks the old cottage, Sebastian was a little surprised, Cathy, because he thought I'd gone off him, see."

Sally giggled again, when her thoughts turned back to the day she had tormented her suitor.

"What did he say, Sal?"

"Nowt, Cath. He just listened to all the plans I'd had for months about it and didn't object at all. I knew he'd been drinking the night before and when I caught him out, he didn't have a leg to stand on."

"Well, it'd make a lovely home, Sal, but it does need a lot doing to it. When you showed it to me last year even I could see it wanted a new roof and one of the floors'd rotted through."

"Since Sebastian has been coming round a great deal I've asked Uncle Daniel to give me his opinion. Cus he had a lot to do with the cottage that he's in with Granny."

"Pa told us that your uncle had been repairing it for years, so that he and your grandma could live there comfortably."

"Aye, Cathy, he's done all that and not missed a day working on the farm and all. He's a fine man, considering his past. Pity he never married cus he would've made a fine husband for some woman."

"Pa said that Daniel had been sent to Australia years ago when he was a youth for some wrong-doing." Cathy paused, waited for Sally to say more, but her travelling companion looked out from the carriage at the passing scenery, saying nothing. "It must have been very serious to be transported to Australia."

"Aye, but we never speak of it now." Sally turned her face back to look at her dearest friend. "It was there he found Jesus once more; and a more devoted man thee could never hope to meet, my dear."

Sensing the need to change the subject Cathy replied, "You said that your Uncle Daniel would have come with us to Ashton if it had not been so busy on the farm, Sal."

"Aye, the large field needed dressing see. But he wants to hear all about it when I get back."

"My heart's all of aflutter for some reason. Like when we go to the fairground in the autumn." Cathy smiled at Sally and their conversation switched to the reason for their travels.

They were travelling in a coach-and-four to attend one of Preacher Wroe's open air meetings in the main market square at Ashton-under-Lyne. Thomas had gone on ahead, having had some business to attend to in Stockport first of all. He was to meet the two young women at the public coach house near to Church Street where the preacher had his abode that was called the Sanctuary. This was regarded by his followers as a temporary temple to him, until the building known as new Christian Israelite Church was completed.

They were a little travel weary as they alighted from the carriage but this was of little consideration to them when they spotted Thomas and their excitement mounted. He was sat outside the inn wearing his best coat and an enormous grin while holding a glass of ginger beer. After hugging his daughter with his one and a half arms, and kissing her cheek, Thomas turned to Sally and said, "By heck, young Sally, that young man of yours is a mighty lucky feller. Thou gets bonnier every time I sees thee."

"How are thee, Uncle Tommy? I can see thou's been celebrating already, eh!"

He grabbed his drink from the table and protested his innocence. "Hey up, lass, this here's just ginger beer. I've been a teetotaller for a while now, tha knowst. That's right, ain't it, Cathy? Tell her the truth now."

Cathy smiled wistfully and answered, "Yes, it's true. Pa won't have strong or weak alcohol in the house no more. Not even a bottle of Uncle Eddy's home brew or his elderberry wine that they make in September. He boils the berries properly and everything like they say." She looked at her father who nodded. "But no matter; Pa says No, so that's that." Then Cathy lifted Tommy's right hand in order to kiss the back of it, indulgently smiling at him.

This demonstration of Cathy's love for her father caused Sally to briefly bear a painful pang at the memory of losing her own dear 'faither'. Nevertheless, Sally also was interested to hear more of this abstinence, coming so soon after her conversation with Sebastian during their Ipstones picnic. "Oh, I see. No strong drink. What's that all about then?"

"See, I reckon it's the ruin of too many working folk, Sally. Specially the men. Too many of them drink theirs wages away afore their family gets enough on it to buy food and clothes and such for the kids, see."

"I think I agree with thee, Uncle Tommy. And I've seen too many blokes lose their rag after boozing. Fighting and what have you."

"And hitting out at the nearest folk to them for no reason... poorly kids, the missus what's doing her best. It's just not right... I joined in with the temperance lot at first, but then, later on like, I found the teetotallers had got it better - to my way of thinking."

Thomas looked down, shook his head gently, then suddenly, he looked up and grabbed Sally around the waist with his one arm.

"That's enough of all that, eh! Thou hasn't give yer Uncle Tommy a kiss yet, lass. And you've both got a treat in store when thou hears Preacher Wroe. Come on; he's holding his meeting near his new gatehouse on Mossley Road instead of the market square."

Sally gave Tommy a quick peck on his cheek and they set off in high spirits for Mossley Road.

***

As Thomas and the two women walked to the meeting they became aware of the many hundreds of people who seemed to be accompanying them. It was like a stream of people that became a river of humanity the closer they neared the new gatehouse. There were traders, mill workers and labourers amongst them. Thomas was at pains to remind them of the sumptuous building, the Sanctuary, that they had left behind.

"Aye, and thou should see it inside, the many fine furnishings, no expense spared I were told by a local man. Did ye notice the Star of Judah over the door?" They asked about it. "Well I were confused about that mesel at first, but it all makes sense when thee gets to understand about gathering the lost tribes of Israel."

The two women remained puzzled but kept silent when the noise from the throngs of excited people made conversation and understanding even more difficult. The area around the gatehouse had a few hundred people gathered there and silence spread rapidly when a small, dark, hunchbacked man climbed to stand on the flat back of a wagon. He raised his arms before speaking and waited. Even though they all could hear the person next to them breathing the preacher kept his arms aloft - waiting, waiting. He waited until the silence was almost too painful to bear. And then when he was sure that all eyes were upon him he called out in a broad Yorkshire dialect: "Hallelujah! Hallelujah, brothers and sisters!"

61

The gathered host shuffled slightly and an embarrassed quiet settled upon them again.

"Is that him?" whispered Sally, straining to see the man some thirty yards distant from them. Cathy nodded; Thomas put his forefinger to his lips to order silence.

"For the Spirit of God is amongst us, as was foretold in the Covenant. If we are to gather the lost Israelites from those gathered here today; and tomorrow… and all our tomorrows… then they must truly seek the redemption of their bodies. For in seeking redemption, then surely those people of Israel are they who would be Christians. In proclaiming Israel's In-gathering then I am simply God's holy conduit; the channel between our Lord God and those whose sins require repentance."

Preacher Wroe paused to allow his words to sink in. Then he suddenly declared in his own strange resounding way, "Do not follow me, brothers and sisters! Must I remind you afresh each day? I am but God's servant, as thou must become. I am his vassal in the fight against sin; the prophet who was chosen to bring to sinners the way they must follow in their search for redemption. Thou must not follow me, but follow the Holy Spirit! For in the Spirit is the way to Heaven!"

As his words echoed across the square the preacher held aloft his Bible and then proceeded to quote from it:

"And it shall come to pass in the last days, saith God, I will pour my Spirit upon all flesh, and your sons and your daughters shall prophecy, your young men shall see visions and your old men shall dream dreams"

And so it went on for twenty more minutes, when Preacher Wroe then announced the time and place for the next public baptism. It would be in the waters of the River Medlock. The river waters were now so polluted, with the recent years of industry that it might well cause some to find absolution at another time or place. No doubt those thoughts would occur privately to many of the would-be congregants present, for no-one spoke out of it. Bringing the meeting to a close Wroe took great pains to remind the assembly of newly uplifted persons that if he were ever to be taken away, there would be no more human prophets to proclaim Israel's In-gathering.

"The method and the way of His Testament have long been ordained, and now the Spirit of God is amongst you in the form of his prophet; for it is to work before the coming of the Messiah." Preacher Wroe raised both arms as before. "Let us all hail the coming of the Messiah - Hallelujah!"

There was a great cry of "Hallelujah!" from the crowd before it slowly dispersed.

***

On their return journey to Thomas' home in Stockport there was much discussion about Preacher Wroe and his proclamations. Cathy and Sally agreed that it had been exciting and even inspirational to them both, and they could see the delight in Thomas' face when they said as much. He declared, much to his daughter's surprise, that after each attendance how he was persuaded to adopt the way of simple clothing and also grow his beard like the followers of the preacher. Both girls were silent, unable to comment for a few seconds.

"See, if I am to show how much I believe in the truth of his words then this is a simple way of showing it."

"Does Ma know about this, Pa?"

"Well, no, Cathy, my dear. Not yet, but after today I reckon she's likely to understand. Specially after she hears how much the both of thee is taken by his words, eh!"

"I'm still not sure about everything, Pa. I mean about the way of Preacher Wroe's followers, or his Christian Israelite Church. His sincerity in his words seemed fine enough, even uplifting at times. But long beards and long hair? And plain gowns on top of it all might not be encouraging to some of your shop's customers. Folk can be a bit… you know… strange, or scared off by such things."

Sally then surprised her friend with her next comment.

"I'm not so sure about those things neither, Cath. But Uncle Tommy's just showing how strongly he feels about his belief in God and the scriptures – through listening to Preacher Wroe."

She turned to Tommy and held his hand for a few seconds as the coach came to a halt on Wellington Road in Stockport. "I wish I had the courage sometimes, to commit myself to something much bigger in life - like Jesus and his good works. Maybe help them as is much less fortunate than ourselves. There's a might too much poverty in this world. Where else can thee get the strength to fight for changing things if it's not from Jesus?"

Cathy was looking very querulous at her friend but her expression changed to one more friendly when Sally continued. "I have thee to thank, Cath, for helping me. *Once I was lost but now I am found*, thanks to thee, Cathy Priestley. And I admire thee, Uncle Tommy, with thy sincerity and new found faith."

Thomas got out first from the coach and as he helped Sally down he held her close and said, "Why, bless thee, Sally. That's very kind of thee, lass." Then he briefly held his daughter with his one hand on her shoulder and looked deeply into her eyes and asked, "You're not going to say anything to yer ma about this are ye, Cathy? Only I must pick me right moment, see."

"No, ye daft lummox, Pa; it's up to thee. I'm not at home so much nowadays and rarely in the shop, so I'm concerned to think ye might lose customers. Does Jack know this little secret of yours?" Cathy was unable to prevent a tiny smirk to creep to her face, half expecting her father's response.

64

"Jack! Why I'd be losing me mind to confide in Jack about anything. Jack's almost a heathen these days. He scoffs at most anything that's not to do with machines and steam power. He constantly reminds us about the future of the country relying on these new engineering inventions. He could be right about that and all but I fears for his place in Heaven, with his contrary way of speaking about the Testaments."

They were walking along the London Road towards Gibson's Store, the family business that was so called after Milly's maiden name. After another twenty minutes they arrived to find Jack and his mother standing in the shop entrance, grim looks on both their faces.

"Why, lass, what's up?" asked Thomas as Milly ushered the group inside.

"I'll stay in the shop with Rachel while Ma explains, eh," said Jack when the rest of them moved into the back parlour.

"We've had Jenny here most of the morning, Tommy. Weeping her eyes out most of the time – worried to death she is."

"Why what's happened, Ma? Has someone died?" asked Cathy.

"No, no, nothing like that, my dear. It's your Uncle Eddy; he's been arrested for robbery."

"What!" yelled Thomas. "Where is Jenny? Is she upstairs? It's got to be a mistake. Thou could never find a straighter bloke in this world, than me brother! Who says it, eh? I'd like a word with them, meself!"

"Please calm down, Tommy," pleaded Milly. "My nerves are already in shreds with Jenny's distress." Tears welled up in her eyes again and she sat down on their old couch, encouraging Thomas to sit beside her. Cathy knelt on the floor beside her mother's knees. "Jenny's gone back to Quarry Bank. A neighbour's been looking after their kiddies and she promised to get back before dark."

Feeling embarrassed to be present while emotions were running high, Sally now spoke up. "I'll just go and see if Jack and Rachel need a hand behind the counter."

No-one really heard Sally, or noticed as she left the parlour. But she heard Milly's tearful whisper as she carefully closed the door behind her.

"They say he robbed from the safe in the manager's office."

"What safe? Which manager, Milly?"

"The safe in the manager's office at Quarry Bank mill."

***

"It will be quite a change for you, Sally, I daresay. When you are married to Sebastian and he is working in his father's funeral business. You will probably need to move to Leek or that other Cheadle, the one near to your farm." Milly paused. "Hm, yes, and you'll live in quite a different house to your farm cottage. A big house as befits an important man in his profession."

Milly was thinking about her own background when she had been a lady's maid in a big house in London. When she had been happy to move north in order to marry Thomas and eventually become a shopkeeper's wife and mother to their three children. They were a devoted couple and had a sound and very happy life.

"There's a house I like very much, near Cheddleton, like I told Cathy. It's a big old cottage that needs doing up. But I was just dreaming - though I suppose, thou might be right, Milly. I hadn't really stopped to think about our future life together."

Sally and Milly had been chatting quietly during her last evening, staying with the Priestley family. It had been a welcome change for Milly after the upsetting morning and afternoon. She and her children had taken the remains of the afternoon to calm Thomas down and persuade him to stay home until the following day. He was all for immediately saddling up Pollen, their pony, and riding to Styal to 'sort this matter out'. He cared nothing for the fact that the pony was trained to pull his cart and had never taken a saddled rider. Over the years Thomas had become very skilful at controlling the pony and cart with his one arm and his teeth, but he knew little about saddling up. When the others reminded him that he would have to return in the dark later he paused to re-consider. Jack had closed the shop and hearing what was said he offered to ride with his father early the next day and to help get to the bottom of things.

"Aye, that's good of ye, son. But it would be more help to me if ye could stay behind the counter tomorrow. I've got some special order customers coming in; and I expect Cathy and yer ma will be taking Sally to the stagecoach station when she leaves for Cheddleton."

"Okay, Pa, but ye promise to take the cart to Quarry Bank, eh? None of this here saddling up Pollen and riding one-handed."

"Of course, Jack… All this is going to be a reet worry and no mistake. I'm sorry about this, Sally. I know I promised to give thee a lift into Stockport."

"Uncle Tommy, it's not that far to walk into the town centre from here. Besides, I can have another gossip with Cath and Rachel about girl things on the way."

"Ma can stay in the shop with Jack, Pa," added Cathy.

"What about school?" asked Tommy, nodding towards Rachel, whose ears pricked up further as she played with her dolls. Then Milly had finally settled things with her calm but very firm words.

"Tommy, will you please find something to do for the rest of the day? We can sort things out ourselves about tomorrow. We are just as anxious as you to know what is going on with Eddy. Probably just one big mistake, when I stop to think about it, eh?"

"Aye, you're right, lass. I'll be in stockroom sorting out that order. Can ye give us a lift with things, Jack?"

The men left the room and Cathy called after them, "I'll be in with a nice cup of tea in a few minutes, Pa."

"And a bite to eat as well," added her mother.

Rachel, who had been sitting quietly in the corner of the parlour, listening to the adults, appeared to be occupied arranging her dolls into height order and swapping their clothes between them. The dolls were to receive one of her stories if they behaved themselves. Then she quietly reminded the adults of her presence with a question.

"Will Uncle Eddy have to go to prison, Ma?"

"No, no, Rachel. Don't be silly. Your Pa will sort things out tomorrow. Now then, you've had your supper so I'd like you to get ready for bed. It might be an early start tomorrow."

Milly had raised her eyebrows behind Rachel's back, when looking at Sally and Cathy, pausing, as she was about to leave the room with her. She made no further comment about Eddy but changed the subject to one about Sally's future with Sebastian, having learned at the start of her visit that she and Sebastian had become engaged. Cathy was also now more curious to continue the conversation with her friend.

"I expect you'll miss working on the farm, Sally, when you're the wife of a funeral director?"

The earlier mention of her future with Sebastian had started a subconscious thinking process in Sally's brain that had slowly fermented and resulted in a conscious conclusion.

"Well, I will hate to leave the farm. I love working with the animals; the horses, the cattle, pigs... Ploughing fields, properly, is so hard, but... It's so, so... fine, when you look back at a tilled field at the end of the day. Or end

68

of season, when crops are ready for reaping. I always feel so useful - so, so fulfilled I suppose the word is."

Catherine and her mother exchanged knowing looks.

"Sally, my dear, I hate to interfere but if you will be unhappy leaving the farm, and all it means to you, then you have to tell Sebastian."

Cathy agreed with Milly and said as much. Sadly, Sally's response did more to cause them concern than to calm them.

"I suppose so, but he is so different to anyone I've met in farming. Sebastian is well educated, knowledgeable about all sorts of things, and with clean, smooth hands, with clean fingernails. Not like any farmer I know – and I'm sure he cares for me. He often tells me so. Do you think I might lose Seb if I tell him?"

Milly frowned. She already had enough to worry about with Eddy's plight and yet she loved Sally almost like a daughter and wanted her to be happy. She felt very awkward asking her next question so framed it carefully. "He is very handsome, and so sophisticated, and caring, as you say, but do you love him, Sally?"

Cathy interjected. "Do you feel happier in your heart, with your pulse racing, every time you meet up with him? Thou knows what I mean, dearest Sally. Surely, thou knows - just as it says in some of those poems we love to read?"

Sally's first response to Cathy's question was anger because she was still waiting for the feelings she had read about. Even though it felt so right whenever she was with Sebastian, with someone who was always so eager to please her, who bought her little tokens of his affection, whose kisses were sweet but whose attentions were patient; she was still not sure if her feelings for him included love.

"Cathy, Milly, I know that I wish to be with Seb more and more, and I always miss him when we're not together. I'm sure that I want to be with him forever... I suppose that could be love. But I love being a farm girl; I always have and I always will. So, yes, you're right. I must tell him. I will, aye I will, directly I get back to Cheddleton."

Cathy smiled and they embraced briefly before the conversation changed again to one about the new railways. Milly kissed Sally on her cheek and left the room to see to the food and Rachel. The two friends were very curious to know when a railway line between Leek and Stockport would be built and now, after hearing Preacher Wroe speak, when there would be a line from Stockport to Ashton-under-Lyne. They were intent on meeting together more often in order to attend Preacher Wroe's sermons regularly. Cathy said she would interrogate her brother Jack about this as he claimed to know so much about railways. Sally was sure that Sebastian would know something since he had become interested in the business of building and investment in railways.

Sally's visit to the Priestleys on this occasion would give her much to think about on her journey home the next day. What would her mother say when Sally told her that Eddy Priestley was in jail for robbery from Quarry Bank mill? She had felt so uplifted in Ashton that she could not stop wondering if she could be one of Preacher Wroe's lost Israelites? Would the development of the railways help her find out by enabling more journeys, more often and more quickly? And not only that but, most importantly for her, what would be Sebastian's reaction when she told him that she wanted to stay on the farm after they were married? Would that put an end to their future plans, to their relationship? Could she face the hurt and the embarrassment? If all that came to be then perhaps becoming one of Wroe's disciples was what she was really meant for in this life.

Chapter 7
A New School and New Understanding

CATHERINE Priestley and James Longton had a problem. Would they be able to work together in a new school that was to be set up in nearby Cheadle Hall? It was said that the charity boarding school, for the needy children and orphans of warehousemen and clerks, currently being run by Mr Macdougal at Shaw Hall in Flixton, needed to be expanded. The charity had intended to open its own premises in Ardwick, in central Manchester. The original charity had been founded in London for a school there and was funded through donations and subscriptions. A similar foundation, arranged by a committee of business men from Manchester, had decided upon the expansion. It would be non-denominational and only admit children between the ages of seven to twelve, with boys leaving at age fourteen, girls at fifteen. Entrants to the new school would be selected by a ballot of the subscribers, which was similar to the London school. The Shaw Hall teachers were surprised to learn that building had already commenced on a large purpose-built home for the new school in Cheadle.

Cathy and James had been asked to be two of the teachers in the new Cheadle Hall Academy. While both Cathy and James felt excited to be part of such an important new project, they had not been co-operating well together lately. They were each to receive a small increase in their salary, becoming promoted to head up their own subject departments and, a little later, they would be involved in the selection of more new teachers. James Longton had continued to show Cathy much more attention than she desired; he feeling that he was being supportive professionally; she feeling embarrassed and resentful at this unwanted 'interference'. Unfortunately, his small displays of affection, with occasional short notes and little gifts left on her desk, became one day the focus of a slight altercation, some of which was also witnessed by Mr Macdougal himself.

Their argument had almost come to an end as the headmaster entered Cathy's schoolroom, unnoticed, with some papers in his hand. Voices had been raised but the details of their conversation had been missed by Mr Macdougal. All that he heard was:

"And so, Mr Longton, I would be most grateful if you did not enter my room ever again, in my absence. Is that clear?"

"Crystal clear, Miss Priestley. In future I will attempt to furnish you with my calling card, attached to a note requesting the honour of an audience with her highness, her majesty, the most sensitive - but amazingly unfeeling - princess Pries-"

Fortunately the sarcasm contained within James' riposte flew out of the doorway and over the headmaster's mortar boarded pate.

"Well, well, well, I must admit as I approached the door of your schoolroom, Miss Priestley, that I thought to find that there was some disruptive pupil of yours, no doubt correctly, receiving a dressing-down for his misdemeanours… But I see I was mistaken. Rehearsals for the school play, I assume, Catherine, ably assisted by Mr Longton directing. Am I correct?"

Although tempers were hot and feelings injured, neither teacher wished to reveal any sort of fracture in their co-operation as educational colleagues. Warm smiles grew wider and warmer with every word from Mr Macdougal.

"Well, yes, in a way, Mr Macdougal. But the script has not been decided, erm, quite yet," replied Cathy.

She felt slightly wrong-footed by his rare use of her Christian name. It was something that had not happened ever since she had been much younger, when still a pupil in some of his classes. James seized the initiative with, "We were also practising the projection of our voices for when we need to address pupils and parents in the new, larger assembly hall. At some time in the future I would… erm, assume, Headmaster."

"Oh, I see… I think. But there's no need for all that for quite a time yet, Mr Longton. I have a much more pressing task that I wish both you and Miss Priestley to undertake. The bishop will be calling in to see me in a few weeks' time to run through our Bible Studies programme for next year's curriculum."

The two teachers looked at each other quizzically and then, smilingly, back at Mr Macdougal.

"Yes, well, these are my thoughts on the matter and I have included a few suggestions of my own. You don't have to include them all, of course – but if you could work together on the new curriculum and report back to me in, let us say three weeks, I'd be most grateful. Yes, most, er, grateful."

The headmaster turned to leave the room, having placed a copy of his notes in the hands of each teacher. Cathy felt certain that rumours of the recent disharmony between her and James had somehow reached his ears and asked, "Ahem, is there a particular reason why you have chosen us to work on this, Mr Macdougal?"

"We, that is, the school governors and myself, have noticed just how well your pupils for Bible Studies have been doing in the end of term exams for the past two years. So, of course, it makes good sense to ask the two best teachers of the subject to write the new curriculum for it." He raised his eyebrows. "Yes?"

"Well, yes, sir, of course. Thank you for the opportunity," replied Cathy.

"And I must reiterate my excellent colleague's comments, Mr Macdougal. We will start straight away if possible. What do you think, Miss Priestley?"

"Why, yes, of course, of course." She paused, blushing, aware that she was repeating herself, then angry that the two men must have noticed her blushes. "And we won't let you and the bishop down. Three weeks, I think you said, Mr Macdougal," Cathy quickly added.

"Splendid! That's the spirit. Teamwork - just what I like to see. Teamwork; yes, I only wish that some of your, more, erm, shall we say 'sleepy' colleagues had such a positive attitude towards the education of our precious young charges, hey! Oh, and by the way the new, more snappy, more modern title of the subject is to be 'Scripture'. I like it… Yes, more modern, snappy, et cetera, et cetera."

Mr Macdougal left the room, muttering to himself, and breezed down the corridor in a flurry of black mortar board and billowing black gown, with surprised pupils along the way diving out of his path into alcoves, empty schoolrooms and under stairs storage cupboards.

***

Cathy and James had been working together for about three weeks on the newly named Scriptures subject. They had firmly agreed upon one thing only; that, despite the headmaster's suggestions, it was going to appear remarkably similar to the original Bible Studies subject. When James said that the best thing that they could do was to shift the balance to include more from the Old Testament Cathy objected. She felt that they should continue to place more emphasis on teachings from within the Anglican Church, from the New Testament, like the works of the Apostles and the Holy Trinity.

"That way, James, we will avoid too much censure from the school governors and, probably more importantly, from the bishop."

James shook his head again. "What is so wrong with concentrating on Moses and the Mosaic laws? Most children find the stories fascinating: Moses in the bulrushes; parting the Red Sea; stone tablets handed down from God and so on."

Cathy looked dubious. James pressed on.

"And what about the story of Noah and the Flood? And David and Goliath? Children love those stories."

She slowly shook her head with each item in James' list. The unspoken truth was that Cathy was trying to avoid any potential discussion with James, or anyone else, about the Christian Israelite Church. The enthusiasm for Wroe that had waxed, after her visit to Ashton-under-Lyne with Sally, was now on the wane. She had heard worrying rumours from some old Sunday school friends about John Wroe since then, though her misgivings were being constantly swept aside by her father.

Thomas had indeed taken to growing his hair longer; it was now in a pigtail down past his shoulders. Not shaving for many weeks meant his unruly beard was reaching down his throat and heading for his chest. He was wearing a long white 'nightshirt' every day, all day, and it was no longer faintly amusing. Cathy and her mother felt things had gone too far with his new beliefs. Her parents argued all the time about this new way of living. They were not allowed to eat pork any more, nor have any alcohol in the house and Tommy was insisting that all the females in the family wore only very full skirts. Rachel wept every day at the idea. Jack had dared to rant at his parents, threatening to move out permanently if his father continued to try to make him only wear 'ridiculous' coats without collars and with seams sewn on the sides.

What was she to tell Sally in her letters? She knew how much Sally felt influenced by Thomas and it seemed to Cathy that she was being disloyal to both, her dearest friend and her father. Cathy found the whole affair too much and welcomed the time soon to come when she and all the teachers of Cheadle Hall Academy would be 'living in' as house tutors. It would be a relief to escape from home, uncomfortable though that thought may be. She dreaded every day that the subject of the Christian Israelite Church may occur in a conversation with school colleagues. The worst thing of all for her was that James Longton was the last person in the world with whom Cathy felt able to share such concerns. Telling herself every day that she should never have agreed to work so closely with him did not help.

Cathy's thoughts would turn constantly each day to the time she and Rachel had witnessed a rare and terrible argument between her parents. The family had been attending the local Anglican Church in Davenport for many years and, on the last occasion, Milly had been unable to persuade Thomas to wear his 'normal' clothes for the Sunday service. His appearance with his long beard and hair and dressed all in white, had invited disapproving looks. The curate had asked them on leaving the church if Thomas had changed his religion to Judaism and was at the wrong place of worship. Thomas' response had been to burst into laughter and walk away cackling and muttering to himself about only the righteous entering Heaven. Milly had promised to explain later to the curate and hurriedly chased after her husband.

Their upsetting disagreement occurred later that Sunday and had ended bitterly when Milly had insisted that Thomas would never be taken seriously, in his efforts to save Eddy, while he was turning up in his nightshirt in front of the authorities. Eddy was still imprisoned, remanded for several weeks, while the criminal investigations continued. The tension and pressure within the Priestley family had become almost palpable.

One day, while Catherine and James were in the middle of a lesson discussion, she was distracted. Both teachers felt under pressure as the end of term approached and they were still to complete the new syllabus before Mr Macdougal's deadline. She was thinking once more about her parents' row as well as the rumours concerning Preacher Wroe. James had suddenly asked her, "A penny for them?"

"What do you mean, Mr Longton?"

He could see she was angry with his question but continued, "Well I asked you a question about the third Scripture lesson, about the Twelve Tribes of Israel. But you didn't respond. You seemed to be very preoccupied with your own thoughts for a few seconds, so that was why I offered a penny for them – for your thoughts. Perhaps I was too flippant, Miss Priestley, but you looked so worried I felt concerned. Can I help at all?"

Cathy's rancour subsided quickly, not wishing to cause a scene in the staffroom where they were having their discussion. She offered a vague excuse about not feeling well and left the room, a hand to her forehead. She suspected that James' concern was genuine, having got to know him a little better during the three weeks they had been meeting about the new Scripture syllabus. At the very least Cathy had begun to respect his knowledge and his undoubted professionalism. To her surprise he had shown quite a degree of flexibility, just lately, about adopting some of her ideas, while adapting his own to fit in with their agreed subject objectives. Even so, she was both discomfited and irritated when James arrived in her schoolroom at the end of lessons to ask her, "Do you still feel unwell, Catherine?"

It was the first time that he had ventured to use her first name and she thought it would have been petty to object. She took it as a sign of his honest concern for her well-being. Besides, she found it a little flattering for some reason, in what seemed to be a growing, but hesitant, friendship. It was something more than their usually cold, but respectful, professionalism when together.

"I am feeling much better, thank you, Mr Longton."

"I wish you would call me James, but perhaps in good time it may happen. However, I am pleased your good health has returned so that we may complete some of the finer details of the syllabus. It is only a few days now before we must see the headmaster with it done, so to speak."

No matter how hard she tried Cathy's usual concentration would not return. She replied, "I wonder, Mr Longton, could I leave the completion of the Scripture syllabus in your hands? There is little more to discuss I think and I have a few pressing matters at home which demand my attention."

Cathy was trying hard not to let her trembling voice reveal her fragile emotions. She could not handle the betrayal she felt towards everyone she loved by wanting to escape from them by living in at the new school. She kept thinking: *What is becoming of me? Have I changed so much into this unfeeling person?* James' voice broke through. "Oh no, Catherine, I cannot do this without you. Your presence, in my thoughts, in our everyday meetings has come to mean so much to me. I can see, even now, how troubled you are, and wish that I could help. Please let me. Just a hint, a word, or something that may enable a helpful suggestion from my lips… Please, let me help. I care so much for you but have been unable to speak of it, lest I frighten you away again."

Could she share her worries with James Longton after all? And then, abruptly, before she was ready, she heard her own words blurt out in one fell swoop:

"James, have you ever heard of the Christian Israelite Church?"

Catherine became yet more stunned on hearing his reply.

"Oh, yes indeed, I am quite well acquainted with the works of that scoundrel, John Wroe. What would you like to know?"

***

It had been many weeks since Sally Sefton's last visit to Ashton-under-Lyne with Cathy and things had moved forward with the engagement to Sebastian. Wedding plans were now in place and her visits to see Parson Trunchman were not just to discuss the words of Preacher Wroe. The clergyman had heard little from his bishop to discourage Sally's infrequent visits to Ashton. From all that he knew he'd explained how Wroe was encouraging the believers in the coming of Jesus as the Messiah, to prepare for a great assembly soon. He told Sally which parts of the Bible to read in order to find out more and told her of the ten lost tribes of Israel; that the ten came originally from Moses' Twelve Tribes of Israel, who were also known as the Israelites. Much of this confirmed what she had heard from Thomas and from John Wroe during the two gatherings she had attended with Cathy and her father.

When she had spoken to Sebastian about her wishes to remain on the farm Sally was pleasantly surprised by his immediate reaction. They were on the road to Rushton Spencer passing through Rudyard and had pulled the pony and trap over to take in the view over the lake.

"My dearest, darling Sally, that news gives me no disquiet whatsoever. If that is thy desire then it is a wish easily granted. I hope it may be amongst many more wishes that you may have and that will come true. For all I wish is to make you happy for the rest of our lives together."

"But how will thou feel about finding somewhere to live on the farm, Seb? Somewhere that befits your position in the community – as a business man, I mean."

"I can change. It is an opportunity I welcome with both hands. To become a farmer next to my beloved, Sally, will be exciting – a new adventure. If you are willing to teach me and we are together, then I can live anywhere in the world where we can be happy – together! I have ideas about business we can discuss later and there are properties nearby needing improvement where we may live."

"Will we be able to afford it if you give up working for your faither, Sebastian? Many folk are leaving the land to work in the mills and factories these days."

He offered a wild speculation of his own: "All of those people working in the towns still need to eat, Sally. And the ones left on the farms, like Seftons Farm, will be the suppliers of that food. So, more demand from the mill workers will put up the price of farm produce, particularly if there are fewer farmers. And besides I am tired of the stink of formaldehyde working and living there."

Sally attempted to make an intrigued, but impressed, look come to her pretty features.

"My business partner tells me I have some investments coming along in the new railway lines between Cheddleton, Leek and Stoke," he lied. "In addition there is an opportunity to invest in that line I told you about from here to Manchester and Stockport. When they mature we will have enough capital available to afford a large house, even add to the farm if that is what you wish, my dear."

Now she laughed, relieved that they were still to marry but feeling slightly nervous that Sebastian was prepared to give up his secure career in Brewers Undertakers.

"I will be satisfied to live in one house, large or small. And, Seb, one thing more I wish to be clear about.

Thou promised we should each be equal in our marriage. If thou truly meant it then I would like to be involved with thee in business matters. I mean it to be in farming as well as your railway plans. Thou can teach me while I teach thee about arable crops and shepherding and such."

It was then he had replied, "Sal, my dearest darling, Sal. I have wanted thee for my wife ever since I glanced across the auction arena and saw you bid for the dairy heifers. *What a beautiful and spirited girl that is*, I thought. And, my darling, I was hooked, hooked like a speckled trout from yonder Rudyard Lake. We two will always be as one, sharing everything, equal for as long as we both shall live."

They kissed and Sally took this as their promise together to share everything, equally, just as he had said. Sebastian could not believe it. His opportunity to get away from his father and brother had fallen into his lap so soon. Of course he agreed willingly to everything that Sally asked. The smaller details he could iron out later. It was the same philosophy he had agreed with the man he had met in the Three Tuns, his new partner in the future dealings with railways. The details could be sorted out later, after he had come up with a reasonable amount of investment capital.

"Sally, when do you think we shall be wed? I would like it to be before summer has turned into autumn; maybe around harvest time? Your beauty will put the summer flowers to shame and for Cheddleton to see the prettiest girl, for miles around, adorned in white and pretty petals will be such a sight to see. 'Twill be a sight to make other men jealous of your man, this Sebastian Brewer, the man who would be proudest of all."

"Why, Sebastian, thou has some poetry in thee after all." She kissed him tenderly and long. When they had paused for breath she added, "I will ask the parson tomorrow when we meet again. I, too, wish it could be soon like thee, my darling."

Chapter 8
The Robbery

THE group of seven men left queuing in the mill manager's office constituted a rather mixed but typical collection of male humanity. Three of them were not the tallest of the mule spinners, much like the three who had already left the room, but all of them were described by their associates as 'sturdy' and a misty cloud of cotton 'flue' hovered about each of the men as they moved around Quarry Bank. Some of their nicknames tended to reflect something of their stature. Stocky Smeaton was the broadest and he often found his way to the front of the queue, except that today he was delayed by his search about the mule shop floor for a cleaner bit of waste to wrap around his burst blistered finger. Rocky Roberts was the eldest, hair and beard looking as grey and white as the rest. But his hair and beard stayed a grubby white after their daily clean-up when their work-shift had ended. Philip Podmore's wild and woolly ginger hair became as white as the others within an hour of starting work each day. His chubby features with their sparse red whiskers, clinging to his cheeks and chin, had led to the over familiar byname of 'Pud'.

The two mule spinners waiting at the wages hatch had much leaner faces, like most of the mill workers. The man bringing up the rear was either called 'Flaggy' or Fred depending upon whether they had known him as he grew up from a boy piecer to becoming a spinner as an adult. Very rarely did the apprenticed boys coming from a workhouse grow to be tall, as had Frederick Grafton. The overseers said he was like a flagpole when he became as tall as they at about the age of thirteen, and so they called him Flaggy. Now, well into his twenties and over six feet tall, everyone still tended to call him Flaggy, which he did not mind as his son was known to all as Little Freddy. Freddy was small like his mother. The man in front of Flaggy in the queue was almost as tall but he was called Steady Eddy.

Steady Eddy Priestley, Tommy's younger brother, had worked at Quarry Bank since being a small boy. When Thomas had introduced him to Mr Greg many years ago he had already advised his little brother to work hard, not complain, and to ask him for advice if anything confused him or made him unhappy.

"That way, mate, thee'll get a reputation for being a good worker, see. Reliable, and hard-working grafters is what they like, so when it comes to promoting lads up they'll more'n likely choose thee. Do ye understand, pal?"

The boy had nodded and remembered his brother's words. Thomas was correct in his assumption, which is how Eddy's nickname amongst overseers and fellow workers became simply 'Steady'. However, later circumstances resulted in Thomas having to leave Quarry Bank mill leaving Eddy to mature and grow naturally, more often relying upon his own counsel. On a good week a mule spinner, a steady worker like Eddy, could take home a few pence over a guinea. The rapid increase in the number of local mills had created more competition and a fall in the price and the demand for yarn. Even the spinners' wages had fallen, though the men were still paid more than double the women. This led to many an argument in the village where the workers lived in their two-up-two-down cottages. A number of them had paying lodgers but Eddy's pride would not allow this despite Jenny's remonstrations.

"How are we to pay for the children's schooling, Eddy, if we refuse to take in lodgers like so many others in Styal?"

"I'll think of something, my dear, like I keeps telling thee. Don't fret so much. I'll not have them work in mill less us really 'as to. Our Tommy's got it reet. It's education what matters these days."

Rocky Roberts collected his wages from the manager, who was standing behind the hatch in the wall. The workers in the queue shuffled forward a little when Rocky had checked his money, agreeing the deductions made for purchases from the company shop in the village. It was Friday, wages day for the mill workers, and as they neared the hatchway the ones at the front could see the large safe door hanging open behind the manager. Not many had been paid as yet and counted piles of silver and copper coin were in rows along shelves and just inside the safe. There were some piles of paper money but not many since few got paid enough to warrant it. Many of them preferred gold to paper payments and were still old fashioned and less trusting in the rapidly introduced new system.

Flaggy and Eddy could see over the shoulders of Rocky and Pud that many more of the hundreds of workers had still to come and collect their wages. They had to await their turn and appropriate permission from one of the clerks who were also employed in the mill manager's office. They sent groups of about ten people at a time from the mill floor to the office on pay-day. That had been the familiar method before Robert Greg took over completely from his father. Robert had always argued with Samuel about the inefficiency of the system with workers leaving their machines to get paid. He was about to change the system to one where everyone collected their pay only at the end of their shift. This had the effect of causing more talk about forming a union since this was in the workers' own 'going home time'.

Mr Howlett, the manager, was about to address Eddy when all hell broke loose in the room, behind the queue of workers.

"Mr Howlett! Oh, Mr Howlett! Thee must come quick. There's bin accidents in the mule room and in weaving shed and all. Look, look! Oh! My God... Blood everywhere there is!"

A very distressed looking young woman held both hands up the hatch, palms facing it. There was wet and dried blood on her hands and apron with grimy streaks running down her forearms as well as her tearful cheeks.

"Calm down, Hazel and tell me what's happened," replied Mr Howlett.

"Thee must come now, Mr Howlett." She turned to the door. "Overlooker said to come immediately, Mr Howlett! Immediately! Jimmy Holroyd's trying ter tend to the lad in the mule room and our Cora's had the shuttle fly off into her face!"

Hazel ran to the door, her tiny body swaying from side to side as she hopped from one foot to the other in an uncontrollable panic.

"There's blood everywhere – everywhere!"

The men in the queue outside and the two inside, Flaggy and Eddy, all had grim looks on their faces. The young woman was wringing her hands, clutching her face, smudging the blood and grime together. She began to moan and groan, somewhere between a scream and a howl. The tiny hatch door slammed shut with a bang causing Hazel to scream so loud it echoed through the building. The mill manager was just behind her, Charles the wages clerk stood in the office doorway, uncertain what to do.

"Come on, Hazel, take me to the worst accident first."

"Ah don't know which way ter run, Mr Howlett! The overlooker said they're both serious. Our Cora's covered in blood - she's on the floor, screaming and screaming!"

"Eddy, go and fetch Mr Robert. He's with a factory inspector in the scotching room – Oh, and the doctor if he's still on site. Charles, grab the bag of cotton waste and clean rags we keep in the office and come with me."

"Where will the doctor be?" yelled Eddy to the trio as they ran out of the mill manager's offices and disappeared around the corner of the mill yard. There was no reply

"Thee'd best get after the gaffer and find out where the doc is, Steady," said Flaggy. "I'll nip down to scotching room for Mr Greg. No time to waste, eh?"

Eddy stood outside, confused for a few seconds about which way to run. "Aye, all right, Flaggy. If thee can do that and…" he mumbled, without finishing his sentence, before racing across the yard, and almost colliding with a group of small boys, apprentices walking to collect their wages.

*****

Eddy had run to the stables and then to the Apprentice House asking everyone he met along the way for the location of the doctor, the Greg family's own surgeon, without any luck. While he tried to catch his breath back after running all the way up the steep hill, the superintendent at the Apprentice House paused for a few seconds to think.

"Now let me think, young Eddy Priestley. The missus did say something earlier about why he'd called today. Cause we wanted him to call in here, see. There's a couple of the girl's with cotton fluff stinging their eyes." Mr Timperley closed his eyes, frowned, concentrating hard.

"It's very urgent," wheezed Eddy with the little breath he had left. "The mill manager's sent me. He's gone in with his clerk. Blood everywhere the lass said."

The superintendent suddenly indicated that he had been listening when he exclaimed, "Oh, dearie me! It sounds serious. I've remembered now, he's gone to the big house to see Mrs Greg. She's not too well today, so I -"

But Eddy had gone. He was running back down the hill to Quarry Bank House before Mr Timperley's concertinaed brow had smoothed itself out. Unfortunately, the doctor was no longer there and the servant who answered the door to Eddy told him that another worker had called just minutes before him. She had said the doctor was needed in Mr Howlett's office and so Eddy raced back there.

The events of the previous day went through Steady Eddy's mind over and over again. He'd had to recall them once, twice, even a third time, but this time in front of a police inspector. On the first occasion it had been for the mill manager who then had sent for Robert Hyde Greg and Eddy had to repeat it a second time for him. He was unable to understand why all three men did not seem to believe him. Within a few minutes of his arrival the policeman had agreed with Mr Greg that there was no obvious sign of a break-in. He was shown that the spare key to the office hung on the wall on the side away from the hatch.

"Hm, so you would need to have very long arms indeed to reach it from that little hatchway," said the inspector. He turned to Eddy, staring at his arms he continued, "Well, Mr Priestley, I am obliged to inform you that we have two witnesses who say they saw you go back into Mr Howlett's office, alone, when there was no-one else about, and leave with your pockets bulging. Plus, you were carrying a canvas sack that appeared to be heavy and that you then ran in the direction of the mill entrance, around the corner. But we can find nobody to back up your story about going into the weaving shed."

"I did go in there – with some clean cotton rags for the doctor. But they'd all left and some of the hands said I was too late. Everyone had gone to the infirmary... I, I..."

Inspector Walter Button was not impressed with Eddy's stuttered repetition of the events. He was a stout man with jet black hair that was severely parted down the centre. He had a bluff no-nonsense attitude to all suspects who were often fooled by his initially amiable approach. His habit of clenching his jaws together and protruding his lower lip eventually gave the impression that he did not believe anything he was told, not even when the Holy Bible was clutched in one hand. Button had been appointed three years before to be criminal inspector, assistant to the Chief Constable of Manchester. When working in London he was successfully doing a similar job in the Whitehall area, inspecting the pubs known as flash-houses, where stolen property was regularly fenced. These 'nurseries of crime', as the magistrates called them, had sprung up all over Manchester and they had requested his help. Inspector Button had moved north with his widowed sister and her three children. Now that it had become a permanent appointment and his pay had been increased, he was eager to show his police masters in Manchester that he was going to be worth every penny. Through his contacts in the city Robert Greg had been able to attract the inspector to the Styal robbery.

"So, where is this here bag of rags you say you were carrying?"

"I dunno. There was a reet mess of things happening in the mill when I got there. Folks rushing about, in and out, all over place. I must've put it down somewhere when I heard they'd all gone off – to the infirmary, like I said afore."

"See, lad, I've been in the mill with the local constable and Mr Greg looking everywhere for this here sack. Nowt! We found nowt and I ain't inclined to believe this story of yours. So thee'd best accompany me to the lock-up in Hawthorn Lane, till I've asked a lot more questions."

"Lock-up? Dost mean prison?"

88

"Aye, in Wilmslow. So come on, no trouble now or my constable here and I will have to chain thee up. I've got two witnesses so it ain't looking too good for thee."

"What now? What about my missus? She doesn't know what's going on, or nothing - and there's the kids..."

Inspector Button looked at Robert Greg and the mill manager and nodded. "I dare say word will be got to your family about your arrest, Edward Priestley."

Both Quarry Bank men said nothing but merely nodded back at the inspector in silent agreement.

It was later the next day during Inspector Button's further questioning of Eddy that Thomas arrived at the Wilmslow lock-up with Jack and a distressed Jenny. His son stayed with their horse and waited nearby. Tommy and his sister-in-law had sat in a very sparsely furnished outer waiting room with just two wooden chairs for seating and six posters of wanted felons decorating the walls. The memory of a visit to Newgate Prison many years ago did not help to calm Thomas down. Eddy's impatient older brother failed to sit for more than two or three minutes before knocking hard on the grubby glass panel of the locked dividing door. Eddy's wife pleaded with him each time that he would only make things worse.

"Tommy, thee's going to upset the constable if thou cracks the glass in his door. Cannot thee knock a bit more gentle like?"

"We've got a right to know what's going on, Jenny. Thee's got more right than anybody. It ain't right putting an honest bloke in jail. Nobody at the mill could tell me anything. Howlett told me it was none of me business and threatened to have me thrown off the premises."

"See, that's what I mean, Tommy. Upset his masters at mill and he'll never get his job back..." The fresh thought of that brought yet more tears to her eyes. "Oh, mercy me, what are we to do if Eddy gets the sack?"

Tommy stood before Jenny, his eyebrows raised, slowly shaking his head, with his good hand holding his new growth of beard.

"Don't you understand, Jenny, if he goes to jail for robbery thee won't see him again for years? Likely the kids'll be grown up afore he comes home – if ever. Tut! Transportation if magistrates in a bad mood." He grumbled as he turned back to the door and knocked yet again, his unhelpful comments initiating another torrent of tears from poor Jenny.

Thomas had arrived at Quarry Bank mill in the morning and demanded to see Robert Greg when he had confronted the mill manager. Mr Howlett had lost his temper after ten minutes of attempting to explain about money being taken from the office safe. He avoided the details, which would have included his failure to close the safe door and also his forgetting to remind Charles to do so. But Charles had turned the key in the office door before leaving to accompany Mr Howlett and Hazel in their race to the mill. Carrying their very rudimentary first aid bag and locking the door seemed to have given Charles an air of sensible superiority. Mr Howlett was painfully conscious of this air so went out of his way to compliment Charles later for his quick thinking. Thus the open safe door was a secret only known to three people, one of them of course being the safe robber.

It was after a wait of almost an hour before the inspector's grim face appeared at the glass, eyes narrowed and lower lip slowly jutting. Then he unlocked the door and stepped out into the waiting room.

"And who might you be, knocking so loud on this here door that thee's interrupting important police work?"

Inspector Button looked Thomas up and down and, although he had conceded to Milly's wishes and not worn his white nightshirt, they suspected he was not impressed by this aggressive one-armed man's long pigtail and unruly beard.

"I'm Eddy's brother and this here's his missus, Jenny Priestley," snapped Thomas.

"I'm worried about Eddy, sir. I've not seen him since yesterday morn when he left for work. Does he get fed? I've got some bread and cheese for him in this bag."

The inspector took the bag from her.

"I'll see he gets this, Mrs Priestley. But we do provide our prisoners with basic rations. I'm sure he'll enjoy this here extra grub when he knows you brought it yourself."

"Hang on there, constable. Are you not going to let us in to see him? Jenny's got every right to see her husband. Specially when thee's got it all wrong and he's innocent," yelled Thomas.

"Inspector."

"What?"

"I'm not a constable. I'm an inspector and I'll thank thee to get it right – as well as not coming in here making demands, Mr Priestley."

"That's as maybe, but –"

"Now then," he addressed Jenny directly, ignoring Thomas. "I haven't finished my interrogation of your husband, and investigating further about this robbery. So, I'll have to insist that both of thee leaves me to carry on with my police work."

"Thou can insist all thee likes – Inspector! I ain't budging until I've seen me brother and Jenny sees her husband. It's only right and proper… and that's that!"

Inspector Button's teeth were as tightly clenched as could be without breaking them to bits. His lower lip had been joined by its upper partner and as he advanced towards them he seemed to grow larger and fill the room.

"Until I see fit to let a prisoner's visitors in to see him then that, as you put it so well Mr Priestley, is that! If you do not want me to arrest you for impeding an officer of the law in his duty, I suggest thee keeps quiet."

Button's eyes were piercing directly into Tommy's and Jenny took hold of his good right hand to say, "Tommy, my dear, I know thee means well but please do as the inspector says. Maybe, wait outside with Jack while I have a quick word, eh?"

"Mrs Priestley, it is obvious to me that you are a sensible and respectable woman. So, if Thomas here takes thy advice and waits outside, then I might grant thee a few minutes with your husband. Though, I must be in earshot and sight of thee both. Do you understand?"

"Of course, Inspector."

A most subdued Thomas sighed, tutted as he walked to the door, and said, "I'll be just on pavement near to the door then. Jack won't mind waiting down the road at farriers."

As soon as the door to the tiny police station on Hawthorn Lane was closed Jenny thanked the inspector, adding, "I hope thee can find it in thysel to understand, sir. Tommy and I know that this must be a mistake. Eddy is not the kind of man to steal from anyone. He's as generous as they come, god-fearing and kindness itself to anyone less fortunate than hissel."

Meanwhile, outside, waiting in the rain, Thomas brooded on his unfortunate day, starting with his trip to Quarry Bank mill. He had intended questioning all of Eddy's work partners about the events that had lead up to the robbery. He met a few but not all by any means. Most of them either said little, expressing ignorance, or refused to comment at all, which excited his curiosity, and even his suspicions, further. This led to heated arguments at various points around the mill site and therefore attracted the attention of the mill manager and Mr Greg. Robert recalled that when his father had been in charge he had dismissed Thomas for some misdemeanour from the past and so asked him to leave immediately. The unhappy memory stung Tommy's feelings and he had finally stormed off, suspicions still intact, claiming he would be back with his lawyer. Jack had suffered his father's ranting all the way back to Stockport but tried to calm him down with an offer to drive him and Jenny to Wilmslow later.

Jenny's tears and more deferential attitude towards the police inspector had resulted in her sitting in Eddy's cell for almost fifteen minutes. They held hands and after much hugging and a few light kisses, when Jenny held back her tears with difficulty, she heard his side of things when he was in the mill manager's office alone. Inspector Button remained nearby quietly making notes in his brand new logbook.

"Well, my dear, thee can understand that when I didn't find the doctor in Mr Howlett's rooms or anywhere else around the mill, then that's when I grabbed an empty sack and began stuffing it with raw cotton from the bails everywhere. See, there's usually plenty about the yard awaiting treatment in the scotching shop. All I could recall in me head was little Hazel - screaming and screaming about 'Blood everywhere! Blood everywhere!'... I knew we needed it to mop it all up, see. It's happened afore, see."

"Where did thee leave the sack, Eddy? Inspector Button said to ask thee about that."

"I dunno know, Jenny. Everybody were rushing about panicking and shouting. I could've left it in the loom room Ah reckon, but I can't be sure."

Button's deep voice suddenly broke in. "What about your pockets, Eddy?"

The couple started with surprise and Eddy said, "What about them?"

"Did you stuff them full as well?"

"Not with raw cotton! I wouldn't do such a thing cus it causes terrible itching and raw patches on the skin. That'd be daft!"

His care-worn wife recognised the signs of Eddy's temper flaring and placed a calming hand on his knee. The flush on her plump cheeks and the moisture in her eyes had already softened the heart of his interrogator, so she quickly interrupted the two men.

"The raw cotton's full of sharp bits of seed and twisted fragments, ye see, Inspector Button. I remember it well from when I was a mule minder as a kiddy, piecing broken yarn and suchlike."

"So you were a mill worker, Mrs Priestley?"

"Aye, that's how we met – few years back now." She smiled at Eddy and patted his stubbly chin. "But I stopped when we had our own children. Cotton flue we calls it and it can be terrible if thee wipes it in your eyes without thinking like." Jenny smiled wryly at Button.

"Aye, and workers are breathing in that fluff and flue every day. Clogs yer breathing pipes up terrible. So I won't have my kids in a mill if I can help it," added Eddy, a little calmer now.

"A couple of your pals at the mill said you wanted to send your children to school, Eddy."

The prisoner frowned but nodded as an answer.

"Could be expensive that, specially nowadays," said Button, now with his own friendly, but askew, smile. Eddy was not fooled and neither was Jenny.

"Which of Eddy's workmates was that then? Were they the same ones as said they saw him with a bag of money?"

"Oh, I'm sorry, missus. I forget. But I'll get their names later when I go back. Thee must understand that I ain't obliged to disclose details of my investigation until we're afore the magistrate."

"Not even to his wife, Inspector?"

The inspector shook his head and tried to smile at Jenny but it still came out a little crooked, competing with his clenched teeth. The couple glanced at each other with a look that said more to them than it did to Button, but it was committed to his memory, nevertheless.

Chapter 9
Cause for Concern

"**PLEASE** don't think that I am interfering in your family's affairs, Catherine, but I would have nothing whatsoever to do with Mr John Wroe. I refuse to call him a preacher and certainly not a prophet."

James appeared to be so sincere that Cathy could only respond with, "Go on, please, James. I need to hear this. Why do you think these things?"

The pair of teachers had finally handed in their completed syllabus for 'Scripture' to Mr Macdonald and it had gone well with many positive responses from the headteacher. They had agreed a few days prior to this that James' explanation about his prejudice against John Wroe would need more time than was available that afternoon when Cathy was about to hurry for the coach to take her home. The following few days had been full of end of term lessons and special arrangements for the pupils leaving. School had closed a little earlier which meant that later the same day Cathy and James could take a stroll together around Abbotsfield Park, the beautiful green parkland which adjoined the Flixton boarding school. The recent busy days at school and her father's constant rants about Uncle Eddy's arrest had left Cathy even more tired and emotional. She was fearful of what James might say about Preacher Wroe and felt deeply disloyal to her father because of his growing commitment to the Christian Israelite Church.

They sat together on the felled trunk of a large elm tree. It irked her that James had instantly placed a large, clean, white handkerchief on the bark so that she might sit there without marking her skirt. She resisted protesting as she knew it would have been churlish and she tried to deny herself the small pleasure of feeling flattered by his attention. Undeniably, there was a brief ripple of gladness inside Miss Catherine Priestley on such a sunny afternoon. James had made nothing of it at all, saying not a word. He was equally eager to explain about Wroe.

"You see, Catherine, I was born and brought up in Bradford where John Wroe began some of his shenanigans. He took up the cause of a woman called Joanna Southcott."

"Oh, I see – well, not really. Where does she live now?"

"She died some years ago; the year before Waterloo. She thought she was about to give birth to the new Messiah, called the Shiloh. By coincidence it was around this time when I was born."

He paused then added, "Though of course I make no claim to have been born the Saviour of the World." Smiling at what he considered to be his little joke, James could see that there was no trace of a smile on Cathy's mouth. She considered his remark most sacrilegious but, at the same time, she was mentally working out James' approximate age. Then she coldly said, "Carry on, James."

"Yes, of course. I digress. Please accept my apologies, particularly if thou found my remark offensive."

Cathy could see in his face and eyes a plea for her forgiveness. James had felt his heart plummet into his boots.

What was I thinking? You idiot James Longton! Just when things have been going along so well. She is even using my first name at last!

"James, please, carry on. You were saying about that woman giving birth to Jesus, the Messiah."

"Joanna Southcott was about sixty four, or maybe sixty five, at the time she claimed to be with child, and ..."

96

"James! Excuse me but did thee say the woman was well past the age when most women go through the change – the menopause to be exact?"

"If you say so, Catherine, but while I realise this is all a little indelicate, I will continue the tale; her wishes at the time were to keep her body warm after her death. I presume in case the babe was still alive inside her body, and still yet to be saved; still yet to become our Redeemer."

Cathy's jaw dropped in disbelief. She was not sure how to react, but said, "Mr Longton, are thou sure that you have the story right? It is a most fanciful tale to be sure."

"Yes, indeed. There is more, just as incredible. I learned much of this from my parents as I grew older. It was well after the time that they too became would-be followers of John Wroe – and lost much of their assets through it." James looked up. "Catherine, if you look towards those dark clouds coming across, I think we may be about to have a shower. Shall we head back to the school and I continue the tale as we walk?"

"No, James, I wish to hear more now, while we are still alone," she replied while adjusting her bonnet slightly against the small breeze that had sprung up.

"Certainly… Well, Joanna Southcott and a man, known as Richard Brothers, became very well known around the end of the last century through their writings, pamphlets, proclamations and books about the lost tribes of Israel. Their supporters included many clergymen from the Church of England. In his younger days Brothers was a Royal Navy man who lived in London, but he spent many of his later years in a lunatic asylum. Both of these people claimed to have had visions and messages from God."

He turned to look at Cathy who was speechless and staring down at her clasped hands in her lap. A confused frown remained across her forehead.

"Joanna Southcott was from Devon originally and had very many followers, known as the Southcottians. Her many prophecies were sealed in a famous box by some of the same clergymen who had followed Richard Brothers. It was intended that 144,000 writings from her believers would also be sealed. Later there were three public examinations of her prophecies; in the first few years of this century in fact, but she continued to publish many books of them in her lifetime."

Spots of rain began to darken their clothing, and were unnoticed by Cathy until James suddenly took hold of her hand and said, "Catherine, let us hurry to the bandstand for shelter before we get soaked by this shower."

"What! Oh, yes, of course, James. Let's run."

The bandstand was about a hundred yards away and they joined a very military looking gentleman, sporting an impressive grey handle-bar moustache. He smiled, tipped his hat to Catherine on their arrival, and then looked up to the equally grey sky. James wished to keep Cathy's hand in his but he let go as they each gently patted some of the raindrops from their clothing. To her surprise Cathy felt a little disappointed when they no longer held hands, then her burning questions returned to mind.

"Was there a child born alive?" she whispered. "And why 144,000 sealed writings, James? What is the significance of this particular number?"

"I daresay we'll be seeing a rainbow very soon," boomed the military man suddenly. He nodded towards the southwest. "Bit of the old sun trying to break through those clouds on the horizon."

"Oh, yes, I daresay you're correct, sir," answered James looking in the same direction.

"Righto, must go soon. Coach to catch, then one of these new-fangled steam trains over that Stockport brick-built bridge structure they've just constructed. Have ye seen it?"

"Erm, no, sir. I'm afraid I haven't but I've heard it's quite striking," said James, smiling, glancing sideways at Cathy.

"Me neither, but my friends called it a magnificent… what was it now?"

"Viaduct? I've read of Stockport's viaduct; I think it's to link Manchester, Birmingham and London through the railway line," said James.

"Yes, that's it – a viaduct! Capital! A magnificent viaduct; a magnificent feat of engineering, apparently. Might invest a little of the old savings in all these railway goings-on, eh!"

"I hope you enjoy your trip on the steam train," ventured Cathy.

"What? Oh, yes; quite. Must go, now the rain's stopped. Look there. What'd I tell you – lovely rainbow."

He touched the brim of his hat again to Catherine, and pointed to the rainbow. "Nice to meet you, Madam. Clever fellow this," he said, holding out his hand to James. They shook hands and James replied, "Thank you, sir. But I must assure you if I may, I'm no cleverer than my companion, Miss Priestley, here."

"What! Oh, yes, quite!" The man briefly waved a leather gloved hand and marched away.

"If he'd glanced at my hand he would have seen that I'm not married," said Cathy, trying to feel affronted.

"I've no doubt it will happen one day."

"What about the answer to my questions," said Cathy eager to change the subject.

"Oh, yes of course. There was no evidence of a pregnancy after a post mortem. And the number refers to the lost Israelites in Revelations, chapter seven."

"And these were the tribes of Judah, Reuben, Gad and so on, were they not?"

"Yes, the twelve chosen tribes, each with a population of twelve thousand. Chosen, so that they wouldn't suffer from thirst, hunger, storm and fire, et cetera, at the coming of the Apocalypse, the End of the World, or words to that effect."

"But James, what does all this have to do with John Wroe? I think I understand that he seeks the ten lost tribes."

"Well, the Southcottians became known as the Society of Christian Israelites and their proclamations and prophecies became more and more popular in areas of poor employment, poverty or low wages. In particular in the north of England, in villages and hamlets spread throughout Yorkshire, where the promise of a better life for believers would have been popular."

"And in Bradford I suppose?"

"Exactly, Catherine; John Wroe challenged to become the leader of the Southcottians around this time. Of course I knew nothing of it as I was only about six or seven at the time. But my parents knew of him when we lived in Idle Thorpe, north of Bradford. They were suffering like so many at that time from the mechanisation of spinning and weaving wool. It was when cottagers in the woollen trade felt it most harshly, when the popularity of cotton cloth grew so fast."

"Your parents?"

"Aye…" James paused. She could see both anger and sorrow in his eyes. "My father's hand loom stood silent for many days as I grew up. That I do remember. We relied on carding and spinning for a while. Father was persuaded to sell it all, loom, spinning wheel and carding brushes, in order to move to Ashton-under-Lyne when I was about twelve years old... As I recall he virtually gave it away."

"What persuaded him to move all that way, James?"

100

"It was John Wroe and his new temple in Ashton. He promised dozens and dozens of families a new life, as the chosen ones, to follow him there. There would be work and new homes for his followers; believers like my parents."

James leaned against one of the supporting pillars for the bandstand roof and stared at the fading rainbow.

"I suppose my father was like so many of us, always hoping to find the pot of gold at the end of the rainbow. I think he regretted the move from Yorkshire for the rest of his life... I recall his stories about the 'good times', as he named them. When the wool markets of Leeds and Halifax were booming and hundreds and hundreds of woollen and worsted cloths were sold every week in Bradford."

"What went wrong, James? How did you become a teacher if things were so bad?"

Ignoring Catherine's question he had more to say about his parents and John Wroe. "My mother told me that at first they both worked in a big Wellington Street loom shop, in Ashton-under-Lyne. It has three floors of hand weaving looms. We lived with friends, trying to make ends meet, and waiting for the promised homes." James broke off speaking, turned his face from Cathy, unable to prevent his emotions for a few seconds. He wiped his eyes on the back of his hand and continued:

"Mother said that all three of her children became ill, factory fever of some sort, and she had to stay home. A child of the other family died and they asked us to move out, suspecting the disease had come from the loom shop... Oh, Wroe was correct about the work in Ashton. The cotton trade was expanding apace. People were using the same skills for making cotton cloth as they'd done to turn sheep fleece into worsted. Only now it was fustian cloth from raw cotton. I was sent to work there as a can-tenter for all three floors. I hated it, but wanted to help."

Cathy reached out a sympathetic hand to James' shoulder. "And you were ill and only twelve?" It seemed to awake him briefly from his angry musings.

"Probably... No, I think it was the putters-out transferring their business from cottagers to the bigger mills that caused most of the problems. Plus, of course, we had nowhere to live. The homes Wroe had promised did not exist. The money Father and very many others had donated to Wroe's cause, was spent building his so called Sanctuary, a place that I would call a palace!"

"I've seen it from the outside. My father claimed it is very splendiferous inside."

"Hm, and now I hear more was spent on it than Ashton-under-Lyne's own town hall... But, nevertheless it is not the main reason that I'm surprised he has the nerve to return to the town."

"He left Ashton at some time in the past then, James? It must have been before the walls around the town were completed and now he's back to see it finished. Don't you think so?"

"I have no knowledge of the reason for his return, Catherine. I only know that the reason he left was because of a scandal. I also heard of rioters in Bradford who ripped out handfuls of Wroe's beard, and I was told that one of his most ardent supporters, one William Lees, hearing of John Wroe's fall from grace shaved off his beard and left the Christian Israelite Church."

"How terrible; and all because of the outrageous spending on his Sanctuary."

James was now in full flow and he was marching about, round and around the raised base of the bandstand, emotional, ranting to all and sundry who, thankfully for Cathy's embarrassed sake, were absent that afternoon.

"There was that of course. Can you imagine how my father and many others felt on arriving in Ashton-under-Lyne to find that his new church, within the walled town, was never intended for the poor and needy. Only the rich and well-off in the local community were welcomed into the congregation. The gatehouses had marvellous residences that were the homes of the high priests and others of the Society of the Christian Israelites. Mrs Wroe lived in great style in the area around the Shepley gatehouse known, can you believe, as the New Jerusalem."

"I see. It was meant just for the rich. What a disappointment for your parents."

"Oh, no, that wasn't it. It wasn't losing his money which caused my father's early death, and that caused great sorrow to both my parents. It was when this so-called 'prophet' returned from one of his missionary tours, with his seven virgins, maidens who were needed to attend to his administration and so-called housekeeping requirements..." He stopped stomping about, paused in his rant, to turn to Cathy to be sure, sure she was listening.

"When he returned to Ashton after several weeks away one of the girls was expecting a child. Although, I have since been told by an acquaintance we knew in Ashton, about another girl also claimed to have been pregnant by the man. "

"Oh, now I see. What a scandal it must have been."

"It was claimed that this child was yet again to be the Shiloh, the new Messiah. Many of his followers immediately left the 'fold', he faced charges of immoral behaviour, and my father made us move once more. To Salford this time where he was promised work in a loom shop, again with three floors of hand weaving looms. He had to work much harder after that as we had little to fall back on."

"Do you come from a large family, James?"

"Two brothers and two sisters, but there's only three of us left now. When we lost my sister, Agnes, Father became even more disillusioned, miserable and never prayed again. Mother struggled with her health after he died. They each sort of faded..."

"And James, tell me, what of your poor mother, in all of this sadness?"

"Catherine," his normally calm and measured voice had developed a tremble, "may we return to the school? I can speak further about my family along the way? I feel the need for a little refreshment."

Catherine agreed and so they strolled back. She learned about James' aspirations to become a teacher, of his younger brother joining the navy, and about his sickly mother who lived with James and his older sister in nearby Urmston. Along the way Cathy found that it felt natural to link her arm in his. He turned to her and suddenly it occurred to James that this slightly built, pretty young woman, with her generous warm nature and sympathetic eyes, was supporting him. This was not meant; it was a reverse of what he had intended. He was now in such a nervous state he needed some comfort from somewhere, from someone. Catherine somehow understood this and his most earnest wish was that she would be there, beside him, forever, one day soon. As the pair passed through the school gates they unlinked arms and the warmest of smiles replaced the tie.

Cathy was pleased to hear that James' father had been a keen proponent for education like her own father. Money had been put aside for the schooling of James and his brother, but during their hard times this had been virtually used up to find rent and buy food. When it became possible to apply for a scholarship at Mr Macdougal's school his younger brother had declined the chance. He intended to join the navy and insisted that James had more brains than he. James was a year older than the usual entrants but Mr Macdougal took a liking to the lad of thirteen and he passed the examination. When he eventually graduated, James was also asked to stay on as a teacher and became highly thought of by pupils and most of the staff.

Catherine and James felt a new closeness after their special day in Abbotsfield Park. He promised to accompany Cathy when she told Thomas about John Wroe if she still had her misgivings about how her father would react. She invited him to her home in Stockport feeling assured that Milly, her mother, would agree when she had explained. However, Cathy was also worried about James' emotional state during the second telling of his story, despite his promise to remain calm this time.

"Please don't be offended, James, if I approach Pa on my own first of all. You can enlarge on things later. We have always been close and I will prepare my mother beforehand. Between us I am certain we may keep him as sweet as he usually is. That is, if Jack stays with you, maybe in the shop, and you could ask him about the new percolating coffee pot, or maybe the sewing machine that Pa has taken in stock. Jack is fascinated as you know with machines. It will help because I fear he may scoff about Pa's mistaken conversion to Preacher Wroe's church and ruin the atmosphere."

"No it's not going to be a problem, and if I ask him all about the new Stockport viaduct as well we could be chatting for hours. You said he was very interested in steam trains and railways and I know a little about them."

"Oh, James, that would be perfect. Jack can find no-one at home to discuss engineering and trains with. Thou will be his friend for life if he can tell thee all he knows about them."

The presence of Jack had been bothering her but now she felt much more settled in her mind.

"And what about thee, Miss Priestley? Will you be my friend for life?"

"Please call me Catherine, James. You are the only one who does and it gives me pleasure. I will be indebted to thee of course. How can I repay thee? I have long worried about this meeting with my pa, but with thee next door occupying Jack's attention, and ready to step in and back up my tale... Well, I am so happy."

"I have thought of a simple payment which can quickly settle the debt thou spoke of, Catherine."

Her eyes narrowed. "Oh, yes, and what might that be?"

"A simple kiss from thee is all I ask, my dear."

Cathy smiled and reached up to pat his cheek.

"It will be well worth it, James."

"We could start right now, Catherine. We could practice, so to speak." He puckered up his lips, hope in his eyes.

She brought his face down to hers with a gentle hand on each cheek and gave him a peck on his left cheek.

"There, James, I think we may manage the rest when you visit us in Stockport."

As she modestly turned away a little Cathy Priestley felt her pulse racing. Was this emotion and this sudden feeling of pride in her heart all because of James? Could it be she would be proud to see James again in the home where she grew up, and where she could introduce this fine man to her parents? Her recent words to Sally echoed briefly around her head.

***

Cathy's next problem was how to explain to Sally about John Wroe's immoral behaviour, his infidelity and his swindling of his followers. She felt very guilty about encouraging her closest of friends to visit Ashton-under-Lyne with her and Thomas in order to restore Sally's lost faith. Remembering their enthusiasm about his sermons and his prophecies, and then how Sally had been so generous with her comments to her father it began to feel like another betrayal; a betrayal of her friend's trust. The dread Cathy felt inside was as intense as the upset she had about her father's potential loss of his new found faith.

106

She resolved inside never to tell anyone anything about God, religion, or faith again. Then she remembered that it was her job to teach the subject of Bible Studies as a teacher.

There was nothing for it but to invite Sally to stay with them soon and speak face to face. Cathy had considered writing about Wroe in a letter but this had felt cowardly. She was forming the words in her head, sat at their writing bureau the next day, when she had news in the post, about Sally's forthcoming wedding to Sebastian. Cathy read it twice more. Sally wanted her to be first bridesmaid during the wedding ceremony. A thrill of excitement shot through her body.

"This is wonderful news! Ma and Pa will be so pleased," she exclaimed aloud. For Cathy it also felt like a lifeboat saving her from drowning in her sea of consternation about speaking to Sally of Preacher Wroe. Now there was no need! Her thoughts raced on ahead: *Thank goodness. With talk of plans about flowers, feasts, bridesmaids and wedding vows – no doubt a hundred other things – we may forget this charlatan, John Wroe forever. Oh, how I do hope so. I will pray to God with thankfulness this very night.*

Cathy kissed the letter in her hand, and was reading it yet one more time when Rachel came into the parlour. She looked around and asked, "Who were you talking to, Cath? I heard thee speak as I came in."

"It's good news, Rachel. Sally and her sweetheart are to be married – soon! I must tell Ma and Pa."

She ran to the shop clutching the letter leaving Rachel's unanswered question hanging in the air.

"Oh! And am I to have a new dress?"

Chapter 10
Just a Farm Girl

SEBASTIAN Brewer was about to have some problems of his own. His father, Jonas, was not pleased that his son wished to marry Sally Sefton. Luke had mentioned it to him the morning after Sebastian had made an announcement in the Three Tuns and they had toasted Sally's health. It was one of many toasts proposed during the evening with their many friends.

"What does he want to marry a simple farm girl for? What do you know of her, Luke?"

"It is beyond me, Father."

"I know he is now of an age to make his own decisions about such things but surely she has nothing to offer. There most certainly will not be a dowry. I think we may be certain of that."

"She is a very pretty girl, Father. You may remember her from the two funerals her family had to bear in recent years."

"I see, so we have done some business with her family then? But he has never brought her home to meet us I think."

"I think Seb intends to put that right very soon. Mother will be pleased, no doubt?"

"What! Of course not, Luke. She is just a farm girl after all... Is it a large farm?"

Luke shrugged his shoulders; Jonas tutted loudly.

"I see, so apart from her prettiness, thou knows nothing about her either. Go and get him will you? I will speak to him now."

When Luke returned with Sebastian ten minutes later their gaunt-looking father was standing at the fireplace, grim, his beetling grey eyebrows almost meeting in the centre. Their pale, and rather dumpy, mother was sitting, dabbing her tearful eyes with an embroidered silk handkerchief. She was obviously flustered and fidgeted with her matching silk cap, about to speak but silenced with a look from Jonas. Sebastian took in the situation with one glance and wasted no time with explanations but came out with a firm statement immediately.

"Father, I am not concerned about a dowry, but I ask you to recall there is her share in the farm. When we are wed I will become a part owner of Seftons Farm!"

"And this share is worth what – a £100?"

"More than double that, Father. Probably around £250 in fact; I overheard some of their discussions some time ago when they were talking about the unfortunate loss of the eldest brother, Gabriel."

This sum was almost a year's salary to Sebastian and equal to the amount of cash that he'd been asked to invest in the new Leek-Stockport railway line.

"I presume this was one of the funerals we handled, Sebastian?"

Determined not to be put on the defence Sebastian replied, "Father, you know full well it was. Although thee did not express it as such, you wanted to see whether I could persuade the family to afford one of the new iron safe-guards for the grave. It was your test of my persuasive abilities."

In the slight pause of this outburst Jonas shook his head and looked furious but before he could speak Sebastian continued, "Yes, it was, Father! Please do not deny it; and when I succeeded - thou said nothing. Not a word! No words of encouragement in my direction – at all – ever! Never can I recall praise from your lips."

"Sebastian! Please do not speak to your father in such a tone. You must show him more respect," said Martha.

His mother was shocked into her desperate plea. His father just glowered at him. Luke felt it was for him to speak, in defence of his father, but also for his brother. He had long understood Sebastian's position and loved him dearly. Afraid a family rift was imminent he said, "Seb, thee is being too harsh. Father is always so busy with the books and he would -"

"Martha, Luke, please do not interfere. Sebastian has something to say, which he obviously feels is important and which I am anxious to hear... You were saying?" Jonas turned to his son and the cold look he gave him could have frozen a funeral pyre.

"There is nothing more to say, Father. I am going to marry Sally in six weeks' time regardless of your opinion about her being just a farm girl. As far as I am concerned she is a clever, beautiful young woman with a share in a successful farm, and I will be pleased to learn from her about farming."

"Oh, there is no doubt in my mind that you are hoping to gain from this marriage in some way. If I'm not mistaken it is in the financial area, and I see no problem with such a plan."

Sebastian exhaled loudly and glanced towards his mother, shaking his head. Martha attempted a smile.

"When are we to meet your intended, Sebastian? Sally Sefton is her name I believe? I should dearly like -"

"Martha! If, thou would allow me to continue!"

"But of course, Jonas. Yes, yes, of course, I'm sorry if -"

Her husband sniffed, ignoring her attempt to apologise, and addressed his younger son again.

"I will give you this piece of advice, Sebastian. Take it or leave it; it matters little to me now. With all this nonsense we hear of, about egalitarianism between rich and poor, business man and worker, men and women, and so on and so forth... Then be very careful that thee retains the upper hand in the decisions made during your marriage. Women are not made to take such things as business decisions and monetary matters, other than housekeeping, into their hands. They are made from a quite different mould to men. Where they are of an undoubtedly superior ability is in the family; while they are bearing children and caring for them, bringing them up."

Sebastian's crooked smile at this remark was a brief portent for his feelings. "Now there I am inclined to agree with thee, Father. It's a great pity that thou has never given me the opportunity to display my talents in the business, in the world of finance and investment. But no matter, I am certain opportunities will come my way in the future. And then... Well, we will see what fortune may bring, hey?"

His father swallowed this retort without any change in his facial expression. As he left the room, however, he made a cruelly sharp comment, "I must thank thee, my son, for assisting me in a decision I was about to make regarding thee and Luke. As thee is about to become an independent business man, there is no longer any need for me to make both of my sons partners in Brewers Undertakers. All that I have to do is tell the sign makers for the new company's title to erase the letter 's' from the last two words. So now it will read: 'and Son', rather than 'and Sons'. Thank you, Sebastian."

Although he wanted to forget every one of his father's words, Sebastian could not get his mind clear of his advice about retaining control once he and Sally were married. How could he allow her refusal to 'obey' him? He had to find a way out of this new quandary. Martha and Luke watched the door of the sitting room slowly swing to after Jonas' exit, remaining silent until Luke got up from his chair and closed it to.

He turned to Sebastian and said, "That was most unfortunate, Seb. I'm sure that once he calms down Father will think again. Don't you, Mother?"

111

"Your father can be very determined at times. But, Sebastian, thou can be very like him sometimes. I hope the both of you will calm down and talk again about this." She dabbed her eyes dry, trying to smile. "When will you bring Sally Sefton here to meet us, my dear?"

Sebastian snorted. "Certainly not while he is in such a disagreeable frame of mind, Mother. But I hope to, soon, because I am sure that thou will learn to like her, and I know how disappointed you will be if we marry and thou never gets to know her."

His mother looked horrified at the thought of such a thing. She clasped her hands in prayer. "Oh, no, Sebastian, that must not happen. I love her already if she is thy intended, but I dearly wish to meet her – as any mother of sons would. The day seems to be set. Can it really be but six weeks away?"

Luke glanced at Sebastian and they both realised what was going through her mind. He tried to change the subject. "And I am to be Sebastian's best man, his groomsman, Mother. So I will appreciate any advice thee has for me on the subject." He smiled and gently held her hand.

"Mother, thou can tell Father my dear Sally is not with child, as I'm sure you both suspect. We agreed to marry some time ago and have spoken to Parson Trunchman about the arrangements. Whether Father wishes to make me a partner in the company or not will not change my mind, not now, it is too late. Tell him if you wish."

His mother forced a smile and said, "Sebastian, my darling son, please come and give your mother a kiss."

Martha reached again for her handkerchief as they parted, and she added, a touch of despair still in her voice, "I fail to understand what it is that comes between thee and thy father, Sebastian. You are so alike. What do you think, Luke?"

"I think it is at the crux of the matter, Mother. Father is always so strict and certain that he is correct in all matters of business. And you, my argumentative brother, find it impossible to accept criticism, or advice, even when you are in the wrong."

Luke held out his hand and as the brothers shook he added, "I am heartily surprised that thou has asked me to be thy groomsman. But I feel most genuinely honoured, Seb."

"Despite our differences, Luke, I have long believed that you will always know what is the right thing to do. You are my brother and I trust you."

"Oh, deary me," muttered their mother into yet another silk handkerchief. "How I wish your father were here now, to see such brotherly affection. It would soften his heart for sure."

"I doubt it, Mother," said Sebastian, shaking his head as he left the room. Luke paused to gently kiss his mother's forehead, and then he followed Sebastian.

***

Later in the evening Sebastian had been drinking heavily with his usual companions in the Three Tuns, disregarding Luke's requests to 'hold back with the spirits'. He was drinking because of the numerous regrets he felt he had in his life. Chief amongst these was the distance he felt was between himself and his father. There was the envy he had for Luke's position and future prospects within Brewers Undertakers. This jarred horribly with his brotherly love; it created hatred and anger against Luke at those times when he was at his lowest. It was then that alcohol became a kind of consolation prize, compensation for his hurt feelings. But it also acted as a buffer, making all of his feelings fade away into a blurred oblivion. He knew, deep down, every time he began a new boozing session that afterwards he would blame himself, for hating his father over making Luke the favourite son. Would he ever be free of this churning hurt?

"Seb, you must believe me when I say how many times I have pleaded with Father to not be so hard on thee."

"Save your breath, brother. I heard thee this afternoon and it will always be there. So it's best I move away from him and try a new life with Sally, in farming."

"But farming, Seb? You know nothing of it. And her family will see through your schemes very quickly. How can you think they will believe thee, when you tell them later how you wish to control their future plans? And how will you do it? With new investments elsewhere - investments in the railways! Which thou knows very little of either – be honest with me, with thyself!"

"You are forgetting one central, vital thing, Luke. My commitment to farming is only because of my love for Sally Sefton. And on this I do not need your opinion or your advice."

"Well, I am sorry, but I'm not convinced of either, Seb. Are you sure that Sally believes you want to become a farmer? Have you helped out on the farm at all? No!"

"We have talked of my investment plans, Sally and I, briefly. When we are married, then I will make the business decisions – as a gentleman farmer. Such people do exist, Luke."

"Aye, amongst the gentry that has land already... I fear for two people, the new Mr and Mrs Sebastian Brewer, who will become very unhappy when thy plans fail. Her family will prevent your gaining control over the farm if they question your commitment - which I suspect they do at present. They will see that you do not love Sally, as they probably think now, and will rush to protect her. Can you not see this? Sally Sefton is an intelligent young woman; she will never hand over the management of their farm to a silky-palmed ignoramus like thee!"

Sebastian could take no more negative advice from his brother at this point. He had been steadily drinking more ale, with more whiskey chasers, throughout their conversation and now he exploded. He jumped to his feet, pushed over the table so that everything on it fell on his brother's legs. Their friends looked across from their game of skittles in the far corner, when the crash and Sebastian's curse reached their ears.

"Damn thee, Luke! I'll thank you to speak no more about my love for Sally or our future together. Keep your advice to yourself or I'll never speak to thee again!"

Luke's first instinct was to strike Sebastian as he rose from the broken glass with bruised legs and bruised pride. But Sebastian lurched towards the door and fell in a drunken, crumpled heap, just as Alf, the landlord, and their friends ran across. Three of them lifted the struggling Seb to his feet and half-carried-half-pushed him outside.

"I'll thank thee not to drink no more, in here, with thy brother again, Luke Brewer. It's happened once too often. He's barred from the Tuns till I've had words with thy faither."

"Let me pay for any damage," pleaded Luke. "No need to speak to our father. I can settle things."

"Master Brewer, thee's tried afore to bring yon Seb down ter heel – many times. Nay, I will speak to Mr Jonas Brewer. Thy job is ter take him home and tell him he's barred from the Tuns, see! G' night to thee!"

The landlord pushed Luke outside and slammed shut the heavy wooden door with a dull thud. Luke joined the small crowd outside and they dragged the senseless, dribbling Sebastian home.

During Sebastian's terrible hangover the next day, he foggily recalled investing an amount of money with Ivor Sheppard, his 'financial man', as a down payment on the new railway line from Marple, near Stockport, to Leek and then on to Cheddleton. The ten guineas he had given Ivor was half of his month's pay. Then, with what felt like a steam piston pounding his skull, Sebastian searched through his pockets for the confirmation document he had hurriedly stuffed there when Luke had arrived to join him and his friends. Ivor and he had briefly met in a corner before the game of skittles and their later serious drinking session. Ivor had confirmed more details, in answer to Sebastian's prior questions, about a new rail connection to run north from Stockport to Ashton-under-Lyne.

"Oh, aye, my friend, work is to start on that northern section of the railway in about four months. The Marple link will touch on Romiley, see, afore it goes past a town called Hyde, then on to Ashton. I can bring thee a map of it when we meet again."

"Good man," said Sebastian, glancing behind Ivor. "I see my brother has just entered the smoke room and he must not see us together. So I must go and join the others."

"Thee wants to keep all the profits to yourself, eh?" Ivor touched one side of his hooked nose and winked a watery eye. "No matter... I'll see thee again in a couple of weeks, Mr Brewer. Don't forget the next ten guineas, sir, and I'll have the map and those documents for thee. Like I said, you're getting in at just the right time, well before the public announcements when it'll cost five, maybe ten, times your sum to invest then."

Sebastian was not listening properly to Ivor. He desperately wanted to avoid Luke's probing questions. When, weeks before, he had excitedly discussed his initial railway investment with him, Luke had spent an hour lecturing him about the wisdom of it. Sebastian had launched into a rant about their father's decision to invest, excluding him but accepting Luke into it. He had angrily stormed off, vowing inside never to ask Luke about railways again. So Luke's earnest opinions later that evening were not going to be received cordially by his very drunken sibling.

While he blearily gazed at the crumpled scrap of paper, that he'd retrieved from his tobacco smoke impregnated frock coat, there was a timid knock at his bedroom door.

"Sebastian, my dear, your father has been asking for you in the funeral parlour. He wants you to organise the cossetting work for the new man today. It's, erm, while he and Luke visit the baker's widow and the vicar about the service. I've had the maid put some breakfast aside for you, dear."

"Yes, of course, Ma. I'll be down soon. Thank you."

Rushing to get dressed, with an upset stomach and a pounding head, trying not to think of his breakfast, a sudden idea occurred to Sebastian. Last night Luke had mentioned he had no farming experience whatsoever. So, he would arrange to speak to Daniel and Wesley about correcting this within the next day or two. What better way to convince everyone, but especially Sally and his father, about his seriousness to learn more of farming? He would become a gentleman farmer despite the doubts of all his critics: his brother, his father, his cronies and even his betrothed.

Chapter 11
Jack and James meet Pud

"**THE** viaduct is an incredible example of man's advance in structural engineering, Jack. What do you know about it?"

Jack could not wait to impart some of the facts and figures he had been mulling over for many weeks."

"James, I wish to know so much more. But I've read that it has twenty seven arches – twenty seven! Can thee believe it? And it stands at over one hundred feet high – amazing!"

"Yes, I believe it is actually one hundred and eleven feet high, and the largest of its kind in the country, possibly the world," replied James.

The two men were chatting in the stockroom and at that moment Thomas opened the door leading to the shop.

"Reet, my customer has just left and your ma has asked me to step into the back parlour for a minute, Jack. So if the pair of thee doesn't mind... I hope he's not boring thee, agoing on about machines all the time, James."

"Oh, not at all, Mr Priestley. I have an active interest in such things myself," replied James.

Thomas pulled a face and said, "Oh, has thee? Right, well, I see. Thought the both of thee were getting' on like a simmering stew. Still, if Jack has to serve a customer in the shop, it might give yer ears a rest, eh!"

Jack forced an indulgent look while James laughed out loud.

"It's Tommy, by the way, James. Or Thomas if thee wants to be a mite more formal."

"Thank you, sir... erm, Tommy."

Tommy grinned and went through to the back parlour with Milly. In the parlour Cathy and her mother had been discussing how to speak of John Wroe, with Tommy. As she had anticipated Cathy's parents were very pleased to hear of Sally's forthcoming wedding and that she had been invited to visit Seftons Farm to discuss the arrangements, but particularly the dresses for the bride and her bridesmaids. When Cathy had explained to Milly, alone one day, about wishing to warn Sally about her findings of Wroe's dubious actions, her mother had no hesitation in agreeing with her daughter. Cathy had told her a little more about her last visit to see Sally, when she'd had some misgivings with regard to her Sunday school friends' gossip but had said nothing to Sally.

"We were sat in the vestry of her local church, Ma, talking about some of the meetings we'd been to in Ashton-under-Lyne. About some of the things we'd heard in Preacher Wroe's sermons."

Milly had looked surprised at this. "In the vestry, Cathy. Are you sure?"

"Oh, yes, Ma. Sally had repeated some of his sayings to Parson Trunchman, who was very pleased to meet me by the way. And he had left us there to talk together. He'd given us a list of references in the Holy Bible and his own Holy Book, so then we could check for ourselves the various beliefs of the Christian Israelites' Church."

"Parson Trunchman sounds like a very considerate and understanding man."

"Oh he is, Ma. In fact Sally's actual words to me after he'd left us to talk alone were about not being married in his church. She said that if she and Sebastian were ever to get married then it might be in Preacher Wroe's Sanctuary – in Ashton."

"I'm not sure I understand you, my dear. There was some doubt about marrying Sebastian then?"

119

"Well, I was a bit confused and so I asked her what she meant by it. Sally said she had decided in the end to marry Seb in Saint Andrew's Church, which was where we were sat talking. The parson had been so kind to her, for such a long time. And she knew her mother would prefer it, as it was where she had grown up and everything."

"Of course. But what was the purpose for the pair of you two girls sat in his vestry? It is the vicar's private room is it not?"

"Yes, and a very dark and gloomy room it was too. Dark wooden panelling around the walls and a big desk, dark oak as well I dare say." Cathy fell silent for a few seconds, thinking back to the occasion, convinced that that was when she should have mentioned her doubts about Preacher Wroe.

"So Cathy, why were you there?"

"I think we both felt a little awkward about refusing Parson Trunchman's offer to sit quietly, going through his Bible with the list he had produced for Sally. So that's what we did."

Milly smiled and said, "So you were both being kind to him, in return, in a way."

Cathy nodded and her mind went briefly back to some of the references, to which Sally had enthusiastically drawn her attention.

It's all here of course, Cathy: the beliefs of his church regarding Satan in the books of James and Ezekiel. And the resurrection of the believers of Jesus Christ's sacrifice; and his return to Earth, in Corinthians and Revelation. Listen, I'll read this out to you...

The recital went on for almost an hour in the church vestry, with Sally's vigorous enjoyment contrasting painfully with her best friend's doubtful misgivings – and her prickling conscience.

"Sally read every page out to me, while I felt awkward with not mentioning my doubts. I just stared out of the very small window – only half listening to her."

"My dear, stop fretting yourself. I think you were, and still are, correct to say nothing before the wedding. It would have been the honourable thing to invite her here, to reveal his immoral behaviour, and to speak personally, yes. But now, with her marriage to Sebastian approaching in just a few weeks, I suspect she wishes to enjoy the talk of all that with you. And with Ellie, her mother, and with her friends of course."

"And, Ma, you do not mind if I am to visit Sally again?"

"No, no, not at all. Your pa and I have agreed to send you with a few swatches of wedding dress material, for brides, and their bridesmaids. Our gift to them will be to have her gown and those of the bridesmaids made at our expense. When you write, soon, to say you can come to stay, you must let her know."

Cathy hugged her mother. "Ma, oh Ma, that is such a wonderful thing to do."

"Save one of your embraces for your pa, Cathy. Perhaps before we embark upon your story of Preacher Wroe? I will fetch him in from the shop."

"Very well, Ma. But it is more James' story than mine and do not forget, he refuses to call him 'Preacher Wroe'."

***

"James, what do you know of a new railway line to run between Leek and Stockport?"

"I think you must mean between Manchester and Crewe, Jack. That is, if you are still on the subject of the new viaduct in Stockport."

"Hm, I did wonder whether my sister had got it right. She mentioned it the other day, in connection with a line that would continue from Stockport north to Ashton-under-Lyne."

"I have not heard anything of that either, Jack. Why? Is it important?"

"I'm not sure. Her friend, Sally, had written of it in one of her letters... I think with regard to one of Sebastian's investments or something like it."

"Well, the Crewe connection will continue south to London. It avoids Leek in that way. Curious? I must find out more."

"Perhaps Cathy or Sally have got things confused with the news about the canals. The canal that runs through Cheddleton, near to their farm was only built a few years ago. It runs north to Macclesfield and that's a few miles south of Stockport."

"Perhaps, Jack, because the canal there brings coal from Norbury and Poynton, and they're only three miles from the cotton and silk mills of Stockport. And there is the recent Stockport to Ashton canal, built to join Manchester, as well as Stockport to the coal mines around Oldham and Ashton-under-Lyne. It terminates in Heaton Norris next to the main turnpike road."

"Yes, James, that's what I've learned. But I've read nothing about new railways along those routes. I've some friends employed in the Manchester-Leeds Railway Company so maybe they've heard something. I'm hoping to gain employment there as soon as I've graduated from the Institute."

James was very impressed with Jack's enthusiasm and had spoken to some of his teachers, at the Manchester Mechanics' Institute in Quay Street, before this visit. Jack was a very capable student and was expected to do well in his final examinations. He would be careful not to upset Cathy about his enquiries in case she accused him of probing into her brother's private life. He had taken to the young man and wanted to help him in his ambitions if he could.

"Of course Pa wants me to run the store now that Cath's become a teacher. I expect he'll object to me going into engineering. I was advised by one teacher to sign up for an engineering apprenticeship with a local colliery rather than work in the shop. What do you think, James?"

"An excellent idea, Jack! They can provide plenty of practical and theory experience; on steam pumps for example, just the thing for steam trains."

"Aye, and there's a couple of collieries not far from here."

"But don't be too harsh on thy father, Jack. If he and your mother have built their business up from scratch, then it will be hard on them to sell the store later if no-one in the family is to take it on... What about Rachel? Your little sister might be the one."

Rachel had been helping her older brother in the shop by fetching items from their stockroom when needed. In between customers Rachel gaily skipped about the shop humming a playground tune. Every so often this music was changed into one that allowed her to dance, while holding various pieces of dress material in front of herself. Then she swayed before a new full length mirror, intended for the use of their customers, which is what Rachel was doing when a portly young man entered the shop with his equally stout lady companion.

"Yes, sir, and what may we do for you today," said Jack, pausing from his railway conversation.

The man, who had an untidy red beard and cheeks to match, said, "Reet, it's about some of your best frock material. And my wife-to-be here'd like ter choose some."

His companion giggled and then asked, "Can I see yer latest fashions, if thee pleases?"

As she was always ready to talk about dresses and suitable material for them, Rachel rushed across to the appropriate shelves and said, "This is some of the nicest we have and it's just the same as what's in the big shops in

Manchester. And it's so lovely – come and feel how silky it is."

The couple followed Rachel and proceeded to examine a few more examples under Rachel's enthusiastic guidance. Jack was happy to leave her to it, while James was quite bemused by her confidence at such a young age. After a few more minutes the man said, "Reet then, young lady, Miss Beatrice Pelling and me will be going to the harvest festival party in Styal soon. And there's to be a dance later, so which is the best like? The most suitable as thee might say, so where's thy mother?"

"Phillip, that is Mr Podmore, wants to be sure we won't look out of place there," explained Miss Pelling. She blushed and giggled again. "You see, there's a dance later on and we've not stayed before. But this fabric, did thee call it damask?" Rachel nodded. "Well it's lovely like thee said but I'd like someone a little bit older for some more advice."

Jack took charge. "That's no problem at all, Miss Pelling. My mother or my older sister will come out to measure you up and advise how much material you will require. They have a little more experience than Rachel about current fashions so you can rely on them for good advice."

He went through to the parlour and returned with Milly, who took over for a few minutes and arranged for a dressmaker. The couple paid for the whole order there and then with the man announcing, "See we went to another shop but they had nothing of suitable quality. But I want the best for My Beatrice, and I'm prepared to pay for it. They recommended your shop, tha knowst."

Then they left, with the lady still giggling over her choice and the expense. James was very impressed and said so.

Weeks earlier Milly had been very pleased when she'd ordered the mirror and Tommy had later been forced to admit to her, very ruefully, "Perhaps a mirror wasn't such a waste of money after all, my darling."

So many ladies had found it useful, in making a decision in the shop, rather than going away to think things over later, that Milly could not resist saying, "Of course, Tommy. Have I not been saying for months that this was just what women want? Since holding material in front of a body is not as helpful as trying on a finished garment in front of a mirror."

At the time Thomas had smiled but said nothing.

"I'm sure we could start keeping a range of hats in stock as well, both ladies' and men's. A mirror is just the thing for that isn't it? And Stockport is the very place for their manufacture and supply of course."

Thomas continued smiling, perhaps not quite so broadly and muttered, "Maybe."

"So, Tommy my dear, what of my other idea? A dressing room, with drapes across the entrance, might be the next thing to add?"

"I'm not sure, Milly. Women undressing! And in the shop? Allowing such immodesty in our store could be harmful to our reputation."

"There is space in the stockroom, Tommy, and a new doorway through to it in the far corner of the shop, away from the counter, is all that's needed."

"Hm, we'll see. Leave it to me for now, my dear."

A retort had occurred to Milly about the possible damage caused to their store's reputation by the proprietor wearing his nightshirt, while sporting a bushy beard and a long pigtail. But Milly's natural diplomacy prevailed in light of their recent arguments. Things were a little calmer in their household and she was not about to cause upset. *Slowly, slowly, catchy monkey,* she had thought. Maybe things would change for the better once Catherine and James had spoken to Tommy. Tommy's wife was so very grateful for the occasion of James' visit and full of both hope and apprehension.

125

When Rachel was out of earshot Jack had laughed at James' ideas of his little sister being in charge. He'd replied, "Rachel! My silly, muddle-headed sister. She's obsessed with dresses and hats and ribbons – but business, figures and accounts? I doubt she'll ever take such a thing on as a business, James."

"Well, whatever will be, will be... I suppose –"

At this point Cathy came into the shop and asked Jack to stay behind the counter while she took James away to chat with Thomas. Feeling a little like a lamb taken to the slaughter he took in a deep breath as he entered the room, accepting the small glass of honey coloured liquid from Milly. Cathy had told James about her father's new ban of alcohol from their home and he attempted a tactful sniff as he raised the glass to his lips.

"It's ginger beer," whispered Cathy.

He sat down at the fireplace facing Thomas who grinned at him and nodded.

"Hey up, James, our Cathy has been telling me some of the tales about Preacher Wroe. What she said has upset me, I don't mind admitting... If, it's true." Tommy sent a piercing look at James. "She says that thee knows a lot more about it. But I won't have somebody defamed in my house by rumours and suppose so's, tha knowst."

"Of course not, Mr... Tommy. What I can tell you is based upon my own experience – and that of my poor parents."

James cleared his throat and began the tale that he had told Cathy a few days earlier.

***

"You see, Catherine, I knew all along that you and your ma were up to summat when thee invited James to tea. So's Jack could have a chat with him about railways – indeed!"

126

"What do you mean, Pa?" Cathy was not sure if Thomas was annoyed with her or if he just wanted to talk seriously about the afternoon's events. It was so very rare that her father called her by her full name. He tutted loudly and the pony's ears twitched back and forth.

"Hey up, Pollen! It's owreet, girl... Walk on! Me favourite pudding an all! And here was I thinking it was about you and James. Tut!"

After supper Tommy had driven James to the town centre for him to catch a hackney cab back to his home in Urmston. He had sat tactfully and patiently waiting several yards away, while Cathy and James had said their goodbyes. On their short journey back to Gibson's Store he was trying to find out a little more, while enjoying one of his favourite pursuits – merciless joking with his eldest child, who he loved more than his own life.

"Huh! Pa, I told you before it was about Preacher Wroe and so James could confirm what I'd heard from my friends at church."

"Right, so thee's not sweet on him then?"

"What! No! James has become a good friend at school. A helpful colleague; we have worked together on a new scheme of lessons for Mr Macdougal."

Glancing to his left, her father smiled at the bright pink blush he had caused to appear on Cathy's face and throat. An earlier glance at the pair kissing as they parted told him all he needed.

"I ain't so green as I'm cabbage-looking, tha knowst, our Cathy. You say thee's not sweet on James, but he's right smitten with thee, lass. He couldn't take his eyes off thee all the time he was in the same room as thee. And I know why, it's cus you're as pretty as thy mother; and as sweet and kind and clever – just the same... I was just like it with Milly, back when I first met her in the big house, where she worked as a maid... and we rescued yer Uncle Eddy... Aye..."

127

Cathy put her arm around her father's waist as they turned into the alley where Pollen was stabled. Thomas was thinking back in time and there was a lull before they got down from the trap.

"Oh, Pa, I'm not so sure that it's the same as with you and Ma. But I do like James an awful lot; and I can tell he thinks a lot of me. And I was going to mention it all, to both you and Ma, when we were together later, without Rachel and Jack present."

They got down and Tommy paused to scratch his head with his good hand.

"See, I am a bit confused, lass, because I thought you worked with this here Mr Longton. And I knew that thee couldn't stand him with his la-di-da ways and know-all attitude."

"It is the same man, Pa. James Longton is the same man I resented when I first worked with him. But I was wrong. He is clever and knowledgeable, but kind and sensitive – and much more understanding than I originally gave him credit for."

"And thee's fond of him. I can tell. Your ma will be very keen to hear all this… Now then, I do respect what he told me about Preacher Wroe, but there's a couple of things I need to check. About who's taking over while he's away on a missionary visit and what have thee."

"Oh, and what's that about?"

"As I says, I ain't rightly sure, but I know that there's a couple of councillors in Ashton what goes by the names of Lees and Stanley. And I think there's another one, name's summat like Squires or Swires. Any road, they supports Wroe with finances and such like, and I heard a rumour, which I wouldn't take no notice of at first – about one of them 'as broke away from the church of the Christian Israelites. But now… well, I'm wondering if any of it's true."

"Where is Preacher Wroe going when he's abroad, doing his so called missionary work?"

"Spain and Gibraltar and them parts, so I was told, but he's got big ideas for Australia next. The son of one of these civic councillors, goes by the name of John Stanley, has become a high priest or some such position of the Christian Israelites Church, see. Well, I think, if I've got it correct, that he will be the main leader of the church while Wroe is away."

"So what is that to us, Pa?"

"I want to know what is going on, Catherine. See how it all fits in with what James has told me. I'm not taking kindly to being tricked. And all those other folks, that might've lost money and all. It's not reet!"

"No, you're right, Pa. It's not what we expect of a religious person."

Thomas shook his head, sad for a moment. "And now we've gotter rescue Eddy again, from these false accusations. I dunno what the world's coming to, I really don't."

"Shall we go in now?"

"Oh, aye, Cathy, darling, let's cheer up thy ma with thy news about James, eh!"

Cathy held his arm tight and gave him a knowing look.

"I know, I know, lass, without thy brother and sister present – for now!"

Cathy gave Tommy a big kiss on his cheek and they proceeded in through their backdoor.

Chapter 12
Buttonholing at Quarry Bank

INSPECTOR Button was in the mill manager's office asking questions. Robert Hyde Greg and Mr Howlett did not take kindly to having the business surrounding the recent robbery made public. Robert was concerned that the article in the local papers would have a very negative effect on the company's reputation, since it had been mentioned in the article that suspicion had fallen upon one of the mill's workers. The mill manager was more concerned that the rumours that had come to his attention were about his failings as a supervisor of people, and of his lack of efficiency in the office.

"Well I can't say how the story got into the *Gazette*, Mr Greg. I have taken care and certain steps with my constables not to make the suspect's name known. But, as we know, people talk, and they gossip. Which, I have to say, brings me to the main reason for my visit today."

"Inspector Button, you have requested a free hand, pretty well, in questioning anyone and everyone who may work here, or who lives in the village where most of our workers reside. I cannot afford to stop production for this. We have contracts to complete and need to keep the looms and mules working."

"I wish to proceed with my investigation, sir, as it's now an official police matter." The inspector's lower lip and jutting chin indicated that he was not about to negotiate. "The law has been broken and I will find the culprit, no matter how much time it takes. It's very likely that the felon is to be found somewhere on this site."

"Of course, I understand that, Inspector. But you make it sound as if we employ a nest of thieves and rogues. I have already had to withdraw a sufficient amount of money for the wages of those who were still waiting to be paid after this wretched robbery. Losing money, our reputation and production is a big worry for me, at a time when competition is most fierce."

"Might I point out, Inspector, that you have arrested Eddy Priestley? Surely, the matter is closed now?"

"I'm not convinced yet of his guilt in the matter, Mr Howlett. There are still things that I need to be sure of. And I would be most grateful, sir, if thee could assist me in this, and accompany me today."

Mr Howlett blanched at this statement and he asked in a more timorous voice than was usual, "B, but, but, for what purpose? How, Inspector? I have told thee as much as I could remember about the matter. I have much business to complete today." He turned to Robert Greg, seated at his side. "I'm not sure that Mr Greg could spare me for the time it will take to go to Wilmslow and back, for however long this will take."

Inspector Button smiled – an unusual event. "I mean for you to accompany me around the mill and the village. It could help me a lot when I'm asking questions; checking the accuracy of the replies, you see."

"Oh!"

"I think that will be in order, Mr Howlett," said Robert Hyde Greg, somewhat impatiently. "The sooner we help the inspector and clear up this matter, the better. Where do you wish to commence, Inspector?"

"I understand there is a company shop in the village, Mr Greg?" Robert nodded. "That's a good place to start. Does it sell alcohol of any sort, ale, and spirits?"

"The shop is becoming more of the co-operative kind, Inspector, and will be managed by the residents of the village. Though I still do not encourage the over indulgence of alcohol on any part of the estate, including

131

Styal village. There should be nothing stronger than beer and cider in stock."

He turned to Mr Howlett, for confirmation of this, who nodded and added, "Though I cannot speak for the Ship Inn."

"I have carried out some of my investigation in the ale house before today. So a visit to that excellent hostelry will not be necessary, Mr Howlett."

"And was it productive in the progress of your investigations, Inspector Button?"

"I am not at liberty to say at this stage, Mr Greg. I would like to know whether your clerk, Charles, is still certain he didn't take a large sack with him when he followed Mr Howlett into the mill."

"No, it was just the emergency bag of bandages and salves, and such," replied Mr Howlett. "Ask him yourself if you wish, Inspector. He's just next door."

"I'll take thy word for it, for now, sir. Now, if I am to interrupt things for as little time as you wish, then perhaps I may start in the next few minutes?"

"Of course, Inspector, and Mr Howlett will show you around as you wish. If you will excuse me I have my own inspections to conduct in the weaving shed. The Plug Riot attacks last year caused some damage to the outer building as well as to a hoist. Repairs have only recently begun and the work was to be completed this morning."

The three men got to their feet, hands were shaken, and they each went their own way about the site.

**

When the Inspector had visited the Ship Inn the previous evening he had kept quiet, leaning on the bar in a shadowy corner, just observing everyone, taking an occasional sip from his glass of cider. He'd noticed a very tall young man and his much shorter, stout companion deep in conversation in another corner. The pair struck

Button as being quite conspiratorial, glancing about them every so often to see who might hear their words. When the tall man had stood and drunk up after about twenty minutes, he recognised him as Flaggy Grafton, so hid himself behind a newspaper. Grafton then left the pub while the fat man commenced to get very drunk and paid for two rounds of drinks for a large group of his fellow workers, who referred to him often as 'Pud'. They had joked with Pud about robbing the mill, which made him angry as he'd claimed that now he was on 'piecework', with a new weaving machine, he was earning 'real money' at last.

"Aye, lads, I tell thee, these new looms they've got in means I can be wed ter my sweet Beatrice afore end of year. And I'm going to treat her to a new frock for the harvest party down at Oak Farm. Thou see if I don't!"

"So long as the Gregs keep taking in new orders, Pud," said Rocky Roberts. "But 'appen business drops off and they'll lay some on us off if it suits them. I've seen it afore, tha knowst. Aye, just like that!" There was a loud snap! of his big calloused fingers at the end of his statement, before he took a long quaff of his beer.

Some of the group were not so sure about the possible truth behind their ribald claims, at Pud's expense, about the robbers of the mill's money. One of them, Stocky Smeaton, who'd had to wait a few more days for his wages, had heard rumours. The delay in being paid had caused him problems at home, where they often lived hand-to-mouth with having seven young children. There had been arguments and much impatience there, about the inconvenience of borrowing money for food. It still rankled with him and he felt inclined to speak out.

"Thy mate, Flaggy, were in a bit of a hurry, Pud. Not often we see him in here, tha knowst."

"Said he had some business to attend to or summat," said Pud.

"I still canner believe Steady Eddy had anything to do with it, though," said Stocky. "Flaggy were the one who says he saw Eddy with that big sack of money, weren't he?"

"Aye," agreed Rocky. "With his lad, Little Freddy. Hard to believe, eh?"

"It was to pay for his kids schooling... So I heard," added Pud. "But I agree... Steady Eddy, eh! Who would've thought it?"

Inspector Button committed their conversation to his memory and wrote one or two names down for his future use. Then he left the Ship, still unhappy that the small boy's earlier statement about seeing Eddy with the heavy sack would stand up in court. He had hoped to discover another witness but nothing further was said. Unfortunately, he missed a big argument which later ensued between Pud and Stocky regarding the likelihood of earning enough money to throw it around buying drinks.

"If thee ever gets enough money to support a family of kids I'll be surprised!" were his final words, but he still finished his free drink at Pud's expense before he stormed out.

***

Inspector Button and Mr Howlett were walking across a field of oats that were ready to be harvested, taking the shortcut to the shop that the mill manager had suggested. The inspector paused to watch the Oak Farm labourers.

"It's a grand time of year, harvest, don't you think, Mr Howlett? When farmers can see the rewards for all the hard work that's been done since spring."

"Yes, I suppose so. Some of the villagers get a bit of part-time work now and then, to bring in a bit extra for their family, I suppose."

"Talking of extra income, how about in the mill?"

"Oh there's a few do quite a lot of overtime when we have a few large orders to satisfy. But that's not been the case for a while. Mr Greg's thinking of laying some workers off while it's so quiet."

"Oh, is that so, Mr Howlett? I got the impression that the new machines, power looms are they called, were making a few weavers very much better off these days."

"Not at present, Inspector. Who told thee that?"

"Well, as I said, I was in the Ship last night and a young chap by the name of Pud was boasting a bit about his big earnings – buying everybody drinks. Made himself very popular of course."

"Pud Podmore! He never makes as much on piecework as his mates. Oh, he can make a big song and dance about how hard he works, but he never produces as many finished cloths as the rest of the line. Rarely does overtime, unless I twist his arm."

"Right, bit of a braggart eh?"

"Well, I wouldn't do the man down or nothing, Inspector; but he's likely to be one of them we lay off for a time. Until things pick up, of course."

"Aye, of course, Mr Howlett."

When, later, Inspector Button noted some of the answers to his questions in the company shop, in Styal village, Phillip 'Pud' Podmore's name figured there in his new logbook once again.

Mrs Taylor was behind the shop's counter when the mill manager and the inspector entered the premises, which was tucked behind the double row of Oak Cottages. She looked up, wiped the palms of both hands on her apron on seeing Mr Howlett, and said, "Good afternoon, gentlemen, if thee's come in for some tobacco we're a bit low. Mr Henshall's gone off to get some more in from Bakers in Wilmslow."

"No, it's all right, Mrs Taylor. We're here to help Inspector Button with his enquiries."

135

"That'll be Bakers in Grove Street I suspect," said Button. "I know it well. I call in once a month myself. Do you know Mr Baker, Mrs Taylor?"

"Oh, no, sir. Never been to Wilmslow mesel. No, it's Mr Henshall as runs things here, see. Same as he's off to Kirkwoods for coffee and to get more soap from… now where was it? Oh aye, from Cromptons. He always tells us where he goes, see, but I could never find them if thee was to drop me in the middle of town."

Her nervous laugh told the two men that she was feeling somewhat unnerved.

"Well now, Mrs Taylor, as I'm here to ask thee a couple of questions - easy questions, I must emphasise – I'll get on with it, eh!" The inspector grinned, trying to put her at ease, but the grimace beneath his nose had the effect of perplexing amusement. A woman customer at the counter, looking at some drapery, glanced at the men, frowned and said, "I think I'll come back later, Mary. See what that worsted's like when it comes in."

"Righto, Nellie. See thee!"

Inspector Button continued, "I hope I'm not causing you to lose custom, Mrs Taylor. And I tell thee what, I might take half a dozen rashers of that streaky bacon when I'm finished. It'd be just right for me bit of supper later on. That is, if I'm allowed, Mr Howlett, with me not being one of thy mill workers."

"Of course, that's quite in order, isn't it, Mary?"

"Happen I can cut it up for thee, while you ask away with thy questions… er, Inspector… Is it about that robbery everyone's on about?"

Mary Taylor enjoyed a good gossip but she was not about to encourage the two gentlemen to outstay their welcome.

"You see, Mary, it would help my investigation quite a lot if you knew of anyone that has been spending a lot in thy shop lately. I mean quite a lot more than usual, you see."

"Oh, right. Aye, that'd make a bit of sense… Hm, well… I suppose the Bradburys and the Bradshawes've been taking quite a lot more sugar lately. And there's a few taking a lot more bread now it's cheaper; it's instead of making their own oat cakes, like they used to do. Of course these days, there's a lot growing their own spuds in the garden. Does that count?"

"Hm, not a lot of spends amongst that range of goods," said Button. "What about special orders? You know, for furniture, or little luxuries for the home; pictures for the wall, or ornaments and knick-knacks; presents."

Mrs Taylor shook her head as she wrapped up the bacon in some tissue paper. Then she added, "It's a nice bit pork that; fresh in from the local farm."

Button took out his pocket book to pay. "So, thee doesn't take special orders for more expensive items then?"

"Oh, I'm not saying that, Inspector. But it's Mr Henshall that deals with specials, see… Come to think on it – he was willing to take an order for that bloke with the red hair and whiskers. Big feller he is. Didn't think much of our fabrics; mainly cheaper cotton and fustian we keep in, see."

Button paused in passing across his cash, his large hand hovering halfway across the counter, Mrs Taylor's tiny palm moving slowly back and forth beneath, as if it was trying to guess where the coins would fall.

"And what was the name of this special customer, Mary?"

"He wanted to see what we had in for dresses, for dancing, at parties. But we don't keep stuff like that in, see. But we order it."

"His name, Mary, was it –"

But Mary was not listening and the inspector had waved his other hand in Howlett's face to silence him.

"It was for his sweetheart, Beatrice. I remember that. Funny isn't it the way your mind can play tricks on thee? It began with a letter P, Ah'm sure on it."

Button was now thinking she expected a gift of some sort. But Mary Taylor was scrupulously honest; the reason she was trusted in the shop. He reached into his pocket book again and said, "If I paid a little more for your memory to recall his name would it help, Mary?"

Mrs Taylor took the correct payment for the bacon from his hovering hand and gave him a withering look.

"I don't expect a bribe for my honest information, Inspector whatever thy name is!"

"I'm sure the inspector was not trying to bribe you, Mrs Taylor," said Mr Howlett.

"Not at all, Mary," added Button, his grimacing smile playing about his features once more. "I wish merely to pay for your time which we have, unfortunately, used too much of."

Feelings a little mollified Mary passed his package of streaky bacon over and added, "We was going to order it from Gibson's Store in Stockport and told him that. We recommended it to the chap – a weaver, I think he said – Pud! Pud Podmore! – Aye, that's what they call him in the mill! Ah remember it now."

Chapter 13
Gentleman Farmer

THE gossiping tongues of Cheddleton were flapping and tutting in a tutti staccato of whispered twaddle. There was confusion and certainty in equal measure passing between various middle class ladies, the ones who took it upon themselves to maintain the appropriate, and acceptable, standards amongst the township. The confusion arose because most of the ladies were unable to accept that Sebastian Brewer would do such a thing. The certainty came about because the original message was uttered by the Lewin sisters; not just one sister but all three, and in different places, and on different occasions. It was fortunate that the rumour, which may have been true in fact, came from a chance encounter one morning when the misses Lewin were taking the air across the village green. Amelia and Jane were just in discussion about who should hold their parasol and Clara noticed a horseman trotting towards them.

"Why, Sisters, look. Here comes Sebastian Brewer on his chestnut mare. My, how fine he looks too."

"Well don't just stare at the man, Clara," said Amelia. "Wave to him. I'd like to know more about the forthcoming wedding to Sally Sefton. It's gone much too quiet lately."

Suddenly, all three were yoo-hooing and waving Sebastian to come across to them. He was in a fine mood having won a small sum at cards the previous evening. He slowed his mount to a walk and then joined the trio, dismounting and leading Duchess his horse by the reins.

"Good morning, ladies. What a lovely day you have chosen for your perambulation. I trust you are all well?"

"My sister, Amelia has her touch of rheumatism again," said Jane. "But she is a martyr to her -"

"Never mind all that," snapped Amelia. "I wish to know your destination, Mr Brewer. You are wearing very fine boots today and your riding jacket is of the finest cut. New, no doubt. Off to see the squire's son? I believe he's back from college."

"Not today, Miss Amelia. I'm about to take my first instruction in becoming a farmer. I'm on my way to Seftons Farm and would not tarry too long here. Charming company though I find you and your sisters, I must urge Duchess into a canter while the day is still young."

This intended compliment caused a tittering flutter of embarrassment and appreciation from Jane and Clara. Amelia was not impressed.

"Away with you then, Mr Brewer. You must save your flattery for Sally Sefton, and no doubt such sweet talk helped thee win her heart. Though I find it hard to know why thou need soil your hands with the loam of their farm."

"Simple ambition, Miss Amelia. I mean to apply my professional skills, acquired of course while assisting my father with his business, in the area of agriculture. I am not afraid of getting my hands dirty in the pursuit of my aspiration to become a successful gentleman farmer."

This boastful revelation caused all three sisters to be taken aback. The surprised look on their faces helped to explain their speechlessness. But it was no surprise that Amelia recovered her composure first.

"Well, I'm sure we wish you well in your pursuit, Mr Brewer. No doubt your family will encourage you to gain success in the future as well. I'll wish you good-day and hold you back no longer."

Sebastian thanked Amelia for her good wishes, returned her farewell and galloped off, with the good wishes of Jane and Clara echoing in the distance behind the chestnut mare's dust. The three Lewins then made haste back to their cottage, eager to write invitations to tea for their several friends and acquaintances. This was news well worth sharing at last.

Such a public declaration of his new ambition was not to settle well with Jonas Brewer, however.

***

"Good morning to thee, Mr Brewer," said Daniel Sefton as Sebastian tied the reins to a post near the barn. Before he could reply, the rider heard a bold remark from Wesley as he strode across the yard to meet with his future brother-in-law. Like his uncle, Wesley was wearing a smock and gaiters.

"Though it's near enough afternoon for us. Us having been up over four hours since!"

Daniel frowned at his nephew and said, "No need for that, Wes. I suspect Mr Brewer has got reasons for't, and the road here from town is in a right state with all the rain and mud."

"Well, I suppose I could've got here sooner, Wesley. I forgot what an early start farmers need to make. And I met the Lewin sisters on the way, for one of their little chats, as you may know."

"Don't know them," said Wesley. "Though I've heard about how they like to gossip... Shall we get started then?" He looked Sebastian up and down. "Thee's going to get them fine clothes and boots in a right state, Mr Brewer – unless you've brought summat else to wear." Wesley glanced at the chestnut mare and pulled a long face.

"No matter," replied Sebastian. "And if we are to be related soon then we must all be on first name terms. I insist you call me Sebastian."

He extended his right hand to Daniel who shook it warmly. "Welcome, Sebastian. I'm Daniel."

Wesley said, "We already know each other, eh!" But he shook hands to confirm his reluctant welcome.

"I hope you're not wearing thy wedding clobber, Sebastian," said Daniel, jokingly. He grabbed three rip-hooks then passed him a scythe and a sickle and they began walking toward the crop fields, away from the farmhouse. "Happen we can find thee a spare set of gaiters."

Without hearing this remark, Sebastian glanced back and asked, "Where's Sally?"

"She's on t'other side of the house int' parlour, with Cathy and our maither. When we got thy message about keeping thy visit quiet from Sal, we didn't rightly know what to do abart it," said Wesley. "But Cathy arrived last night with silks and fabrics, for the wedding frocks, so she's took care on it for us. They're measuring and marking and all sorts. Granny and a couple of Sal's best mates are in there and all. Reckon they'll be nattering for hours about it."

"Aye, Wesley's likely to nip back soon – just to check they're keeping Sally busy, and away from windows this side of the house," said Daniel with a wicked grin and a wink of a sparkling eye.

"Am I?" asked Wesley. "Why's that then, Uncle Dan?"

"Like I said, to check on things, Wes. Oh, and to check on Sal's friend, Emma. Make sure she's happy."

Wesley frowned, opened his mouth as if to reply, but then thought better of it. His blushes told Sebastian all. But Uncle Daniel was in a playful mood.

"Ah, thought thee was a bit sweet on young Emma, our Wesley. Hair the colour of the corn we'll be cutting and eyes like the fine blue sky over our heads, eh!"

Wesley ignored his uncle and began marching smartly on, clutching two more scythes, in the direction of their six acre field. Sebastian and Daniel smiled at each other.

"So thee wants to keep this labouring a secret from Sally then? What's that all about, Sebastian?"

"Not much, Daniel, but I suspect she doesn't think I'm serious about being a farmer when we're wed. So, if I can prove it today – maybe on a few more fine afternoons as well – then perhaps Sally will start to believe in my objective."

"Hm, I see... But there's no need is there? If you stay in the funeral business, won't thee be earning enough to keep thee both very comfortable in tha future life together?"

"I mean to leave that behind and become a serious investor in the new railways while raising my expectations in agriculture."

Daniel nodded, looked thoughtfully at the sky, saying nothing for a few dozen yards as they drew closer to the fields.

"Well, I expect you know what you're about with the railway investments. I canner say I do... but, I do know that thee can work hard all thy life in farming and still wind up with very little – except the land, if thou is lucky. Too much depends ont' weather, see. But I can help thee with it so long as you're capable of some hard physical 'toil on the soil', as me boss down under used to say."

"Down under is what they call Australia isn't it, Daniel?"

"Aye."

"You must tell me more."

"Perhaps another day, eh, Sebastian, over a couple of pints. Too much to do today, mate. Are thee sure thee doesn't want me or Wes to nip back for a smock frock and some gaiters?"

"No, I'm fine. I'll put my jacket under a tree. A bit of mud won't hurt these leather boots."

Wesley had reached the field well ahead of them and was calling back.

143

"Come on, Uncle Daniel, Sebastian! While the weather's this good we should clear a couple of acres between the three of us!"

"Aye, Wes, we're right behind thee. If you and Sebastian go round ahead of me, reaping into sheaves, I'll follow thee building up the stooks for threshing later."

***

It was a very grimy and sweaty experience reaping under a hot sun for more than three hours. The dust and perspiration tended to mix and cover everything, skin and clothing, in a film of abrasive slime. Sebastian's calf hide riding gloves protected his soft hands quite well, for the first hour, but now they were shredded and clung unpleasantly to his hands and wrists. His fingers and palms were scratched, sore and blistered, but he was determined not to complain. His back and neck ached terribly and there had been moments when the novice farmer had almost succumbed to a fit of swooning. Sitting in the dusty furrow and staring wildly at the horizon, for a minute or so, seemed to bring his senses back to him. The thought of a pint of best ale, with or without Daniel, had a great appeal for Sebastian at that moment. When a shout went up from Wesley, some fifty yards away, Sebastian looked up and wiped his brow with a sweat soaked kerchief.

"Hey up, Peter! Thee's a sight for sore eyes. I hope that's grub and a drink thee's carrying in your sack!"

"Aye, Wesley. It's a bit late, Ah know, but there was a bit on a fuss sorting out the animals for a while back. But I'm here now and there's plenty of ginger beer to slake thy thirst, tha knowst."

The three reapers gathered to eat while Peter, the hired labourer, chatted on. The three farmers had all noticed Sebastian's distressed and exhausted state, and amused but slightly concerned looks had passed between them, though nothing was said.

"Ah could hear a bit of skirring of wings in the heather and brushwood on the way across, Daniel. Reckon there might be a few grouse or mebbee pheasant there, if we was to wait in the next day or so."

"Righto, Peter," replied Daniel, his cheeks full of bread and cheese. He swallowed his drink in one go and continued, "If you're up for a bit of shooting, Sebastian, you could join us, eh?"

"Perhaps," came the dry and breathless reply from Sebastian.

"What were up with the animals, Peter?"

"Well now, Wesley, it's the fault of that blooming new goat thee's so fond of, see… Ah were just seeing to the pigs and thy goat comes up behind me and butts me in the rear end - straight into the sty! Blasted animal! Ah told thee she doesn't like me."

Wesley and Daniel burst out laughing while Sebastian found just enough energy, in his raw turnip and cheese, to smile a little.

"That ain't the end on it, though! Oh, no! Them two babby piglets got art again while I was struggling ter stand up… Course I ran after them, after I closed the gate to the sty. And would thee believe it? They ran away reet around the farmhouse, with me after them, round and around, like the merry-go-round at the fair."

Now all three reapers were laughing; knees were slapped; heads were shaken from side to side, and tears of joy ran down weary cheeks.

"Thee might well laff at us, but all the ladies were gathered at the windows laffing their socks off at us and all. Reet embarrassing it were!"

"So that was it, was it, Peter?" said Daniel.

"No, see, Sally comes out to help me catch them by running in the opposite direction, which she does. But Missus come art with one of her friends to try and get

145

Sally ter go back in again. But any road she'll have none of it, see. Says she's going to check on Boulder, while she's out by the barn."

"Did she notice Duchess, my chestnut mare?" asked Sebastian.

"Aye, Mr Brewer, she did. I'd stabled her and give her some water and a few oats, when I saw to Sally's horse see. Such a fine horse thee's got there and all; but I didn't know it were some kind of secret. Mrs Sefton told me off about that, so I'm reet sorry if I've upset things… See, Ah would not –"

"No matter, Peter," said Sebastian. "Please don't trouble yourself about it. Sally, would've found out soon, when she took a look at my hands. I've no doubt."

He held out his injured and blistered hands, palms upward.

"I could bring thee some grease and salve or summat if they're sore, Mr Brewer," said Peter.

"Not at all. You've given us all some fine entertainment in a break from our toil. Although if you were to include a flagon or two of cold beer next time, it would be very welcome I think. Don't you agree gentlemen?"

"Aye," said Wesley. "But not if our Sally has out to do with it – not since she last spoke to Tommy Priestley, Cathy's faither."

"Oh, yes. What's that all about then?" asked Sebastian.

"We all reckon he's took the pledge or summat, since he got this new preacher feller under his skin," replied Daniel.

"Well, since then she won't have nothing stronger ginger beer in the house. Trouble is, Granny and Maither agree with her, see," added Wesley.

"I see," mused Sebastian. "Well, I certainly haven't taken the pledge, and I mean to keep some wine and best port in the house when we're wed."

146

The others laughed and Wesley said, "No ale then, Seb?" He had been warming, somewhat, to his future brother-in-law but his doubts returned at Sebastian's next remark.

"Beer, cider and strong spirits, if I so choose. A man has to put his foot down sometimes, specially when entertaining friends and I hope to include the both of thee. Aye, and you too, Peter. You'll always find a welcome drink in Sebastian Brewer's house."

"Thanks for the invitation, eh, Wes." Wes nodded but it was more tactful than genuine. "I'll say good luck to thee about winning Sally round, regards that, my mate," said Daniel. "She may be but a slip of a girl in her stature, as thee might say; but she has a mighty strong opinion abart some things, including alcohol."

"And a cast iron will to go with it, and all," said Wesley.

"Nevertheless, a subject's all to be decided in the future. For now, good honest labour is needed if we're to complete two acres. You said you'd like to commence threshing the corn this week, so I'll get back to it, I think, gentlemen."

Sebastian got up, grabbed his tools and walked back to the furrow where he had been reaping. Wesley said, "By the heck, Peter, I would've paid good money to see the antics the goat and them piglets led thee."

"Aye, so would I," agreed Daniel. "And I'll give Sebastian his due he's done well all things considering. Eh, Wes?"

"Aye, I suppose so. We might be well into a third acre done, in another hour."

"Ah don't know what it's all abart," said Peter. "But yon, Mr Brewer is a game one, I must agree."

Unfortunately, for the suffering Sebastian, compliments and congratulations from his father were not awaiting him when he returned home later.

147

***

"Sebastian, what were thee thinking about? Working in the sun without a hat, for hours and hours, like that! Thy face is as red as a lobster! And your hands! Look at thy hands – cut and swollen, red and blistered. I'll fetch a bowl of fresh lavender water, and thee must soak them for twenty minutes." Sally was not happy with her fiancée.

"I hope thee doesn't get a touch of sunstroke, Sebastian," said Ellie, turning to run to the water pump in their yard. "Stay here, Sally, and roll back his shirt sleeves. Tut! What a shame, such a fine shirt. I fear it's ruined."

"Yes, I think so as well, Sally, such a shame," agreed her Granny Esther.

While Sebastian was not averse to the fussing and concern over his health, given by the female section of the Sefton family, and he had surrendered to it for the required number of minutes, it was time to say farewell to them. He waited until Sally and he were alone and insisted upon returning home before the sun was setting.

"Duchess is still uneasy on these poor rutted paths and roads in the dark, Sally, and it was my intention to steal away before now. While you and the other ladies had thy attentions focussed on wedding matters."

"Cathy is staying for another day and my other friends have been collected by Charlotte's father… Why the secrecy, Seb? How come you can visit our farm and not wish to see me?"

With his inflamed hands immersed in lavender water, it was difficult to enfold Sally to him – to kiss away the single tear on her cheek. And in that moment his selfish heart went out the beautiful, auburn-haired, farm girl who was to become his wife in a few weeks' time. Sally, in turn, discovered just how much she wanted to take care of the 'silly man' before her – whatever his reasons.

148

"Sally, my darling, can you bear to kiss me first? I will explain but I need to know you'll forgive me... Please."

He was sat at the table in the scullery and Sally had been affectionately treating his sore face, following advice from her grandmother, with cool butter from the pantry. She halted in her busy ministrations, looked down at him, and another tear fell. But this one landed on Sebastian's cheek as she bent to kiss him.

"Oh, my poor, poor Seb," she murmured with every delicate caress of her lips on his burning face. She paused to stare for a horrified moment at his cracked and peeling lips, and then she placed her own mouth over his lips with the lightest, but longest kiss of all. Their first most-loving look passed between them as Sally sat down on the chair opposite Sebastian.

"Well, Seb?" she whispered.

"I wished to surprise you, Sal. It was as simple as that. I knew, you see, you doubted me when I said that I would learn from thee about farming. So I thought that if I came to you, after a few days of secret instruction from Wesley and Daniel, then your faith in me would strengthen. There was no ulterior motive, I promise."

His last lie turned his stomach. He mentally dismissed the feeling immediately, but wondered how it had suddenly become so difficult to lie to Sally. Lying had almost been a part of his nature for recent past years. Sally had a confused frown on hearing his promise.

"I never considered an 'ulterior motive' would be the reason, Seb. I merely thought it strange for thee to be here and we would not meet at all. That's all." She smiled and added, "But it is so sweet of thee to suffer this way for me. I love thee dearly for the thought, my darling."

"No matter, no matter," he insisted. "Kiss me again, Sally. For if I have just one more from you, then I can face the journey home in the gloom of this cloudy night."

149

She laughed and said, "There's a cloudless sky, my dear. Perhaps we may share it while you saddle up Duchess?"

Sebastian groaned and said, "Just one more kiss?"

Sally smiled and shook her head. "More kisses like that and I will be insisting you stay the night," she joked.

His eyes lit up. "And where would I sleep? In your room, Sally?"

"Certainly not; Cathy is sharing with me tonight and I think there would be several of my family who'd object and throw you down the stairs."

"I suspected as much in fact. Right, if thou can bring me a towel to dry my hands, I'll be on my way," he said, feigned sadness in his voice.

"You should have a little refreshment first, Seb. Maither has set it out in the parlour specially."

"I durst say there won't be a pitcher of ale to go with it, as a consolation for no more kisses?" He wanted to test Wesley's earlier statement.

"Ginger beer or water; and that's the way it will have to be in future, my dear. In any case, horse riding and beer should not go together; at night time, in the dark."

Sebastian did not feel it would be a good time to say how it was his usual way of returning home most nights. Even so, he frowned at Sally's words and some misgivings returned to bother him about who would be wearing the breeches in their future household. Later his father's comments would add fuel to those thoughts.

Chapter 14
Suspicions and Decisions

THOMAS looked up from the box of candles that he was pricing to see who had entered the shop, and a large sigh escaped from his lips. He attempted to be sociable.

"G'day to thee, Inspector Button, and what can I do for thee? Is it about our Eddy?"

"And hello to thee, Mr Priestley. I need some information from you if it's not too inconvenient. I am following up on a piece of information in my enquiries, you see; details of which could be vital to the investigation of the mill robbery."

Thomas was immediately suspicious. He was reluctant to tell the inspector anything, which may be interpreted as evidence against his brother.

"Oh aye, and what sort of information might that be then?"

Milly and Rachel had entered the shop, quietly, from their back parlour and were unaware of the identity of the man with the prominent lower lip. They assumed he was a customer. Milly took down a box from the shelves behind the counter and spoke aside to her daughter.

"These are the new bonnets that I told you about, my darling. There's certainly some in your size and I thought that we might all choose ones of a similar fashion for the wedding."

Rachel, as usual, was very excited to be wearing something different and to think she could be choosing for her mother and elder sister filled the girl with pride and pleasure.

"And you're sure Cathy has agreed to this, Ma? She won't scoff at my choice and make me feel silly?"

151

The conversation between the two men at the other end of the shop had been continued in lowered tones, when Milly and Rachel had entered, but it became apparent that Thomas was beginning to be angered.

"I'm sorry, Inspector, but you can't expect me to show thee my shop books without more details. Not when it might help thee keep Eddy in jail even longer. Dust think I'm daft or summat!"

"I quite understand thy worries about Eddy, Mr Priestley, but you must believe me when I tell thee that it might help to prove his innocence in the matter. I'm all about the truth and finding justice. There's nothing to be gained by punishing someone through falsehoods and lies, I think thee must agree with that."

"Aye, well, that's all right on your side, but I've had a few mates of mine suffer in the past what've been innocent. I ain't forgot about Peterloo – and never will, see!"

Tommy waved the stump of his left arm as if in explanation of his point. Milly was looking and listening, ready to jump to her husband's defence if matters got out of hand. At the same time she was curious to hear more from the inspector, apprehensive in case Tommy's temper got the better of him and he made things worse. Rachel could see that it would be better if she remained silent but suddenly, to the adults' surprise, she decided to apply a little guile, something Rachel was quite accomplished at. She rushed to inspector's side and stared up at him – hero worship in her eyes.

"Ooh, are you a policeman? I've never met a policeman before. I think thee must be ever so brave, catching criminals and robbers – and murderers! Just like in a story about Gentleman Jack I've been reading, it's so exciting! Have you caught any murderers? Shouldn't thee have a special uniform? My pa knew a special man in London what caught robbers and killers. Have thee told him about it, Pa? He was so brave – like thee I expect."

She paused for breath, smiling at her pa and Button, who were quite taken aback for a few seconds. Rachel was careful to avoid eye contact with her mother who was frowning at her daughter.

"Rachel, I don't suppose the inspector has time to tell you about his adventures. But... I would like to hear how we could help your Uncle Eddy. What is it you need to see, Inspector erm...?"

"Button, Mrs Priestley, Inspector Button. I need to know whether anyone from Quarry Bank Mill has placed a large order with you recently. If so, then I need their details if you would be so kind?"

"Well why didn't thee say so in the first place?" interjected Thomas.

"Tommy, my love, I don't think you gave the inspector much chance to speak really. Do you?"

Since Milly was usually the calm arbiter in most of the family squabbles, and most often correct in her judgement of settling them, Tommy sheepishly agreed and muttered, "Aye, perhaps so. What is it thee wants then?" But he was also aware of Milly's frowns at Rachel's reading choices so he said to her, "What's this here book thee's reading, Rachel? I hope it's not one of them penny bloods that Jack buys, eh!"

"It's not a book, Pa. It's just a story about highwaymen. Jack said it was alright. It's very exciting!"

"Hm," said Milly. "I'll be having a word with Jack when he comes home later."

Button grinned his crooked grin at Rachel and said, "Maybe I'll come back later, and ask thee about yon story you're reading, young lady. Sounds most exciting." He turned to Thomas to say, "If I could have a couple of names and addresses that will do for now, Mr Priestley."

"If it helps our Eddy I think we can manage that, dust think, Milly?"

"We've a couple of large orders but we don't know if they're mill workers; although, their addresses

153

may be in Styal village, of course. I'll write them down for you, Inspector."

Rachel was still determined to be helpful, particularly if she was in trouble about the penny blood story.

"That fat man with the ginger beard was from the mill in Styal. The dress was for his sweetheart to dance in at the harvest festival party. I remember them. Is that helpful to your inquis – No! inquaros – No! investations, Inspector?"

"I think thee might mean my investigation, my inquiries, Rachel. And, yes, it is very helpful indeed. I'm much obliged to thee, and to your ma and pa. If I'm correct in my suspicions – and I'm not claiming I am – then your Uncle Eddy could be released by this time tomorrow."

There was a sharp intake of breath from all three Priestleys and they hugged each other. Rachel said, "I knew that word from the story, Pa. And it did help the policeman, didn't it? Please don't make Jack mad at me."

Her mother and father had to smile at each other and then at their daughter. "We'll see, eh?" said Tommy. It was just at the point when the shop's bell rang and a customer came in. She paused, looked confused at the three smiling Priestley 'waxworks' and the tall man with the protruding lower lip, then spoke.

"I can come back later if thee's busy, Thomas."

"No! No! Not at all, Mrs Cumberbatch. Is it for the box of starched collars for Harold?" She nodded. "I'll just fetch it for thee." He turned to the inspector. "Will that be all then, er, Mr Button?"

"Aye, there's just them details from Mrs Priestley."

"Of course, please come over this way, sir" said Milly leading the way to the other end of the counter where the account books were kept. Like Thomas she avoided using the word *inspector* in front of their customer.

"Please don't take what I've just said as gospel, Mr Priestley. Keep it to thyselves for now. That's important, very important. You'll find out soon enough the truth of the matter."

When he'd read through the details that Milly passed to him he muttered the words *Podmore eh!* and *a fair sum of money that* under his breath a couple of times. He thanked them again and moved to leave the shop adding, "Has Mr Podmore taken delivery yet?" When Milly shook her head the inspector said, "Hang on to it for now, Mrs Priestley, and the cash."

Her reply of, "As you wish, sir," was to a closing door because the inspector had rushed away.

Mrs Cumberbatch was unable to resist exclaiming, "Well I never!"

Rachel said, "Can girls be policemen when they grow up, Ma?"

***

In Cheddleton Jonas Brewer was not pleased with his youngest son's announcement 'to the world' about working on the Sefton's farm.

"Did you do it to embarrass me and thy mother on purpose, Sebastian?"

"No."

"Then why speak to those awful gossips, the Lewin sisters?"

"Idle conversation."

Sebastian had decided in the previous week not to argue with his father when his mother was in the room. He knew how much it upset her but his short responses seemed to be annoying his father. This gave Sebastian some pleasure but he resolved to leave the room without another word if the matter became explosive and upsetting.

"And the landlord's ban from the Three Tuns, was that idle conversation too?"

"No."

"No, it certainly was not as simple as a conversation, idle or otherwise. It was due to a drunken brawl, in public!"

"There was a disagreement with Luke."

"Luke is loath to discuss it with me. He seems to think he is shielding you from my displeasure. He wastes time protecting you, when you are not worth saving, Sebastian. I regret you are a waster – in every way I can think of."

"Oh, Jonas, what a terrible thing to say about your son," said Martha, tearful and heartbroken.

Sebastian got to his feet, shrugged and said, "I take it there is little point in inviting you to our wedding, Father?"

"I have a respected position in this community and mean to maintain it for as long as I can, Sebastian. When my son takes on the job of farm labourer and marries a mere farm girl, it damages my standing, and that of my business; and it affects the reputation in society of your mother! I can't bear to think of you wedding the wench!"

Jonas' voice had risen to an angry shout. Sebastian was now at the door and said, "You forget that I mean to become a gentleman farmer, Father. Sally is not just a simple farm girl but a land owner and I will take control of it when we are wed."

"Pah! Stuff and nonsense! She will never relinquish her complete control of it to you, Sebastian. Not if she has any sense."

"Nevertheless, for my mother's sake and for the sake of appearances you are both still invited to our wedding, Father."

Sebastian looked down at his feet, shook his head with genuine regret and left the room. He and Luke had some organisation of two funerals to attend to. His part in things mainly involved the horses and carriages with assistance from their two stable hands. As Sebastian was no longer allowed to discuss final arrangements with any of the more distinguished members of the local populace, Luke was taking care of that part of things. He had appointments to keep with the two families concerned: the owner of the large flint mill nearby and a magistrate whose mother had recently died.

Distracted and annoyed Sebastian could not wait to see Ivor later on. He'd arranged to visit a different tavern, the Speckled Sow, the same evening. It was somewhere on the Leek road. He expected Ivor to present him with the last six railway share certificates and so would take all of his remaining cash with him to pay for them. Then all that he had to do was watch his initial investments grow and grow, until he could use some of Sally's share of the farm. He realised it could be several months away but he could wait, since meanwhile he'd have the task of persuading his new wife of the wisdom of further investments. Sebastian was convinced that the future success of the railways from Leek to Stockport, and to Ashton-under-Lyne, would make it so much easier to get Sally to agree. He still had to figure out how she would let go of the idea of omitting the 'obey' part of her wedding vows – just to be sure he'd have the complete freedom he needed with the farm's funds.

***

The documents were impressive. At the top of each page, in flowery script, there was the company name: *The Chester Rail & Canal Investment Company*; below it the address in Chester. Sitting alongside that was an emblem, which depicted a magnificent eagle grasping a scroll in one talon, and what appeared to be a section of railway track in the other talon. Ivor's somewhat elaborate coiffure was arranged, as Sebastian had come to expect, in the early Regency style, demure but as impressive as the company emblem. His shirt and frock coat were also of the earlier fashion but of the highest quality.

"It's such a pity that we have to meet like this, my good friend," said Ivor. "But when you are always so busy with your father's business and I am often on my way south to London or Oxford, it cannot be helped I suppose."

"Not for much longer, Ivor. Soon I will be free of the ties to my father's trade in coffins. And when I have access to further anticipated funds then I will be investing much greater sums in the railway business."

"Good, good, and then maybe we may conduct our commercial affairs in the more salubrious surroundings of my office in Chester."

"Excellent idea, Ivor. I shall look forward to it."

"Now, if I may suggest we continue with the business at hand, Sebastian? Have you brought the entire sum of money outstanding?"

"But of course, it's here," replied Sebastian, placing a leather pouch on the table. It contained many coins of gold and silver and Ivor felt its satisfying heaviness with one hand before peeping inside.

"Well, it only remains for us both to sign at the bottom of each document, together with my own receipted parchment for the company's records. They will be kept safe in Chester for you to inspect at any time you wish in future."

Sebastian smiled, hesitated briefly, and then looked quizzically at Ivor. He was anxious not to appear too naïve in the matter.

"Before we complete these signings, Ivor, should there not be a legal person of some description present, in order to witness the matter?"

"Of course, of course, my friend. I was forgetting, but it does not need to be a solicitor who witnesses things."

He looked up and waved his index finger to someone on the far side of the room. This attracted one or two looks from the drinkers nearby but they resumed their conversations when a very large man with greying hair and enormous mutton-chop whiskers arrived at Ivor's side.

"Evening, gents," said the man. Sebastian assumed he was the landlord of the Speckled Sow when he saw the grubby white apron that struggled to cover the man's expansive waist.

"Thank you for doing this, Jeremy," said Ivor to him and then to Sebastian he explained. "The witness, herewith Jeremy Bancroft, needs only to be a man in some recognisable occupation – which of course Jeremy is."

"Oh, I see," replied Sebastian. "Good evening to thee, Jeremy." The landlord nodded.

"Shall us get to it then?" he demanded. "I've got to attend to me other customers, tha knowst."

"Naturally," said Ivor and, having somehow produced a small pot of ink and a quill pen from about his person, showed Jeremy and Sebastian where to sign on each of the documents. Jeremy Bancroft then remained at their table, silent, his hand outstretched.

"Oh, aye, I was forgetting, Sebastian. I told our good friend here that you might show your gratitude to him with a small remuneration in his direction, so to speak."

Sebastian felt that he was in no position to argue the point with either man and he reached into his pocket for his two remaining silver coins.

"Thank you, Jeremy," said Sebastian, rather uncertainly, as he placed one of the coins into his giant palm.

"And will thee be requiring any more drinks, gents?" the landlord demanded, staring at Sebastian's last silver florin.

"Why, yes," answered Ivor Sheppard. "We must celebrate the conclusion of today's important transactions, must we not, Sebastian?" Sebastian hesitated to reply but Ivor did it for him. "Two more pints of ale, with brandy chasers to follow, I think. And one for thee, Jeremy!"

Without the slightest hint of any more ado, whatsoever, the landlord snatched the last florin from Sebastian's palm and left them, saying, "Righto, gents, drinks coming up, in two shakes of a gnat's whiskers!"

***

Inspector Button had decided that he was going to confront Phillip Podmore with his findings. The stoutly built inspector and his lanky constable waited near the path that led from the cotton mill to Morley Green, which was on the way to Wilmslow. The two policemen had spoken earlier to the landlord of the group of very small cottages there.

"Hey up, Inspector, here he comes now."

"I doubt he can outrun either of us, Higgins, but just in case get thee ready for a bit of a race, eh?" replied Button.

The thought of taking to his heels did cross Pud's mind when he spotted the inspector about a hundred yards ahead. He was tired after finishing his work shift and had just rounded the bend around a field of hops ready for reaping. Usually he would have gone for a rewarding after work drink at the Ship Inn. However, his promise to meet Beatrice had meant he was on his way home to get ready for their stroll later.

"Good evening, Mr Podmore, I thought we would accompany thee on thy way home, while we have a little chat."

"Oh aye, and what might thee want to chat about?" he answered, a threatening gruffness in his voice.

The inspector wasted no time and got straight to business, but Higgins walked silently on the open side of Pud, while Button was on the side next to the field's muddy irrigation ditch.

"Well, it's like this, Mr Podmore. A couple of weeks back when I spoke to thee and Mr Grafton about the robbery, both of thee, and his little lad, told me what you witnessed. Which was... seeing Eddy Priestley sneaking out of the building... with a heavy sack... and with his pockets bulging. Correct?" The protruding lip was very evident.

"Aye, that's about the top and bottom of it. What's wrong with that then?"

"I've been looking into the affairs of Mr Grafton and it seems that he has made some arrangements with a school in Congleton, for his lad to attend there; Freddy is it?"

"We all call him Little Freddy. What's wrong with that then?"

"The thing is, Mr Podmore, I don't believe Mr Grafton saw Eddy sneaking about. He told me that Eddy was always on about sending his children to a posh school, see. Thereby implying that that was why Eddy needed the money. But it was the other way about wasn't it?"

Pud was not sure where this was going, so tried to answer without implicating himself at all.

"Are thee sure about that, Inspector? Ah don't recall any talk about schools."

"Oh, aye, definitely, I wrote it down, see. I write most everything down just in case I need it in court. In fact, you agreed with Mr Grafton about all of that – we call it a statement in police matters. And I need thee to sign it later. There's other things in here that affect thee. About buying an expensive dress for someone called Beatrice, who I must assume is – Whoa!"

161

They had walked almost the length of the oat field and Button was waving his logbook about as he spoke. Pud panicked and shoved the inspector with his left shoulder into the muddy ditch. The logbook flew out of Button's hand into the field and Constable Higgins made a grab for Pud's right arm. The fat man was ready for this and used his extra bulk to drag the gangly Higgins to himself instead and, with a quick trip of his foot, had the second policeman flying into the ditch to land on top of his senior officer. Then Pud was off down the road towards Wilmslow, running surprisingly quickly for such a big man.

After his initial exclamation, as he was launched into the mire, the inspector's second blurt was more of an ejaculated breathlessness, "Oof!" when Higgins landed on top of him. They spluttered and coughed up stagnant, slimy water for a few seconds. Button found his voice first of all and his third exclamation was more of a bellow, "After him, man! Quick now, before he disappears into those woods!"

Chapter 15
Home Discomforts

"**WHICH** of these cottages is it, Higgins?"

A very wet and muddy Inspector Button and his equally wet and muddy constable were hiding behind a tall blackthorn and willow hedge. A foetid odour of ditch hung over them and to say that the two peace officers were unhappy would be a great exaggeration. They were very miserable. The constable had run after Phillip Podmore through the wood but rarely caught sight of him with so much dense greenery obscuring the fugitive as he fled many yards ahead. However, Higgins' sense of hearing was most helpful in the chase. Whenever the policeman paused he could hear the large man crashing through the undergrowth, cursing, gasping for breath and groaning as though he was about to die. He had caught sight of Pud just as the fugitive emerged from the trees onto the Altrincham Road and then he furtively approached a group of small cottages. Looking around and back towards the woods, Pud made his way to a particular cottage and knocked desperately on the front door. He was let in by a matronly looking woman who expressed distress when she saw how breathless and weak the perspiring Phillip was.

"It's the last one on the right, facing us as we look, sir."

"Good work, Constable. It was a sensible ruse to wait for me. He's a big bloke and it might need the both of us to take him in. I was delayed looking for my logbook and we might need it when we confront Mr Podmore, eh!"

Button was also concerned to find his new silver pencil with a slider for the lead. He'd bought it especially for his police notes, and was very happy to retrieve it from the mud in the oat field.

"Aye, that's right, sir. I reckon he's still in there but I can nip around the back to check if he's hiding in the privy."

"Right, give me a minute to get into the cottage, Higgins, and have your handcuffs ready when I get them to let thee in through the back. It'll show them we mean business, see."

"As you say, Inspector, and does thee reckon I'll need this?" He produced a newly varnished cudgel from one pocket of a heavy great coat and the manacles from the other pocket.

"It all depends on how much bother he gives us. Best produce it if he makes another move to run for it. Come on, let's get over there."

As they crossed the road the policemen noticed the curtains twitching in the window. This encouraged the constable to move smartly around the back of the cottage and watch the back door. Before Inspector Button had rapped his first tap on the front door it was opened and the matron frowned down at him.

"Yes?"

"Good evening, Madam. I'm Inspector Button and I would like to see, Miss Beatrice Pilling. If thee would be kind enough to fetch her here."

"Oh, thee would, would thee? And what does thee want with me daughter, then?"

"It's about a serious matter that could concern her, at the cotton mill in Styal up the road: Quarry Bank Mill to be exact."

"Ah knows where Quarry Bank is, young man. No need to tell that to me. I ain't puddle headed tha knowst."

He restrained from heaving a heavy sigh and his lip and chin became more prominent.

"I do not want to waste your time or mine, Mrs Pilling. I assume you are Mrs Pilling? We are in pursuit of

164

a Mr Phillip Podmore and know he came in here. We saw him. I must warn thee that if you impede me in my duties as a police officer... Well it could be very serious for the both of you – you and Beatrice... I must insist thee lets me in! Now! Without delay, if you please."

"No need to come all high and mighty with me, Inspector. I'm only –"

"Let the inspector in, Missus. I know what it's about and I don't want to cause thee any trouble on my account."

It was Pud's voice from the scullery where he had been hiding, thinking of running again; that is until he saw the constable through the scullery window. Higgins in turn had glimpsed Pud and he held up the cudgel in one hand and the heavy iron manacles in the other.

"Best come in then. And don't be dropping all that mud across my clean floor. Policeman or no, thee smells worse than me old dog out the back."

The dog had not stopped barking since Higgins had arrived at the back garden. He was very happy that Chip was securely chained up to the side of the privy and he sidled very carefully past the large mongrel's snapping and growling jaws when Mrs Pilling opened the door to admit him. When everyone was present Inspector Button made an official announcement.

"Phillip Podmore, I must ask thee to accompany me to Wilmslow police station for further questioning with regards to a recent robbery of cash from Quarry Bank Mill. Do you come quietly or must we use force and the handcuffs?"

Beatrice pleaded through her sudden tears, "Oh, Phillip, what hast thee done? Tell the inspector here what he needs to know. I cannot bear the thought of thee being locked up in prison... Inspector, he can tell thee here, in my Ma's parlour, surely?"

Pud was sat on a rough, wooden, bench seat, along one wall, it being the only piece of furniture in the room that could accommodate his bulky frame. He did not look at all well; perspiring, red faced, tousled and half fainting after his unusual exertions, he was content to sag there. He waved a weak arm and wheezed, "Ask away. Ah'm done in!"

The two ladies, also being rather plump, together occupied an old sofa. This left a rickety, wooden, upright chair that Button moved, for him to be sat facing the fugitive; lip and chin challenging all-comers. Higgins was content to stand, grinning at Pud, still holding aloft the 'tools' of his trade.

"Ladies, I'll not attempt to deceive thee. Considering Phillip's unhealthy look I will interview him here. But! Depending upon his answers he may still have to accompany us to the lock-up in Wilmslow. Are thee both clear about that?"

Mrs Pilling was still not ready to be intimidated in her own parlour: "I'll trouble thee, Mr Inspector… what-jami-callit… to be a little more considerate of the poor chap. Take a luke at him, man! He's in no fit state to walk nearly two miles into Wilmslow. What have thee done to him, to get him into this state?" She stared disapprovingly at the muddy water that continued to trickle beneath the police officers making small puddles wherever they remained for more than ten seconds. Her wrinkled up nose told its own story about the smell.

Button sighed and turned to face the women.

"We met Phillip on his way home to Morley Green, where I would've been quite content to put my questions. But on the way he assaulted the both of us and that is how come we wound up in the ditch! That assault is a serious matter all by itself, Mrs Pilling. But there is still the matter of the robbery…" He waved the damp logbook. "And I've a few things written down which I want to put to him, see."

Beatrice wiped away her tears and said, "Inspector, will thee object if we ask a kind neighbour

166

who's the owner of an 'orse and cart to take all of thee into Wilmslow – if that's how things turn out of course?"

"What dust think, Constable?"

"Ah cannot see what's wrong with it if we chain the man to the cart and all, sir. Just in case he's a reet good actor, if thee gets me drift."

"What!" interjected the matron again. "He's in no state to run up the stairs, let alone the road to Wilmslow, man. Has thee lost all sense of sympathy along with the brains thee were born with?"

"Well, I think any more decisions must be left with the senior person in the room, eh! And that being myself, I would appreciate it now if I could get on with things – without ANY more interruptions!"

"Well I never," muttered Mrs Pilling. "The squire will hear of this nonsense."

"Hush up, Ma!" hissed Beatrice. "Please carry on, Inspector, while my mother goes out to speak to our good neighbour, Blakely. Go now, Ma, it'll save time later, eh! And don't gossip too much."

"Ah'm going, Ah'm going, don't fret thesen. Harried out of me own house, by me daughter and all," grumbled Mrs Pilling as she gathered her shawl about her shoulders and left.

"Now then, Mr Phillip Podmore, according to thy landlord you have always been very slow in paying the rent but since the day of the robbery you've paid for a few weeks in advance. In addition to this you've asked him about taking on a bigger and better cottage for when thee and Miss Pilling here are married. What have thee got to say about that?"

Pud groaned and his eyelids closed and his chin fell to his chest.

"Hm, we might come back to this item later," said Button.

Beatrice put both her hands to her cheeks and murmured, "Oh, Phillip, for us… And what have thee done?"

"I have confirmed with Gibson's Store in Stockport that you made quite an expensive purchase there, to whit a length of damask silk and the services of a dressmaker. Again, this is since the day of the mill robbery. Any comments regarding that item?"

A deeper groan came from Pud.

"Oh, Phillip, my lovely, lovely dress." The distressed Miss Pilling was now weeping, almost uncontrollably, into one of the many handkerchiefs she had hastened to fetch from another room.

"I see, well to continue with these questions, I have observed yourself and Frederick Grafton meeting up in the Ship Inn, where… Where, Mr Podmore, I am given to understand thee drinks regularly, and, on the occasion to which I am referring, you were buying several rounds of drinks." Another groan.

"Nothing particularly wrong with that – but I heard thee say ye see, it was due to all the extra money that you had been earning as a machine weaver. Is that true?"

A feeble answer came from Pud, speaking to his knees, "Aye, the new looms and overtime, see."

"No, Phillip, that's not true, not according to the mill manager. And he showed me the records of production with payments to thee, to prove it! So that's not true at all!"

"Oh, Phillip, thou's been lying to me, about all your overtime. Thee must've been boozing it away all the time. Oh, Phillip, Phillip."

"So, Mr Phillip Podmore, it's time to tell me the truth about the money and the robbery. The more helpful you are then I might put in a good word for thee, in court! For that's where you are bound, I promise thee that!"

168

At that moment Mrs Pilling returned to say it had all been arranged with Mr Blakely. She went straight to her daughter to comfort her and Beatrice said, "Oh, Ma, Phillip has been lying to me all this time. What are we to do?"

Torrents of tears from both women ensued after Beatrice told her mother more details in a hushed voice. Every so often they glanced across at Pud and tutted. He remained unaware of their opprobrium with his eyes closed, mentally rejecting the world from his person. This state of mind was shattered by Button's loud clap of his hands and his demand for attention:

"Right, Phillip, now's the time to tell me, just how the money was stolen? If that is, you want my good word to the judge, when thee faces a jury. I'm certain that's what it will mean."

Pud half opened his eyes and blearily asked, "What now? Can it not wait until I've had a bit of shut eye? I'm knackered, man; ten hour shift today, tha knowst!"

Inspector Button turned to the ladies and drew out a handful of copper coins. "Can I pay thee for a cup of tea for us all, please, Mrs Pilling? It'd be most convenient to my investigation if Phillip were to spill the beans now, as thee might say. While it's still in his head, see. I'd be most grateful and thee'd be helping the police in their inquiries – an important civil action."

"Oh, I see, it's all 'please, Mrs Pilling' and 'most convenient' and 'helping the police'… now it suits thee, Inspector Button…" Then her voice softened a little. "Reet then; it's no trouble and there could be a bit of lardy cake and all. Yon poor Phillip looks like he's on his last legs, eh!"

She went out to her small scullery, calling on Beatrice to help her, but could not resist one last comment.

"Best get his information now, afore he goes to meet His Maker. Reckon he ain't long for this world, Inspector Button!"

***

With Pud safely locked up in Hawthorn Lane the inspector and his constable returned to Quarry Bank Mill the next day in order to test out some of the details of the robbery. This was as a result of Pud's confession statement but he also intended arresting Flaggy Grafton and interrogating him back at the police station. On this occasion they used a wagon to travel to the mill and took Eddy Priestley with them. Button had officially released Eddy the night before but omitted to tell him until the morning, since in his mind offering a lift was a kind of compensation for any inconvenience caused to the mule spinner.

Once they had dropped Eddy off in Styal village and asked him to say nothing for an hour about Phillip Podmore, the inspector went to see Robert Hyde Greg about interviewing Flaggy Grafton again. This was the main reason for bringing the wagon as it was his intent to arrest him for further questioning at Hawthorn Lane.

"I'm sorry, Inspector Button, but according to Mr Howlett, Grafton has not turned up today and we've put someone else on his mule. But his lad, Freddy, has still clocked in as his scavenger."

"That seems very curious to me, Mr Greg. Does it happen often? I mean with Grafton not turning up for work?"

"Oh no, it's very rare. My workers understand they are to be diligent at all times; not turning up means they don't get paid; and if it happens too often then they get the sack, and so they will lose their cottage as well!"

"Right, I see. But I suppose Frederick Grafton could be off sick today?"

"Normally I'd agree with you Inspector but Mr Howlett seems to think he's gone to Congleton."

"Why's that then?"

"We have no idea, but that's all his little lad would say. I'll be interested to hear his reason because AWOL is not something we approve of!"

"I'd be interested to know the reason myself, Mr Greg. Keep it to thyself for now but Grafton is top of my list for the robbery, you see. I'd like to speak to his lad in the mill manager's office. If thee could send for him I'd be grateful?"

"Of course, I'll get Mr Howlett to fetch him – and 'mum's' the word, hey!"

An idea had struck Button about changing his original plans for seeing Flaggy Grafton. It would involve Little Freddy if he could get it to work. Higgins gave his inspector a sly wink and a touch of his own nose, but he'd no idea himself of what was going on in Button's brain – as usual.

Ten minutes later, in the small anteroom with the serving hatch and in the presence of the constable alone, Button was having his 'little chat' with Little Freddy. It was important to be on the 'wrong side' of the locked door to Mr Howlett's office.

"So you can see why I sent for thee? With thee being so helpful last time we spoke, Freddy, when you told me who thee saw leaving Mr Howlett's office on the day of the robbery, eh?"

The boy nodded.

"Well, this time it's because I've left an important book of evidence in Mr Howlett's office and we'd best be on our way soon back to Wilmslow. And you're the only lad that I can trust to get it for me. Mr Howlett's gone off to keep his own important appointment, but I need that book. It's a special policeman's book, it's blue, very important and I need it now. Do you understand, Freddy?"

171

Under his greasy mop of mousey hair the boy frowned but still he nodded.

"Right, so it's in there somewhere." Button pointed at the small serving hatch where the wages were given out on pay day. "But the door is locked, and like I say, Mr Howlett's gone off somewhere. But I need to go back now with my blue book."

Little Freddy advanced a little, reached up to the hatch and tested it with a push of his tiny hand. He said nothing but looked up at the inspector.

"Oh, I know the hatch is closed to, Freddy, but if I use this," He waved an opened pen knife, "To jiggle the hatch open I reckon thee could climb inside to the office and find that blue book for me, see. What do ye think, lad could thee do it?"

"Easy as pie! Just like me pa asked me to, afore."

"There you are, Constable Higgins. What did I say? This lad of Mr Grafton's is as a bright as a new silver florin. In fact I might try and find one of them for thee, Freddy, if thee gets me important book back." He started prising the hatch doors apart.

"Well, I never did see a more helpful and clever boy of twelve year old," added Higgins.

"I'm only nine according to me pa, mister," replied Freddy climbing on a stool which was conveniently close-by. "And when I did it afore for him he said Ah could have a new toy if Ah did it proper." He was already half-way through the hatch. "That's where Pa's gone today. To Congleton, where we might live. He says he's bringing me a rocking horse back for me new toy, see." Little Freddy's pipey little voice was now coming out through the hatch as he searched for the blue logbook for Button. "Where did thee put it, Mister?"

"I think I dropped it somewhere on the floor. Oh, if I could only come in there and help thee, but I've got no key and this blessed door's locked!"

172

"The keys in here hanging on the wall like it were last time. Only it's too high up for me. That stool was in here then, and I climbed on it to get it for me pa, see."

"I see, that's how come ye knew what to do, hey, Freddy? Clever lad. What if I pass the stool through this hatch?"

The little boy ignored Button and was jumping up over and over again, trying to reach the large key on the hook about six feet from the floor. His breathless sighs and groans came back to them.

"No luck, Freddy? Here you are lad," said Higgins as he pushed the stool's seat through the narrow opening. Then it got stuck as the wider lower end with the slightly splayed legs jammed themselves in each corner of the hatchway. Freddy tugged the seat and Higgins pushed the legs and between them they succeeded in jamming it completely!

"Oh, no," exclaimed Button. "You'll have to stay in there all night till Mr Howlett comes back in the morning. Did ye spot me book, Freddy? Because then I could go back to Wilmslow."

"Ah'm not staying in here all night, it's too spooky," was the reply. The policeman heard a loud juvenile grunt and a clanking of keys, as Freddy took a small run and jumped up to unhook the keys. "Done it," he said triumphantly. He came back to the hatch and passed the keys through to Higgins. "Here you are."

"Why don't ye let thesen out?" asked Higgins.

"Locks too tight for me, see. I had to pass them to me pa last time."

"Oh aye, is that right, lad?" mused the inspector softly, nodding to Higgins, his lip and chin moving into position, his right hand concealing the blue logbook behind his back. The constable opened the door to the office and they both entered. Button walked to a far corner, dark and shadowy, and as he stooped he exclaimed, "Why, here it is, Freddy! No wonder thee couldn't spot it in the gloom, eh!"

"Can I go now then? Ye've found yon book thee lost."

"Not quite yet, Freddy. I've still got one or two questions to ask thee and thy pa."

He waved his blue book at Freddy and began writing in it. The constable was standing in the doorway that exited from the building, no longer friendly but stern looking, his hands on his hips. Then all three went to see Robert Greg, with Little Freddy being obviously escorted, since his skinny left arm was firmly grasped by Higgins large bony fingers.

"Now I'm able to tell thee a bit of information that I've gleaned so far, Mr Greg. But I'll have to wait in Frederick Grafton's cottage in Styal village before I can leave. On his return I'm going to charge him with the theft along with his mate, Phillip Podmore. I'm pretty sure there's no-one else involved."

"What about the boy, Inspector?"

"Constable Higgins, will thee take the lad outside until I've finished talking to Mr Greg? Hang on to him though, in case the master wants a word with him later."

"Right ye are, Inspector. I'll shut the door and all, eh?"

Higgins left the room still holding on to Freddy and Button explained a few things with Mr Greg, before they all walked over to the village for a few more words with Mrs Grafton. The scene in the cottage was very upsetting for them all, with Little Freddy and his mother tearfully hugging for over an hour. Mr Greg left and the policemen waited well into the dark hours of the night in Styal. Come midnight, the inspector and the constable returned to Wilmslow, angry and without Flaggy Grafton.

Chapter 16
Some Tales to Tell

"**WELL** I never," repeated Milly for the third time. She sat back in her chair and looked at Tommy, wondering if it had been a dream. Her husband assented with just as much wonder in his eyes but his periodic comment was, "I said all along as how our Eddy was innocent, didn't I?"

"You did, Tommy. Let's shut up shop a bit earlier and get Jack back in here with us so we can tell him what the inspector said, hey? He's back to college tomorrow and Cathy's back from Sally's the day after. She'll be happy about Eddy's release."

"Aye, and I'll wager Jenny's right pleased that he's out; and then he'll soon be back to work on the mule, Milly. I'll fetch Jack in."

"I'll make us a fresh pot of tea, my dear."

It was a relief not to have the worry about Eddy's imprisonment in the back of their minds for the next two or three weeks. They would be travelling to Cheddleton for Sally and Sebastian's wedding soon and planned to stay over for a few days. This was in spite of none of the Priestley family really wanting to go, the dragging down feeling affecting each in different degrees. Previously, the thought of being long away from Jenny while she was so distressed felt disloyal. But now, that downhearted pressure was gone – thanks to Inspector Button's visit.

He had explained how Flaggy and Pud had seized upon the chance to get into the mill manager's office, while the wages money was all set out, ready for paying the workers. The safe was open but the hatch and the door to the room closed. Both men knew that it was impossible for either of them to squeeze through the tiny hatchway but Flaggy immediately thought of his son. Little Freddy was waiting in the yard outside with his friends so, while Pud kept watch, Flaggy collected the boy and persuaded him to slip into the office through the hatch and get the keys. This much was what Pud had owned up to. Inspector Button needed to be convinced that it was possible for the little lad to get in that way. Once he'd seen it with his own eyes and heard the truth behind the various lying tales, the inspector wanted Grafton locked up in his jail, awaiting trial with Pud.

Jack was just as amazed as his parents. Some questions occurred to him. "What about the boy, and what about the money in our till, Pa?"

"Well, there's a sight more to it than that, Jack. The inspector ain't convinced the lad's guilty, see, just a bit green and foolish. He's left Little Freddy under Greg's supervision, still an apprentice scavenger, maybe, to live with his mother – but they're out of their cottage. They'll 'ave to find lodgings with another mill worker if they can. We've handed the money back to the police, he says it's evidence or summat."

"And all the silk they ordered?

"We'll have to sell it later if we can. I don't mind about any of the expense, Jack. It's worth it. We'd 'ave paid double to get yer Uncle Eddy out of clink. Ask thy mother."

Milly had agreed and added, "But the other thing is, Jack," she paused. "The boy's father, they call him Flaggy I think, he's still not come home – to his home in Styal village."

"Someone's tipped him the wink, eh, Pa? There'll be some of his mates seen what's going on and warned him off."

"Aye, that's what I think and all, Jack. Probably took a back hander to keep quiet, from his stolen cash. The inspector said they're going to keep watch around the

176

village and the mill, but they cannot keep that up for long."

"So, do you think Mr Greg will just have to say goodbye to all the money, Tommy?"

"Aye, I do, Milly. I feel sorry for Grafton's missus, and his boy I suppose. Ye have to wonder how she's going to cope. The lad's money for scavenging won't pay much for rent and food, eh."

"Won't she find a job in the mill, Pa? Then she and her son might get to stay in the cottage where they lived?"

"I doubt it, Jack. Inspector Button suspects she knows where her husband's gone but she's saying nowt. And I reckon, when it comes down to it, Greg'll never trust her or the little lad."

Flaggy Grafton was never seen again in the region around Styal or Cheadle or Stockport. It was rumoured by some that he had moved to Nottingham and worked there as a machine weaver in a mill. Others said that he used the money to buy a variety of goods, soap, medicine, new gadgets for the kitchen, knick-knacks for the mantle-piece, and became a pedlar, constantly on the move but never around Manchester or the north-west of England.

***

Sebastian Brewer was distraught having returned home after journeying by coach and rail for three days. He had travelled north by stagecoach to Macclesfield, where he stayed overnight, then on the coach yet again to Manchester. His intention was to ride aboard the new railway from Manchester to Liverpool. However, his idea of getting off near Chester would not work as there was no connection. So he had to find another coach to travel all the way back down the country to Crewe, having been informed in Manchester of the recently opened rail line from Crewe to Holyhead in North Wales. At this point Sebastian experienced no sad feelings of time or money wasted, because his first two railway journeys were both thrilling and informative. It was easy to convince himself that this train, the one from which he was pleased to alight in Chester, was but a small part of *The Chester Rail & Canal Investment Company*. He had noticed the very many passengers aboard it and felt somewhat smug, thinking, "Every fare paying traveller I can see will be contributing to my investments. One day I will be able to gloat when I tell my doubting father how I became rich!"

Unfortunately, in Chester a gross, cancerous, weight seemed to have landed in his gut. The address in Chester of Ivor Sheppard's office in Claires Court had been difficult to find. When he had finally discovered number nine Claires Court, it was not at all splendid. There was a distinct smell of sewers coming up from the uneven and broken cobbled street. The inhabitants of the slum had never heard of Ivor or his company.

Determined not to give up his search, Sebastian wandered about the town for a couple of hours asking questions. The sinking feeling in his stomach became heavier and heavier when each person he spoke to knew nothing of the correct address. Three people of a respectable appearance, who had a shop or office of their own in the town centre, told him of other visitors to Chester that had enquired about *The Chester Rail & Canal Investment Company*. Their search had also proved fruitless and the weight in his stomach grew and grew, to become almost unbearable. He needed Luke; he was the only person he dared to confide in, but it was so painful to admit his suspicions to his brother. Had he lost everything? What else could he do with the wedding just a few days away? Sebastian drowned his depressed feelings in alcohol, after arriving home and on later days, by visiting the Speckled Sow for a few hours.

***

"Sebastian! Sebastian! Wake up, you drunken slob! My God, man how much did thee put away last night?"

The brothers had taken a room in the Speckled Sow on the night before the wedding in Saint Andrew's Methodist Church. It had been Luke's idea because there had been few days since Sebastian's return from Chester when he'd appeared to be completely sober. Sebastian had poured out all of the details of his losses to Luke five times in three days. The unending regrets about being ruined and about how he could never tell Sally, even about calling off the wedding, had become a constant insect drone in Luke's ears. There were moments when he'd 'swatted' his drunken brother to sober him up. It had little effect on Seb's drinking but it had felt so satisfying to Luke at the time. Sebastian was not responding to his brotherly advice about how to cope with his immediate future: with Sally as his wife; with being a farmer; with his father at home; and even with standing at the altar and repeating the wedding vows. There had been an opportunity to rehearse with Parson Trunchman but Seb lost his nerve ten minutes before the appointment. Luke apologised to everyone concerned and Sally accepted this, but she could not help but suspect that Sebastian had another hangover after another night drinking. She and her family had lots of things to attend to regarding the wedding so it was forgotten. The unfortunate Luke was fast losing the small amount of patience he had left for his pathetic brother.

It was too much for Luke to stand. Now, on the very morning of the wedding, Sebastian was still pleading in his semi-conscious state about what to do.

"Ye see, Luke, I'm ruined... Ooh, hell... All that money I had saved for investments... Ooh, my head... Well it's gone! Gone!"

179

"Seb, how many times must I tell you? When you marry, all of your wife's property, all of it, becomes yours! So you will not be impoverished, as you keep insisting."

"Oh, aye! I keep forgetting. That's right, Luke... Dust thee know, brother? I told our pa that. I told him just what you said then. How I'd own some of that farm... what's it called? Ooh, my head!"

"Seftons Farm, Seb! God, you're in such a state! Clean thysell up and get into that clean shirt and your suit. Our mother has had it cleaned up for thee – though it should've been a new one for today!"

"Couldn't afford it, Luke. See, I'm ruined! I'm relying on advances on my salary all the time... Oh, my word, Luke! Ye didn't tell Ma did thee? Oh, God, it'll finish her off – and Father! Is he coming to the wedding? Haven't spoken to him for days!"

"Never mind all that now, Seb. Just get cleaned up and into that suit, so that we can be in time for your wedding – your wedding, Seb! Sober up for Heavens' sake!"

Sebastian was descending into a very sorrowful and capitulating state as he washed and dressed.

"You're a fine brother to me, Luke! I don't deserve thee – but I do love thee... and Sally, I love her as well. But I fear she may tell me I can never drink another drop and I can't have that."

"That sounds like a very good idea to me, Seb."

"Oh, aye! But thee doesn't know the half of it, Luke. Sally... my dear, sweet, lovely Sally... told me... Ooh! My blessed head... What was it now? Erm –"

"Sebastian! Will thee concentrate on getting ready? We must be there, in the church, at the altar, before everyone. Come on, Seb!"

But Sebastian was not listening. He merely continued with his rambling chatter: "She's never going to say she'll obey me, see Luke… I think I need a drink before we get on that pony and trap."

"What! Are you mad? No, Seb!"

"See, I agreed about that – a moment of weakness in the head it was – about… about being equal, and Sal refusing to obey. Then our damn father told me! Told me I'd need complete control over her share of the farm, and, and –"

"Sebastian, how many more times? I've said it so many times before. You are such a clot! What on earth is it now?"

"She won't even let me have an occasional little tipple when I need it! It's not right – not fair! And now thee's stopping me from having a drop of Dutch courage when I need it – probably my last drop… Forever! Oh, God!"

"You'll survive! Come on get your hat and coat, while I make sure the stable lad has our horse and carriage ready in the next ten minutes."

Luke left Sebastian and went downstairs and out into the courtyard, before checking with Jeremy Bancroft about ordering a light breakfast. When Sebastian managed to find his crumpled frockcoat, lying in the bottom of the wardrobe, he was delighted to discover his silver hip flask in the pocket. He had thrown his coat down before collapsing asleep and very drunk.

"Oh, thank you, thank you, God! Just a little snifter of the hair of the dog first," he told himself. The flask was still half full of juniper gin, so he paused, took a deep breath, and then drank the lot.

"That's better, Seb. Now thee's ready to face the day and take the hand of your beautiful new wife. Maybe I'll have a little surprise for you, my darling Sally!"

Carefully balancing his top hat on his tousled mop of hair, he lurched out of the room and went downstairs to get married. His white tie had caused him problems and

Luke had to re-arrange the loosely knotted tangle into an acceptable but sagging knot.

At the altar of Saint Andrew's Methodist Church, in Cheddleton, Parson Trunchman had been interrupted by Sebastian while delivering the first few words of the marriage service. Sally and Sebastian were accompanied by Cathy and Luke, both of whom were instantly shocked by this abnormal break in the ceremony. A deja vue event had arrived:

There was an audible gasp from everyone in the church as they waited for Sebastian's next words.

"Shally Shefton, I love thee very much – and – and I always will, hic! But I've been thinking and thinking... And thou must agree to obey me as my future wife, see. And that's it, see! Yes, that's it! Love, cherish and obey, see."

He giggled and swayed towards Sally, who stepped back, swaying in her turn, but away from the groom. Feeling embarrassed and angry, the bride was determined not to shed a tear. Fearing she was about to swoon Catherine Priestley, dutiful as first bridesmaid, stepped forward to protectively enfold Sally in her arms. Before Cathy had taken two steps, to the astonishment of all those present, but to Sebastian's astonishment in particular, the beautiful bride grasped her beautifully weighty bouquet in both hands to fetch the groom a powerful swipe across his left cheek. This felled him instantly, pulling his groomsman down with him so that they both lay, correctly, on the right side of the altar.

***

The congregation of stunned wedding guests were completely silent when they had watched the bride run down the aisle and out of the church. She'd heard that her drunken fiancé had been banned from the Three Tuns Inn and her panic stricken brain told her to seek refuge there. Sitting in the gloom alone, Sally was reminded of the time, a hundred years ago it seemed, when Sebastian had sensitively entered the small backroom in order to comfort her during Gabriel's funeral. The room had then been quietly provided by Nancy, the inn-keeper's wife; and she had done so again on this awful day, this tragic un-wedding day. But now Sally was dabbing her tearful cheeks hating him, desperately not wanting to see the man who had sat beside her before. The irony was not lost on Sally. Here she was seeking sanctuary from Sebastian in an inn; a place whose function was to provide alcohol, the very substance that made her hate Sebastian.

Nancy was tentative in her second approach.

"Are thee feeling a little better my dear? I don't know what went on in the church but thee's going to need different clothes. Thee can't go out like that – unless it's back to Saint Andrew's. Folks'll be –"

"No, no! I'm not going back there. Please don't let anyone in here, in particular Sebastian Brewer. Have you locked the door?"

"That's not going to happen, Sally. Alf, the master, banned him afore, but for today he was happy to let the two of thee entertain thy wedding guests. It's... well, it was meant to be your day, thy special day. I've told him it was all cancelled like thee said."

Sally continued to stare at the door. She asked again, "The door - is it locked? He won't let him in now though, will he? I... I can't..."

Sally broke down again and floods of tears, deep sobs and painful moans prevented any more words. Nancy sat beside her and held her gently, trying to soothe her pain. "Don't thee fret, me duck, the master won't let no-one in unless thee says so, I promise... Shall I see if I can get some clothes for thee to change into? Perhaps, thy maither? She might..."

Sally shook her head vigorously. "No!" was her strangled reply. She felt so deeply embarrassed she wanted to stay there until darkness would hide her and then she thought she would slip away and take a coach to somewhere, anywhere, away from Cheddleton and Leek. But she had no money and that knowledge crept into her mind. Perhaps, Cathy might help? Nancy was still whispering words of comfort and Sally became aware of her surroundings almost afresh.

"God will surely comfort thee in times like this, my dear. Stay in here for now and I'll…"

"May I take a room here for the night, Nancy? If you could send for my dearest friend – her name is Catherine Priestley – she may bring my clothes, and money to pay thee."

"That's the spirit! Stay here, Sally. I'll make it clear there's to be no-one but me may enter with thy friend, Catherine. Leave it with me, my dear. Here's the key, lock the door after me."

It was at this moment that Sally knew what to do; where to go; how she might find a new cause worth living for:

What was it, Nancy said? Ask God for comfort; and he has spoken. I will join Preacher Wroe in his quest for the Christian Israelites. Surely I may serve him as one of his missionaries? That's it! I will travel to Ashton-under-Lyne without delay.

In the world that was outside the gloomy backroom of the Three Tuns Inn, the small world that was the Cheddleton community, all kinds of chaos had occurred. Sally's rapid exit from the church left behind various groups of argumentative people. Jonas Brewer came forward to drag his drunken son to his feet. Sacrificing all semblances of respectable appearances, he commenced to loudly chastise the dazed Sebastian for many minutes. When Luke tried to intervene Jonas began

184

to blame him for allowing his brother to cause such a scene in church. This prompted the parson to protest about the raised voices and while that distraction was happening, Wesley stepped forward in his turn.

Wesley made a show of 'assisting' Sebastian to leave the church in the lurch; although close observers along the aisle noted that the shamed groom's feet hardly touched the floor. It was more of a drag that the powerful young farmer provided when he grabbed Seb's left arm to take him outside. Once they had exited the church and were several yards down the path the gathered observers there, from around the village, were treated to their own piece of entertainment.

"Don't come near me sister ever again, thou boozy sot!" yelled Wesley, and he punched Sebastian square in his face. It was hard enough to send him 3 or 4 feet backwards and to lay him out flat on the grass. Sebastian's lip and nose began to bleed and the stunned crowd looked from one man to the other, wondering what to do. Wesley strode off wondering where Sally had gone.

At this point Ellie and the rest of the Sefton family came out and hastened after Wesley, with the Priestleys and James Longton following them. Cathy was worried about the bride and asked her mother what she should do.

"Cathy, dear, I have no idea. We'd best follow Ellie and Esther back to the farm I expect. We may find Sally there."

Thomas agreed and so the two families took carriages away from the chaos, but without either Daniel or Wesley. Wesley had angrily disappeared into the narrow streets of Cheddleton. Daniel Sefton hurried to the Three Tuns to cancel the food arrangements. However, the 'unseemly scenes' were to provide food for village gossips that would last for years to come.

Wesley had reluctantly hired a horse from the Three Tuns stable and ridden to the Red Cow Inn, where he knew that Cathy and her family were staying. His sister had refused to let him into her room at the Three Tuns even though he'd left almost all of his money with her. When he'd turned up at the inn to explain about the wedding being cancelled and that food was no longer required, Nancy's husband, Alf, told him that his Uncle Daniel had already been but left for home.

Feeling confused, Wesley said, "Oh, right. I'd better make me way home as well then." Though his temper had subsided a little he sat down, rubbed his bruised knuckles in his other palm, and went on, "I might have a pie and a pint of thy best ale while I'm here, Alf."

"Reet thee are then. I'll get the lass to bring it over to thee, Wes. Will thee want to speak to Sally while you're here?"

Wesley jumped to his feet and said, "What! Sal's here! Why didn't thee say so? Does Uncle Dan know?"

"I ain't supposed to say nothing but with thee being her brother and all… Ah've never got on too well with Daniel so I didn't let on. And any road up, Nancy said it were to be kept quiet from the start. But the lass has been here for hours now and I thought… well… tha knowst, it ain't reet."

"Where's our Sally, Alf?" Wesley's temper was rising and the landlord was quick to say, "Calm down now, Wes. Sit with thy drink and I'll send Nancy to speak with thee. She knows all abart it, see. She'll have me guts for telling thee this much!"

"Get Nancy to come here now, Alf. I ain't got patience for all this!"

Nancy arrived at Wesley's table within a few minutes with his beer and explained about Sally refusing to speak to anyone other than Catherine Priestley.

"Well, that ain't going to happen till tomorrer I reckon. They've all gone home by the sound of it and the Priestleys are staying at the Red Cow, down at Cellarhead."

Initially, Nancy was angry with her husband for speaking of Sally's presence in the tavern, but felt some relief about having her brother there to explain things to Sally. He took a quick bite of the pie and downed half of his pint then accompanied Nancy up the stairs to her room.

"I doubt she'll let thee in, Wesley. She's reet upset and won't see no-one, like I said, unless it's her friend Catherine."

The pair arrived at the door and Nancy knocked gently.

"Sally, it's Nancy. Wesley's here and he says Catherine's gone home, and he wants to explain…"

There was no response. Wesley tried the door – locked!

"Sal, let us in, eh! It's Wes here… Cathy's gone home with 'er family. It's gettin' dark now. Ah doubt Uncle Tommy will let 'er come over till tomorrer, see."

The pair on the landing outside heard a big sigh and a sniff come from inside the room. There was a sound of movement and then Sally spoke:

"I don't want to speak to anyone except Cathy, Wes; not even you or Maither. I cannot face it. Please go and leave me here." She then had a thought. "Have thee got any money?"

"Aye, loads of cash; cus I was expecting to be buying lots of drinks after… well, after, thee knows… the wedding, see."

"Good," said Sally, her mind racing ahead of that moment.

"And, well, there's no need to be troubled in thy mind about that drunkard – Sebastian Brewer! Ah've seen him off for good; I can promise thee that!"

It went quiet. Sally was unsure about that news. Then she spoke, "Wes, if thou really wants to help me, then give Nancy all thy cash. I have to pay for the room, and I may be here more than one night. I cannot decide yet. And I want to buy clothes so's I can get out of this blessed wedding frock!"

"Let me in, Sally, please! I fear for thee in thy distress; please."

"No, little brother, I really can't. Go, and come back with Cathy and maybe some different clothes. Our maither will help 'er choose. Go and give Nancy thy cash, please, if thee wants to 'elp me!"

There was no more response from Sally no matter how much Wesley pleaded. Nancy received no answers to her questions until he had gone and she'd returned half an hour later. She was paid for the room and board from the money Wes left. With her Nancy had a small selection of clean clothes she had obtained from her two girls, who worked in the inn. Sally chose a couple of items and asked her to thank the girls and paid a nominal sum. Sally then asked to speak to the landlord about transport to Ashton-under-Lyne early the next morning. Having thought more about things, she still could not face the group of people that would no doubt return with Wesley. She was sure that Cathy alone would be the only one to understand her decision to go to Ashton. So she would leave a message, in a letter to Cathy.

Alf was relieved she was going and was happy not to charge her for paper and ink. He was very happy to confirm that the stagecoach would be leaving just after dawn, and informed her that she would need to change coaches at Macclesfield, then Stockport. Arriving late in the evening at Ashton, with very little luggage, did not seem to concern the young woman. Hard man as he was, Alf knew the Sefton men and did feel some responsibility towards Sally. He'd imagined if she had been one of his two daughters, and knew how he and Nancy would fret about them, alone, in a big town like Ashton-under-Lyne.

Sally did not sleep well with thoughts about Sebastian and her family going through her head all night. But by morning she had eventually convinced herself that

188

this was the best course of action. Becoming a missionary and assisting the Preacher John Wroe was something that would serve God and help to salve her conscience for leading Sebastian on to believe she could love him. Sally had decided finally that she had brought all of this trouble on herself and that she needed to find absolution through her newly discovered faith.

Chapter 17
Saviours and Lost Souls

TIRED and hungry as he was, Wesley had ridden to the Red Cow Inn from Cheddleton before returning home to the farm. It was quite late into the evening and he had to persuade Mr Hawker, the innkeeper, to permit his interruption of the Priestley family. Thomas and Milly had stayed there quite often over the years when visiting the Seftons and the innkeeper remembered them well each time.

"Ah can't go disturbing me guests just cos thee says so young man. Mr Priestley told me clear, they've had a bit of a shock and they weren't to be disturbed after they'd ate and gone to bed."

"Aye, but see, I know all about it! I was there and I've got important news for Catherine Priestley, see. Cannot thee not go up and tell them that?"

Mr Hawker agreed, reluctantly, and went up to the room where Tommy, Jack and James were staying. When he returned to speak to Wesley he was accompanied by Thomas, Milly and Cathy who were anxious to hear the news. Cathy was first to speak after Wesley had explained.

"But I can't understand why she wouldn't open the door to thee, Wesley. You're her brother."

"Cathy, I'm telling thee; you're the only person she'll see! She said she feels too ashamed of what's happened to see any of her family or friends except you."

"Well," said Thomas, scratching his head, "I doubt we can do much tonight, tha knowst. Perhaps we can sort it all out in the morning, hey? Sally's going to be needing her sleep just the same as us. It's been a reet strange, very long day, and no mistake."

190

"But Pa, Sally's had no-one to comfort her since she ran off. I want to help her, poor lamb."

Milly took hold of her daughter's arm and hugged it to her. Then she spoke, "Cathy, my darling, your father's right. It's been a very long day for us all, and Sally's probably asleep at this very moment. We'd best get rested and start off early to see her in the morning."

"To be fair to Nancy, back in the Tuns," said Wesley, "She seems to have been a good friend to Sal, today. And she has grown daughters of her own, so's tried to comfort her right way, Ah reckon. I'll go off now and get me some shut eye at home, and I'll see thee in the morning, then."

"Aye, thee did the right thing to come and tell us, Wes," said Tommy.

"Have you eaten?" asked Milly, having taken in his weary, worried and dishevelled look at a glance.

"Aye; I had summat in the Three Tuns, Aunty Milly. Thanks for asking," replied Wesley. With that comment, he accepted kisses and warm embraces from the two women, a firm handshake from Uncle Tommy, and he left quickly, tears in his eyes, to ride home.

There was enormous consternation the next day when Wesley, Cathy and James arrived at the Three Tuns in a carriage together, only to find that Sally had gone two hours earlier. They had expected to take her back with them to Seftons Farm, wrongly assuming that in the clear light of the new day she would be able to explain what had happened between herself and Sebastian. Cathy read the letter to herself first of all and then to the two men. It had been pinned to Sally's wedding dress, which had been carefully and neatly folded by Nancy. With moist eyes, the landlady had persisted for all the time it took to fold, and when saying her farewells, in asking Sally whether she was sure that she was doing the right thing. Her reply was sorrowful and sincere.

"I cannot give thee an answer to that, Nancy. All I have for now is hope. Thou will be forever in my thoughts for the comfort I was lucky to receive from thee, and thy daughters of course. I beg thee, thank them and your husband for me."

Ten minutes later she was aboard the stagecoach bound for Macclesfield. Cathy's letter from her began with Sally's wish for her friend to accept the wedding gown as a gift if she and James ever decided to marry. Cathy felt too shy with James present to read that part out but when she came to the next part, regarding Preacher Wroe, Cathy was unable to hold back her exclamations and distress.

"Oh, no! Oh, my Lord, forgive me, please! Oh, Sally, what have you done? And the fault is all mine. It's all mine – Oh! James, James you will never believe where she has gone and what she intends to do!"

The men were both shocked to hear Cathy's outburst and Wesley immediately insisted that she read it to them. She read:

'… I am full of regrets about leaving the church and everyone gathered there so hurriedly and will never face them again. After thinking long and hard about what I must do I have prayed to God and he has provided the answer to my question. The solution for me is to join Preacher Wroe and assist him in his good work for the Lord. There are more lost souls in this world to be saved than mine. The lost tribes of Moses that we read of Cathy are sought by Preacher Wroe and his message is one that I can help convey to the world. I can only hope to find salvation for deceiving poor Sebastian by doing this work. I know that you will understand my reasons for travelling to Ashton-under-Lyne, Cathy, being of like mind to myself.*

Please convey my love to my family and yours.
Your loving friend and sister in life,
Sally.'*

"So thee's been encouraging our Sally to do this?" demanded Wesley. He had noticed the worried looks that had passed between Cathy and James.

"Not at all, Wesley," insisted Cathy. "We talked about the Christian Israelites for quite a long time when we were in Parson Trunchman's office a few weeks ago. There was no discussion about joining John Wroe, or his community in Ashton-under-Lyne. But –"

Cathy was prevented from saying more by a touch on her arm from James. Wesley had noticed the brief movement.

"What is it that James stops thee from saying?"

"Well... It's awkward to say more, Wesley – without your family present as well."

"What on earth do ye mean? If it affects me sister, I want to know, Cathy. It's a reet distance from here to Ashton and I need to start off today. Soon as I get times of the next stagecoach north. I'll do it on horseback if I have to."

"Don't do that, Wesley. Surely you're still in the middle of a busy time on the farm? The harvest; reaping and threshing?"

"Uncle Dan and Peter can sort that out while I'm away. So what is it? What's the big secret the pair of thee is keeping from Sally's brother? Her brother!"

James replied. "Wesley, it's very difficult for Cathy to tell you, now the marriage is not to take place. I know something of John Wroe's past life and told her and her father some time before Sally's special day – her wedding."

Wesley's temper was rising with his impatience to chase after his sister. "So what is this big secret thee's keeping from her family? Cathy, thou's supposed to be her friend! Her truest and greatest friend!"

"That is still so, Wes! Please, you must believe me. I would do anything to prevent Sally from being hurt... and... Well, I didn't want to spoil her wedding day

193

by telling her James' news. Please tell me you understand."

Wesley looked down at his feet, deep in thought. "I'm sorry, Cathy, I can't do that. I'm going to find her in Ashton-under-Lyne come what may."

As he walked to the door James took hold of the big man's arm and said, "Wesley, I worked in the cotton mills of Ashton as a child and I probably know the town much better than you. It's best if I come with you to help find Sally. In fact I have a good idea about her destination."

Wesley paused then said, "Then what's to stop us leaving now, James?"

"All of your family need to hear about John Wroe. In my opinion and that of many others he is a charlatan, a rogue. But will you promise to come with us first of all – back to the farm? Then we can tell you and your mother, and grandmother, what we know and what's in this letter to Catherine?"

"Please, Wesley, it's for the best," pleaded Cathy.

For an answer he said that they would be best returning to Seftons Farm immediately so that he and James could set out for Ashton-under-Lyne while it was still morning.

***

Sebastian had stayed in his room in the Brewer's house for the remainder of the day intended for his marriage. Luke and his father had scraped him up from the lawn outside the church and bundled him into their carriage. Martha had spent the whole journey home weeping while mopping up the blood from around her son's face. The semi-conscious man mumbled and moaned the whole time with his father wasting his words of admonishment to Sebastian, both along the way and for hours later in their drawing room. When Sebastian finally had enough strength to look in the mirror, his bruised face with its swollen nose staring blearily back at him, sent him to his bed – seeking sanctuary from the world, but especially from Jonas.

Luke tried to side with his parents about the 'disgrace and scandal' that the Brewers had experienced in front of 'half the village'. However, deep down inside Luke was worried about how unhappy his brother was and had been for many recent years. At the same time Luke found the incident extremely amusing and looked forward to sharing it with his drinking friends, in whichever hostelry would accept the brother of Cheddleton's new pariah.

Luke sat at the bottom of Sebastian's bed chuckling to himself, listening to his snoring and his groans. *The real pain – within his heart – is still to come,* thought Luke. He spoke to him in his troubled sleep, "Seb, my poor slob of a brother, what's to become of you, eh? Now you've let everyone down in your little world; not only the lovely Sally, but father and mother, me, and all of the so-called respectable society in Leek, as well as those who live here in Cheddleton. For I've no doubt the gossip about your wedding has spread to there… Probably on its way to the whole of Stoke-on-Trent even as you sleep it off!"

Luke doubted whether 'it' could be slept off for months and predicted that Sebastian would be heartbroken when he fully realised that he had lost Sally for good. Listening to him speak in sombre mood, in the last few days before his wedding day, Luke suspected that Sally meant far more to his brother than Seb had realised. On the morning of one of those few days, before the day of their nuptials, Sebastian opened up to Luke during his slow recovery from yet another hangover.

"You know, Luke, over the many weeks and months I've struggled to gain Sally's heart, I have come to realise something about her that is rare. Rare in most of all the people I have met in my miserable life. Within my drinking company there's not one person I could identify as having scruples – well no! Thinking again – there is one I could name. Oh, lots of men have principles, like our father for example. He has a misplaced idea of what is the correct way to go about in society; it includes making a success of business, regularly attending church, tipping your hat to the gentry or local councillors and so on. But we all know many of these will send away the needy poor from the workhouse if they are too ill or injured to work, even on cold winter nights. Sally would never do such a cruel thing. That much I have understood about her during our few pleasant outings in the countryside. I feel desperately guilty when I am with Sally for I'm unworthy of such a beautiful person."

"Perhaps you are too hard on our father, Seb."

"He is principled as I said, on the correct appearances in society but he would snub you in the street if he suspected that you did not conform to his ideas of respectability. I've heard our poor mother ask him many times to give a few pence to a begging mother in the street, but his response is to direct them to the workhouse or to the prison."

"I've never seen you take Sally to the Tuns for a few drinks, Seb. So, who is this ideal person, this drinking partner of yours?"

"He's the only person in the world apart from Sally that I would trust with my life." Sebastian turned to look Luke full in the face. "It's you, you fool! Thou awkward, uncompromising, annoying – oh! so annoying, clod of an upright citizen!"

Then he softly punched his brother in the chest. Luke's response was to shake his head and say, "I see. And you are a rogue, loveable sometimes, but a rogue nevertheless. You must stay off the drink, Sebastian. I fear it has shrunk your brain and excluded all sense of reason."

"We may be kinsfolk, Luke, but not kindred in the way Sally and I are. We talk of poetry and books, and the world in ways that no-one I know, not even you, can match. To begin with I found Sally attractive in so many ways; but mainly, as you so rightly accused me some time ago, as my escape from our father and another route to riches."

"And now she is… what, Sebastian?"

"I feel quite certain and I hope she may be my soul mate one day. But there is an obstacle, a principle of hers that she's read of in a book by a woman called Mary Wollstonecraft."

"The principle, as you call it, is about the rights of women to be equal to men. I've read it, Seb."

"You have! Well, you'll understand exactly then. She demands to be equal in all things, and so she refuses to say 'love honour and obey' when we are at the altar."

"Would that be so hard for you? If you truly love Sally as you say?"

Sebastian chose not to hear this because he had moved on to his more immediate fear.

"And she has taken against strong drink, Luke; so this means… Well I can't, I couldn't…"

"You will not do that – not even for Sally?"

"It troubles me a lot. If I want to be with her forever, then I must give up one of the few small pleasures left to me in my miserable life!"

"It has to be your decision, my brother – no-one else's. Maybe your life won't be so miserable when you are with Sally."

"But I've lost everything now to that rogue from Chester, or wherever he came from. I'll need control of the farm if I am not to remain a pauper forever."

***

Sally had made her way to the Sanctuary, Wroe's personal refuge from the unenlightened world. She was desperately tired after two long coach journeys and it was very late in the evening. Telling herself that she should be strong she knocked again on the stout wooden door.

"Yes?"

The young woman who opened the door to Sally made it clear with that one word that she was not welcome. She wore a very plain, pale blue, linen dress that reached to the floor. The woman's hazel eyes stared at Sally from behind a veil and movements of her head indicated that she was inspecting the tired traveller from head to toe. Her mode of dress held no surprise for Sally as she had witnessed similar clothing amongst the converted, during the few visits to Ashton that she and Cathy had made with Thomas Priestley. The other colour allowed by the preacher had to be green, with no mixing of colours or materials allowed to the women. The only other fabric allowed, apart from linen, was silk with the lining and sewing thread to be of the same yarn as the item of clothing. On festival days both men and women attended the Sanctuary wearing white linen. The men's hats were broad-brimmed and the women's bonnets made of straw in the Leghorn style.

"May I come in? I wish to speak with Preacher Wroe."

"And who are you? Does thee have an appointment with the prophet?"

"I regret I have no appointment but I have travelled far to see him and need to rest soon. The journey was long and hard. I fear I may – Ooh!"

When Sally swooned on the doorstep, before the young woman attendant had time to close the door, there was a gruff question hailed from within the building. It was responding to the young woman's exclamation of, "Mercy me!"

"Who is it, Betty? We are about to commence our prayers and John Stanley is waiting for thee."

Betty heard his approaching footsteps and opened the door wider. The tall bearded man who arrived at front door looked down at Sally and said, "Oh, my word, I see. I think it's best we help her inside, Betty. She may explain herself in the kitchen after a glass of water, maybe. If you take her feet I'll lift her under her arms."

A few minutes later Sally came out of her faint sitting in a large Windsor chair, with Betty and Henry sat facing her. She began to apologise for the inconvenience she may have caused them but the man silenced her with a wave of his hand. He introduced himself and Betty as John Stanley's servants, insisting she drank some water from a cup on the table and restored her strength by eating the 'simple repast' of cheese and unleavened bread on the wooden platter. Henry was dressed similarly to the way that Thomas Priestley had been on the last few times she'd travelled to Ashton with him. It had occurred to Sally on Thomas' arrival at Saint Andrew's church that he was once again clean-shaven and wearing a fashionable coat and shirt. Before her, in addition to the unpopular 'nightshirt' of Uncle Tommy, Henry was also wearing a high-buttoned, collarless, jacket together with a white ruff around his neck.

"What brings thee to the Sanctuary, my dear?"

His voice was deep and calming, for which Sally was grateful as her pulse was still racing. She nibbled slowly at a piece of bread and replied, "I am Sally Sefton and I wish to join the preacher in his missionary work."

"Henry, we are missing prayers," insisted Betty. There was very little sympathy in her voice.

"Have patience, Betty, we might all attend soon. John will understand, be thou sure of that. Bring our visitor a veil, Betty, so that we three may enter together." He turned back to Sally. "I see; finish a morsel of food more, Sally, and after prayers we may talk more. Are you strong enough now, if I offer my arm to support thee? Surrounded by the Love of God, as you are here in the House of the Lord, I'm sure thou will overcome a temporary weakness of the body."

His smile was an encouragement to Sally to stand, shakily and uncertainly, but she was determined to show that she could belong there. Betty returned her veil to cover her hair and hid her disapproving, unfriendly, scowl. As the three slowly made their way to an inner sanctum, Henry whispered to Sally that John Stanley was to be the new Master in Ashton-under-Lyne, during the prophet's tour of Australia.

After the prayer meeting, Sally explained more to a group of men, and then she was escorted to the prophet's rooms. The dwarfish figure of John Wroe was sat at an enormous oak desk in his office, poring over miscellaneous papers, muttering to himself and occasionally scratching at a document with a quill pen. He looked up briefly at Sally when she entered with Henry on her left and the towering figure of John Stanley to her right. All of the men wore white gowns and Sally noticed that Wroe's was much fuller and more elaborate. He was even smaller than she remembered and his mass of untidy, shaggy, hair and beard left very little of his face showing. Looking up from his papers again he peered at them then he spoke. His highly pitched voice had a very distinct Bradford accent:

"So, Sally Sefton, Henry has explained to Master Stanley and me that thou wishes to help me in my missionary work. You are aware of my journeying to the other side of the world? To Australia?"

"Aye, yes, I mean, yes, sir."

"Why? Thee will not see your family for many, many months. Maybe we will be gone for a year. I cannot have those who are weak in mind or body along with me. What has determined this wish of thine?"

"Preacher Wroe, I've attended a few of your meetings and become convinced that I may become someone whose soul needs to be saved. I want to join one of the tribes of Israel. I am strong, having worked on a farm since a small child. I can read and write well, and have read the verses in the Old Testament in an effort to understand the causes that you preach. I wish to atone for my –"

"Enough! When you confess thy sins it will be to the Lord God Almighty. Have thou been baptised, Sally Sefton?" She nodded. "It may be necessary to give thee a new name. If we are in Australia thee must submit to that performance by myself in one of the many great rivers there. That is the time to beg forgiveness for thy sins." He paused in his speech and stared intently at Sally. She realised he expected an answer.

"Of course, if that is a requirement in order to enter the Kingdom of God, then so be it."

"I am in need of a good scribe while I'm away, and so thou could fit that bill well, Sally. Time is of the essence as we leave for Liverpool on the morrow." He proffered one of the documents on the desk. "Sally, make a decent copy of this and show me tomorrow. Henry will find fine paper and ink for it and provide a bed in the women's dormitory for later. Henry, is that clear?"

"Yes it is, Master."

"And one last thing, I am informed thee had very little baggage with thee, Sally. Do you have money to pay for thy passage aboard the ship to Australia?"

"I have some, not much, but all of it is yours... erm, Master."

"Well, as you will be working to pay for acceptable clothing – that will not do at all! Thou hast the look of a barmaid... Hmm! I suppose employment as my assistant and scribe may pay for thy passage to Australia as well."

Wroe had pointed to the clothes she wore that had been bought from Nancy's daughters. Suddenly he sat back in his chair and began to moan in his high droning voice. This continued for many minutes while the others watched, totally accepting the strange vision before them, with the exception of Sally of course. His eyes began to roll in his head as he swayed and foamed at the mouth. She looked at Henry.

"The prophet is in a trance; no doubt the Spirit will be sending him a message about you."

"Aye," added John Stanley, nodding wisely. His father had provided much of the funding needed to build the Sanctuary and the gatehouses. He felt the need to act the sage as often as possible. "We will know more tomorrow. Let us leave him now, Henry."

"Aye, Master. Come with me now, Sally, Betty is to explain to thee which prayers are to be used before sleeping. She's not been here long but is proving to become most loyal and very special; a good friend to thee no doubt before long."

Chapter 18
Worrisome Times

THE Digby, a brigantine ship, was expected to set sail from George's Dock, Liverpool, for Sydney in the late afternoon to early evening, when the tide was high enough. Most of the day was spent loading up her cargo and passengers were steadily arriving and boarding as convenient to them. Once on board most of the passengers found their cabin and settled as best they could. Some preferred to rest in their berth but most stayed on deck to idly watch the cargo procedures from a distance.

Wroe's small group had taken the 'new steam train' from Ashton-under-Lyne via Manchester to Liverpool. It had become possible recently for railway passengers to travel in relative comfort now that second class and some third class carriages were enclosed, and not open to the elements. Some of the seats even had armrests and were upholstered. However, their leader had insisted that they deny themselves 'these fripperies' and so they travelled in a third class carriage sat on hard wooden benches without armrests. Liverpool was just one of a few large cities in England, and several others around Europe, where John Wroe had attempted to reconcile Jewish and Roman Catholic churches. It had proven to be very unpopular.

In order to while away some time before boarding the Digby, Wroe took them on a small tour of local graveyards to survey the headstones, pray over them and then noting any biblical names connected to Moses or Abraham. Sally had passed her writing test and was allowed to use a pencil to record the names and their location for the future. John Wroe was keeping a record of his travels, divine revelations and proclamations, known as the Divine Communications. It was for this 'great journal' that Sally's literary skills were mainly required. Betty's attitude towards Sally had become friendlier now that she did not see her as a rival. They had conversed quite a lot at various points on the journey to Liverpool. They both were expected to complete more mundane tasks; preparing food; washing clothes; cleansing the prophet's feet for example. Betty had been told it was she who was 'chosen' to give birth to the new Shiloh after all. She was relieved that it was not to be Sally as she had suspected when she'd arrived. As scribe therefore, Sally was no challenge to her future special role. Betty had revealed to her new friend that it would be on their return from their missionary tours, according to the preacher's prophecy.

***

On the afternoon of the previous day, hours before Sally had been praying for the first time in the Sanctuary, Wesley's close relatives, his mother, grandmother and uncle, had expressed great astonishment to Thomas and Milly. Ruffled feelings of betrayal were shouted out, and disbelief repeated over and over, that they were capable of hiding the information about the 'John Wroe scandal' – keeping it secret from Sally all this time. James was somehow made to feel most guilty by Daniel, for merely possessing the information, without revealing it well before the wedding ceremony.

"Now come on, Daniel," complained Thomas, "That just ain't fair on James. What he told me persuaded me to give up on the Christian Israelites completely. At the time, that had nothing to do with Sally's wedding, mate. What worries me now is Australia could be John Wroe's next trip abroad."

"What! Tommy, surely not! I know just what it can be like on that long journey. Terrible hard if thee ain't got sea legs; thee suffers such sickness, never wanting food. Scurvy's an awful disease if you get it, loose teeth, gums that bleed if thee is tempted to eat… And when you're there the heat is something fierce – and snakes and monsters that can drag your strongest ox or horse into the swamp."

Ellie was terrified to hear this. "Daniel why have you never told us any of this in all the years you've been back with us? Oh, my poor daughter. The thought of it; will she ever return?"

"Well, I never wanted…"

Ellie's mother-in-law, Esther, spoke up, "It's my fault, Ellie. Daniel told me sometimes in the past the hardships he had to endure when he was sent to Australia. It upset me so much each time I made him promise to keep it to himself, pet. I saw no point in horrifying the children or yourself with his tales."

Unknown to the two women there had been times in the past, when Wesley had been a boy, that his uncle Daniel had thrilled him with tales of crocodiles and seven foot kangaroos. Today, however, was very different and Wesley could stand this delay no longer. He began to stamp about the room waving his arms at Tommy and Cathy, shouting, "This is wasting time! Owreet, Cathy and her father chose not to tell Sally about this fraudulent holy scoundrel, under the mistaken thought that it would upset her too much to get married! When all of time it was that damned drunken reprobate she should have been warned of! I knew it all along. I should blame myself for it all! We should leave now for Ashton! Now!"

His mother spoke up again, "Stop thy shouting, Wesley, please... Tommy, I know that you and Cathy would never do anything to hurt Sally. I believe that you both wanted what was best for her."

Milly stepped forward to hold Ellie's hand and earnestly say, "It was my advice that Cathy sought about this, Ellie, my dear. I agreed with her that Sally's excitement and happiness during the preparations for her wedding to Sebastian would suffer terribly if she learned about the scandal at that time. I said to tell her later, but only if it became necessary."

"I can understand that and... I think I would have said the same thing, Milly," replied Sally's mother. "Don't fret thysen about it, me duck."

"If it helps, I agree with both of you, Milly and Ellie," added Sally's grandmother.

The three women turned to Cathy and her father, and Ellie spoke up yet again, "We all believe that not telling Sally was meant well. The problem now is to stop her leaving the country for the other side of the world with an unscrupulous scoundrel whose immoral behaviour puts her in danger."

Granny Esther asked, "Tommy, love, how come you think John Wroe is soon bound for Australia?"

"Oh it's just summat I heard from folks in Ashton-under-Lyne recently. He aims to establish a temple in Melbourne I were told. Dunno how soon he's going, but – "

"What are you saying? My dearest Sally is leaving for Australia! No! No! Never!"

The loud interruption came from the doorway to the farmyard, making everyone turn to look. It was the 'damned drunken reprobate', Sebastian, who stepped forward from the shadows. Wesley reacted first of all.

"Who let thee in, thou drunkard no-good?" he growled, dashing across the room, only to find Luke barring his way. Daniel rushed to grab Wesley's shoulders from behind.

"Hold on, Wes! We ain't gunner cause a ruckus in yer maither's parlour, eh!"

Shaking his shoulders free from his uncle, Wesley said, "I don't want this man anywhere near me or my family. He's a disgrace!"

"Wesley, I will speak for my family; stay silent, please!" Ellie's tone and fierce look told everyone present where Sally's spirit came from. "This man has hurt Sally so much, that even I do not know the measure of it. I want to hear him speak. What is it he thinks he can say that can ever, ever appease the pain in my heart? Sebastian speak!"

"Maither! Uncle Dan! Granny Esther, listen to me - not this smooth-tongued snake! He's a vermin that wants destroying!" He took a step towards the brothers.

"Be quiet, Wesley, or get out!" ordered Ellie.

Sebastian glared at Wesley, his look challenging despite the fear he felt inside. He knew that he would not fare well in a fight with him but after hours of discussion, with Luke and his mother, Sebastian's realisation of his feelings for Sally made him resolve to get her back. He was intent on doing this, if not for his own aching heart, then for her family and the farm that he knew she loved. *I owe Sally and her family that much*, he'd thought.

Luke said, "Mrs Sefton, will thou allow me to speak first? It may help." She nodded without taking her eyes off Sebastian. "Everyone here has been wronged by his recent actions and he's truly repentant. He wants to put things right and help find her. If she has left the country – and let us all hope that she has not – then we will follow her –"

"To the other side of the world if I have to," interjected Sebastian. The tension in Sefton's farmhouse had never been greater, not since Joseph's disappearance, during his fatal illness, many years ago.

"Look," said Tommy, "I have to agree with Wesley on the point of not wasting time, not at all. I say actions speak louder than words and Sebastian can prove all his fine promises by joining the rest of us to Ashton. James and I know exactly where we may find Sally; where

John Wroe's temple and all that is. So, let's away now…
But –" Thomas walked right up to Wesley to continue.
"I'll not have thee accompany us if you're gunner delay
things arguing and fighting with Seb. Reet, Wes? Agree to
that and thee can come."

"Agreed. I've always respected thee, Uncle
Tommy. I ain't gunner change now."

Next Tommy walked straight up to Sebastian and
said, "And thee, Seb, I ain't properly done with thee yet.
But we need all the help we can get to make sure we find
her – including thee. Agreed?"

"You have my promise, Mr Priestley," said
Sebastian.

"Aye, well, we'll see what that might mean in the
next few days, hopefully. Even so, here's my promise to
thee, Mr Brewer." Tommy paused, in order to wave his
one good arm under Seb's nose. "If I so much as smell any
alcohol; ale, wine or spirits, or whatever, on thee, while
we're looking for Sally; or if thy behaviour with Wesley
causes us a problem – then I'll break thy neck for thee!
Understood?"

Thomas turned to Wesley and added, "That goes
for thee and all, Wesley Sefton, big as thee might be. The
job in hand is to find Sally and persuade her to come back
with us – that's it, see!"

The threats from the one-armed, ex-mule spinner
were particularly significant, considering he was much
older and six inches shorter than either of his targets. The
atmosphere in the parlour calmed down after Thomas'
intervention, with Wesley and Sebastian avoiding eye
contact with each other and a 'nice cup of tea', appearing
with the help from Granny Esther. This meant they could
settle the arrangements quietly for their quest. Ellie and
Esther took Sebastian aside into the scullery while the
others talked about the quest. The door was firmly closed
for ten precious minutes and Sebastian begged forgiveness

208

as he tried to convince the two women of his love and future devotion to Sally.

It was agreed that Daniel would stay behind to tend to the farm with Peter's help. Milly would live on the farm and help where she could since their Stockport store was being managed by Eddy while they were at the wedding. This meant that the search party consisted of Tommy, Jack, James, Wesley, Sebastian and Cathy. The men were reluctant to take Cathy at first, but when she insisted that, as her closest friend, she would be the one most likely to change Sally's mind, they relented. Luke would return home to inform his parents of the plan and calm them both down.

James and Jack were now able to contribute to the plan of action, having kept themselves up to date with the latest railway developments. It made hard listening for Sebastian who kept his comments about his losses to himself, with curses under his breath of which only his brother was made aware.

"Unfortunately, the first travel is the slowest, as we must make our way by stagecoach to Ashton. There is still no steam railway link from Leek or Cheddleton, northwards to the town or to Stockport," said James.

This caused Jack to glance, unnoticed, at Sebastian and Cathy before adding, "But the new Lancashire and Yorkshire line will take us directly from Ashton through Manchester all the way to Liverpool."

"Why Liverpool?" asked Granny Esther.

"That's the most likely port for ships to Australia, Ma," said Daniel.

"Look, everybody, we mun not get ourselves into a fretting state o' worry for nowt! Could be we'll find Sally safe an' sound in Ashton, see. We need clear heads, reet? If we do that we'll have more chance o' finding the lass. Believe me, no-one here wants that more'n meself."

Ellie grabbed Thomas and kissed his stubbly cheek. "Thank you, Tommy, there's nobody in the world I'd trust more than thee to find her, duck."

Money for their travel was clubbed together between them, with some more coming from Ellie and Daniel. If they needed much more for their sea travel Luke wrote a promissory note for Tommy, who agreed to add it to his own and he would seek more cash from a bank in Liverpool. That was something they all secretly hoped would not happen. Refreshed and eager to set off for Liverpool docks if necessary, the five men and Cathy left the farm to catch the next stagecoach for Macclesfield, and then on to Ashton-under-Lyne. Eager they all might have been on the surface but under their skin, each person felt as glum as ever they had in their lives. They all feared what may have happened to the beloved Sally while she was in such a distressed state.

***

The young handmaiden, Betty, who was now travelling to Australia with the preacher's group, had not been working at the Sanctuary very long and was about ten years Sally's junior. When they had been sleeping in adjacent beds in the dormitory the previous night, Betty told Sally the reason for her apparent dislike of her at first. Wroe had indicated to Betty a few days earlier that, when she had proven her devotion to his sect, through diligence and her studies of the Christian Israelites' message to the world, she would be privileged to be chosen. As the new scribe then Sally was no longer a competitor for this and she warmed to her. Despite her nervous disposition at that time Sally thought the girl to be sweetly innocent and wondered about her past. Both young women were very tired and fell asleep without further explanation of the term 'chosen'.

Sally and Betty had become separated from the others for a few minutes as they wandered around the graveyard of the parish church of Saint Nicholas. Although the new scribe was feigning the copying of notes at the foot of various graves, she could not resist asking Betty what she understood by the words, 'chosen' and 'Shiloh'. The virtuous girl was unable to hide her enthusiasm for the 'blessed role' as it had been described to her by the prophet.

"Why, Sally, I'm to have a baby when we return to the Sanctuary in Ashton and he'll be the new Jesus, known as the Shiloh. Preacher Wroe had a vision from the Holy Spirit who told him that I had been chosen, just like the Virgin Mary. It is a great honour, of course, and I'll be baptised anew in Australia."

"Of course," mused Sally, but with little enthusiasm.

Sally had been a farm girl all her life and was fully conversant with the natural mechanics involved with adding young to their stock of sheep, cattle or pigs. It occurred to her that tupping time would be fast approaching and that, normally, her uncle Daniel and she would be seeking a suitable ram to mate with their flock of ewes. One of Sally's favourite times of the farming year was lambing in springtime and a small pang of regret ran through her heart. But in that Liverpool churchyard she felt sure that Betty was quite unaware of the major experiences that probably awaited her.

"Betty, it can often be difficult giving birth to a baby, particularly if it's thy first child."

"I know that, Sally. My ma had three more bairns after me and they weren't all easy for her. I could hear her cries of pain when the midwife was in." She smiled at Sally, then continued, "Ma had morning sickness every time, so I know what to expect."

"How long was she expecting before giving birth, Betty?"

"Ah, canno' tell thee how many weeks and months, Sally. Why? Is it important?"

Sally sighed and looked across the churchyard to see Wroe and one of his priests approaching. She started to walk to the rear of the building. "Betty, ye need to hear what I have to say. Follow me this way, quickly now."

"What is it?" demanded Betty. There was an enormous wall now screening them from John Wroe and the priest.

"We don't have time to put this gently, my dear, but tell me have you ever lain with a man?"

Betty looked shocked. "What a question! Of course not, Sally. How could I have a virgin birth if I... if I... went with a man? I've had boys kiss me, but never became with child."

"Kissing will not make thee pregnant! And if you don't become pregnant thee won't give birth when we return, Betty. So what happens then? Thee hasn't been 'chosen' as you were told."

"Why are ye telling me these things? You are jealous of me after all – as I suspected all along. The Master has said that may happen and he promised to take care of it."

"Did he tell thee how? How he would 'take care of it'?"

"Well, no, but…"

They stopped talking when the preacher came around the corner and seeing them he said, "Ah, my new recruits in the fight against persecution. Betty, will you join the others please, while I examine Sally's list of names? They are gathering near to those many cotton bales."

The top of the man's shaggy head came up to Sally's shoulders and he seemed to lean in to her as he surveyed the paper in her hand. His smell was not pleasant and she felt embarrassed. His hand was placed gently on her back as he patted and congratulated her.

212

"Very well done, Sally. You have a perfectly clear way of writing and setting out. A talented young woman like thee deserves special opportunities in life – particularly in the service of Our Lord God. It occurs to me that we might give thee the new name of Joanna during thy baptism. What do you think?"

"Why the name Joanna, Master?"

"Well, because it was Mother Joanna Southcott who was first chosen to give birth to the Shiloh, years ago now. But she failed... Whereas, thou... thou is so much younger and stronger; and much more likely to find success – once the pregnancy is confirmed of course."

"I see, I am to become chosen for this once I am baptised, with my new name of Joanna. When will that be, Master?"

"While we are in Australia I expect, Sally. I must consult the Spirit of course, to find out... I will let you know soon."

Sally's skin was crawling with horror and suspicion. She wanted to flee and hide but spoke again, trying to sound calm and even a little excited, "It sounds a great honour but I understood from Henry and Betty that she may be the one chosen. How can that be?"

"This is not a random occurrence my dear Sally. When the Angel of The Lord told Mary she was to become the Virgin Mother the decision came from on high of course, from God. And so it will again. In Mother Southcott's time it was believed, mistakenly, that the Shiloh would be born during the millennium year... However, I have been fortunate enough to be the Holy Spirit's vessel for his message this time. I await it with much anticipation. Betty and thyself will be first to know."

Sally could feel the hairs on her nape rising with the dread that jumped to her throat, finding it almost impossible to speak. She swallowed deeply then asked, "If I may complete the task in hand, Master?" She pointed to two large monuments in a far corner of the churchyard.

213

"There are several notes to make about the graves over there and then I may join thee and the rest on the dockside, if I may?"

Preacher Wroe was beaming with pleasure and he squeezed the top of her arm, saying, "Thy diligence does you great justice, Sally. I will walk across to the Digby and look forward to reading the rest of thy notes before we board her. A fine sailing ship, do you not think?"

"Yes, sir; I cannot wait to sail with everyone on such an exciting mission."

Sally began to hurry away to the first monument and John Wroe left the churchyard, walking slowly and reverently, in the opposite direction. The Mersey flowed beside the parish church and Sally watched the high tide of the great river rising steadily against outer walls of Saint Nicholas. Each faint lap of the mingling seawater was like a ticking clock, swallowing time. Panic gripped her stomach; there was no time to waste. She was worried about Betty but had to escape from the whole situation that she was now in. What was she to do? To answer the buzzing bluebottle question that now flew around her head, Sally ran into the church seeking refuge in the nave. Kneeling at the altar she prayed for guidance, anxiety and regret influencing the words she whispered to her Maker. Fear clutched again at her heart when behind her she heard an iron clang at the entrance, and the heavy wooden door creaked open.

Chapter 19
Conflict and Cooperation

THE train had stopped to pick up more passengers from the recently named Manchester London Road station, although there were few vacant seats and very little room in any of the carriages, second or third class, in which the group of six (plus one!) travelled. It had previously been called Store Street station and was built on top of a 30 foot high viaduct. They were all quite thrilled to be there, in particular Jack and James who exchanged a few facts and figures. The excitement stopped when the guard's whistle pierced the air to remind them of their quest, and any smiles vanished. They looked across at the smoke and greyness of Cottonopolis, which their lofty position afforded them, and wondered what might await them at their new destination, the great city of Liverpool.

Hours earlier the group of six had attempted to interrogate John Stanley, the new master of the Sanctuary in Ashton but had little assistance from him. And then, as they stood on the doorstep, arguing about entry, they received tremendous help from another surprise visitor who had come from Flixton. The help was of a more official kind and it came from Inspector Button! Thomas was so surprised to find the police inspector appearing beside him that, for once, he had nothing to say when he was asked, "Gooday to thee, Mr Priestley, we meet again, hey. If you could just excuse me for a moment, I need to ask this gentleman to be allowed indoors?"

When the policeman tried to shuffle his way through the search party to the front door there were grumbles of objection, particularly from Sebastian. Jack was the only other person to recognise Button and he held Seb's arm to say, "It's alright it's the police inspector, let him through."

Sebastian flinched as though he had been stung and allowed Inspector Button through.

"Thank you, sir. Now then, who might you be? I am Inspector Button from Manchester police and I'd like to come inside, if you would be so kind."

He was addressing John Stanley directly who stood in his way at the door, but was now feeling flummoxed. He did not want to let anyone into the Sanctuary until they had completed their meeting about Wroe's departure and future proceedings.

"I am John Stanley, the Master here, and well, I'm sorry, Inspector, but as I was just explaining to these people we are in the middle of a very important planning meeting. I have been called from it this very minute because they would not take notice of our servant girl's instruction to request they return later today. So, I'll bid thee, Gooday, and see you later, sir."

Inspector Button's lip was stuck out and his teeth were clenched! His chin jutted and his large boot was now in the doorway. His notebook was held high!

"Right, sir, in that case I'll have thy name in full, since I may well have to call thee to the magistrate's court. This is a very urgent matter that I wish to pursue with regard to a missing young woman, still a girl in my opinion. But, no matter, I will come in now if you please, or see thee in court!"

The others, on hearing this, all began to speak up loudly and insistently. John Stanley did not wish to appear in court for any reason, in case that information was to ever come to the notice of Preacher Wroe on his return to England. What was he to do? The clamour of voices from Thomas' group added to the perplexities crowding the Sanctuary doorway. They all wanted to know: *How did Button know about Sally's disappearance?*

216

Stanley had held many public meetings for the Christian Israelites, consisting of large numbers of excited followers. Raising one hand, or sometimes two hands aloft, he could hold sway over the crowd. But that technique meant nothing to the confused six – until the inspector stepped up into the porch, turned, and raised his right arm. John Stanley looked up to the sky for heavenly guidance and waited for him to speak.

"Sorry, everyone, but I'm not looking for anyone called Sally. The young woman I'm seeking was named Elizabeth but is known as Betty. It is certain according to her close family that she fled here, to join the Christian Israelites, just a few weeks ago."

A heavy, disappointed, silence fell over everyone. He was not there to seek the whereabouts of their beloved Sally after all? Before one of their voices piped up once more John Stanley spoke:

"I regret to announce to you all that you are too late. Each of those young women was here as followers of Preacher Wroe, but…" He paused to clear his throat. "But they left early this morning for Liverpool. They are to assist him in his missionary work in Australia. It will be a glorious enterprise for them to be a small part of – believe me!"

A volcanic eruption of outrage was slowly pouring from an invisible crater within the six people staring up at him. Then it exploded into demands for details of time and travel, which Button quelled once again with his right arm raised. He turned to face the newly appointed Master of the Sanctuary, his nose just a few inches from this preacher's bushy beard.

"If that be true, Mr Stanley, and I've no reason to doubt thy word – yet! Then, ye can have no objections to me and one of these good people to enter here and confirm the women are nowhere inside. I would suggest Mr Thomas Priestley here." He pointed. "He's a well-respected businessman from Stockport and the senior person regarding age and experience."

John Stanley stood aside and Tommy nodded to him as the pair rushed past him. Tommy had suddenly warmed to Inspector Button; a mutual admiration was burgeoning from out of nothing as they traversed the long corridor.

"It's likely we'll be a lot faster if thee shows us around, Mr Stanley. We've no time to waste if we're to catch the next train from Ashton station, eh? Besides thee'll want us away from under thy feet, an' all I reckon!" He was chuckling to himself as he followed Button.

Within a few minutes Inspector Button and Thomas returned to the others to confirm the women were not present anywhere in the Sanctuary. They all had then raced across town to Wellington Street where they caught the last train to Liverpool.

**

The man wearing religious robes who came down the aisle to speak to Sally was obviously not Preacher Wroe. He was the rector of Saint Nicholas and was curious about the young woman dressed in simple green clothes, kneeling at the altar. She looked back at the entrance door behind him many times as he drew closer to her.

"Hello, I am the rector here. Are you in fear of someone or something, my dear? Your constant glances to the door lead me to believe you are in hiding."

The middle-aged clergyman was clean shaven and had a kind face, with grey eyes that smiled as he spoke. Sally's trust in religious leaders had wobbled in recent years, but Parson Trunchman had restored it with his direct honesty and this man spoke in a similar fashion so she wanted to trust him. The way that the Preacher Wroe had explained things about the Shiloh, to Betty and her, had shaken her judgement and past misgivings had returned.

"There is someone I don't wish to find me here, Rector. I was to sail to Australia with him and his followers... but, I'm fearful to do so... and... they may try to force me or take me on board the ship, against my will...and –"

She was unable to continue. Desperately looking at the church door and then around the sides for the curtains that hid the vestry, Sally continued, "My own parson had a place of refuge where we sometimes spoke in private. I, I wonder... whether I, we..."

The rector said nothing but retreated to the church door and locked it with a large key. His voice echoed as he returned.

"This is quite irregular but I wish to help. I am Simon, what is your name?"

The resonance was disturbing and she whispered it, her eyes widened, fearful. He continued speaking but more softly. "I assume, Sally, you're meant to be sailing on the Digby. She has a good record, you know, so if you're frightened of her sinking I can assure thee there's nothing to fear. Is that it?"

She shook her head, unable to explain to this stranger, unable to explain to herself. Sally thought, *What a mess I'm in. What is wrong with me?* She blinked back stinging tears and bowed her head. She felt broken once more.

Rector Simon could see that she was in a state of confusion and said, "The door will remain locked until you wish to leave, Sally. I am in the vestry if thou needs to speak to me. For now continue thy prayers to God. He will bring thee strength and guidance in your divine solitude, believe me."

She watched the rector as he pushed aside deep blue velvet drapes to leave her alone. Slowly her inner panic subsided as, with eyes closed, she knelt and prayed.

219

Very slowly something of her usual confidence and clarity of thinking returned. Her thoughts turned anew to Cathy and the way they often counselled each other when they were troubled by one of life's uncertainties. Sally was certain that Cathy would be unable to abandon a young girl, such as Betty, to the suspected wiles of John Wroe. She had to at least try to persuade Betty to think again; to ask her why she wanted to follow him. Yes, she would go to the dockside and speak to Betty!

This decision forced her to question her own motives:

Why are thou here, Sally Sefton? Will you do good when thee takes up their cause? Or is it atonement or retribution thee hoped to find if you joined the Christian Israelites? What is the sin thou has committed? Running away; deceiving Sebastian about thy affections? Can these be sins?

Sally was still unsure about leaving the Christian Israelites because she remembered how much it had meant to Uncle Tommy. Preacher Wroe's words had helped her return to God through the misery of losing Gabriel and her father. However, she could face up to him about not becoming the mother of a new Messiah. She felt it was morally wrong, and that gave her renewed strength to convince Betty to change her mind too. She arose, thanked God for his help and approached the vestry to tell the rector her decision. Some anxiety seized her again as her hand reached out to the blue drapes and the handle of the large church door rattled loudly – and then again. Could it be the preacher? She was not quite ready to see him yet. She needed to confide in Rector Simon first of all – maybe? Sally wanted to scream suddenly. It was all so confusing! Perhaps she could hide behind the drapes for now?

***

During their journey to Liverpool the police inspector had revealed more concerning his own quest to find Betty. She was his niece, his sister's girl. They all lived with him in Flixton. Betty had run away from home after a disagreement with her mother about returning her to a large house nearby. It appeared that Betty had been indentured there on behalf of her mother, by her uncle Walter, to serve there as a scullery maid. After only one month she disliked her duties and treatment by a strict cook so much, she had fled back home. Scouring floors, stoves and pans, cleaning vegetables, waiting on the other servants were all too disagreeable to her, so she had claimed. Button had traced her to Stockport and then to Ashton where he was told by John Stanley she had begged to become one of the Sanctuary community.

"And do you think the girl will willingly accompany you back to Flixton, Inspector Button?" asked Cathy, trying not to shout against the rattle of the steam train.

"I've known my sister's children from when they were tiny bairns, Cathy. We always got on well and Betty played her games with me from when she just toddled about. I blame myself for being away for a couple of days in Wilmslow, when I should've gone home each night. It couldn't have helped. Besides, I feel an obligation to them, since I told Olivia, her ma, about the apprenticeship, see."

"It's to be hoped that James' story about Wroe'll stop her from boarding that ship – when we find her," added Thomas.

"Aye, and let's pray to God we get to the docks before she departs," said Wesley.

They arrived in Liverpool thirty minutes later and made their way as fast as they could through the congested roads around the docks to the pier head of the Mersey.

When the group of searchers had exchanged the railway's odour, of steamy cinders and smoke, for the fresh dockside aroma, of salty air and seaweed, they agreed to split up into three groups. Thomas and Sebastian made their way to the taverns immediately facing the Digby, while Button accompanied James and Cathy on the northern side with Jack and Wesley looking for them southwards. They were all aware that a small group of bearded men wearing 'nightshirts', with women in plain green skirts was to be the sight they sought. Thomas reminded them that the preacher was a very small man with 'a great brushwood of tangled hair and beard', so spotting him would confirm they were not disturbing unwary strangers.

Thomas and Seb had looked in two of the inns, only to be confronted by densely crowded, and tobacco smoke-filled public bars, and were beginning to doubt the likelihood of finding teetotallers present. Tommy said he would book rooms in the next inn if it was more respectable, while Seb could carry on looking along the pier. It was at this point that the harbourmaster had agreed with the captain of the Digby that he could weigh anchor. The searchers' only indication of this was the ringing of a great brass bell informing all who wished to board the ship to get on board within the hour.

About fifty yards from Seb and Tommy the preacher had instructed Betty to hasten back to Saint Nicholas Church and to fetch Sally quickly. As she ran past Sebastian he noted her clothing and attempted to speak to her.

"Excuse me, miss, but I would –"

The maiden merely gave Seb a startled glance as she ran even faster to the graveyard where she had left her new friend just minutes ago. When Betty had run around the rear of the church, to discover that Sally was no longer there, Sebastian had caught up with her and asked again, "Excuse me, I am Sebastian Brewer seeking to find a young woman by the name of Sally. I assume you are with a group waiting to board the Digby bound for Australia and she may be with you. Am I correct?"

Now Betty was completely confused about her next move. The brass bell was telling her to return soon to Wroe and the rest; but how could she return to the preacher without Sally? Would he be angry with her? And now this stranger, who knew Sally, was also looking for her. Perhaps they might help each other?

"I'm seeking Sally as well, sir, and she was here, but has vanished in just a few minutes!"

"Let's look in the church then. She may be in there."

They walked round to the front of the building and each tried the door only to find it locked. As they returned to the dockside Seb ventured to ask, "Do you have a young woman, like yourself, by the name of Betty with your party of people? Her uncle is very vexed to find her and he's with us?"

Betty's eyes grew wider and she stared at Sebastian.

"What might be the name of this man, this uncle?"

"Forgive me, miss, for I only know him as Inspector Button. I believe he –"

"Uncle Walter! Oh my!"

"This must mean that you are Betty after all... Betty, please, believe me when I tell thee that you must not leave with this man, John Wroe! It's for the same reason that we need to find Sally, as you are both in danger."

"Preacher Wroe has been kindness itself. Why should I believe thee – a stranger? If you don't mind, I'll return to him now and I'll thank thee not to accompany me, no more!"

She ran off as fast as she could to the dockside near to the Digby. But Sebastian's long legs kept pace with her from a distance; he was not about to give up the chase now, not now he was so close to his sweetheart's

223

whereabouts. As she ran from him Betty was reminded of her uncle Walter, and how kind he had been when they had lost their father to a drunken killer. He had taken them all into his home during the trial. She had grown to love him and trust him as she grew up, so why was she running away now?

On the shore side of the ship's gangway John Wroe had left a sparsely bearded young man to show Betty and Sally the way on board. The rest of the Christian Israelites had found their way to their cabins but Wroe had come back on deck to speak briefly to the captain. Looking down from the side of the ship he called to Betty to hurry aboard but Betty was catching her breath at the bottom of the gangway, watching her uncle running to catch up with Sebastian. When Seb turned to follow Betty's eye-line he saw Button and shouted, "Inspector, I think I've found her! Betty's here!"

When the panting Inspector Walter Button embraced his niece he said, "Thank God I've found thee, Betty. How could I ever face thy mother if I'd let thee run off to t'other side of the world?"

It felt so good to the young woman to be in his arms. He had always been like a father to his sister's children. She felt safe and secure with him, but what of the preacher? She looked up at Wroe who was waving and gesticulating for her to join him on the splendid sailing ship. Cathy and James had now caught up with the inspector and were smiling at Betty, who just looked even more confused. Who were these people?

"Listen to me, my dear. Thy ma and me have agreed thee doesn't have to stay as a maid in the big house. We'll get something sorted more to thy liking, right?"

Betty smiled up at him and he kissed her cheek. "Now, listen to James, here. His story mayhap will change thy mind about boarding the ship. Please, listen to him."

The wetness in Button's eyes made Betty nod. While the three spoke, Sebastian and Cathy drew away and agreed to meet at the inn. He pointed it out and explained that Thomas had entered to book it for later refreshment for them all. Sebastian set off again to find Sally further along the dockside and Cathy wandered over to Saint Nicholas' church. She wished to be sure that Sally was not inside even though Seb had told her the door was locked. Cathy had put herself in Sally's shoes and assumed that she would seek advice from God in prayer. However, she still had to be certain she was correct in the strong feeling she had about that. Pausing for a moment to admire the wonderful edifice that was Saint Nicholas' church, Cathy tentatively tried the door.

Chapter 20
Farms, Families, Futures

THE rector of Saint Nicholas and Sally approached the large wooden door of the nave. He had encouraged her to speak directly to Preacher Wroe and tell him that if she were to remain as one of the followers of the Christian Israelites then, neither she nor Betty could be his wife and mother to his children. Simon knew of John Wroe and said that he was married already, with five or six children. They both agreed that it would be immoral in the eyes of the Lord.

"Are you still sure of your commitment to their cause, Sally? It's a very big decision to make… in view of the situation that you say you left behind in Cheddleton."

"I'm not sure of anything anymore, Rector. I thought I was in love… I thought Sebastian loved me… How can I know?" She paused to listen. "The bell rang some time ago for boarding, so time is short. Perhaps when I speak to Preacher Wroe about this, then I'll know what I want?"

"And I will accompany you, to be with thee, as I promised, Sally."

"Yes, and that will help – I think." She paused again and then she froze. The door handle was slowly being turned but this third time it was gentler somehow. There was less of an urgent rattle; and then a gentle voice:

"Sally, Sally, my dear. Are you in there? Can it be I've found thee at last?"

Rector Simon opened the door and Sally fell into Cathy's embrace. He gently shepherded the weeping pair back into the church, where they sat in one of the pews. As things became calmer Sally explained to Cathy that she still wished to assist Preacher Wroe with his missionary work but needed to explain something to him. The Rector asked her whether he was still needed for moral support now that her best friend was with her.

"I thank thee from the bottom of my heart, Rector Simon, but I need trouble thee no more, now, as you say, that Catherine is with me. I hope thou's not offended." She instinctively reached out her hand to him. The rector clasped her hand warmly in both his and said, "Not at all, Sally. Go with God's blessing, my child. I am sure that with His guidance you will discover the right thing to do."

***

Wroe and his small entourage of followers were all gathered on the deck of the tall ship watching as the gangway was about to be hauled aboard. The Digby was departing, bound for Australia within minutes. He spotted Sally and Cathy approaching so shouted to the sailors, "No! Wait! We have one more passenger!" He frowned, furious to see them both enter the inn.

Thomas had paid for the use of a private room in the dockside inn where they were to stay that night. He closed the door to the noise from the adjacent taproom so that they could speak. Cathy had persuaded Sally to come with her to see her friends and family for *just one precious minute*. Still in a daze Wroe's new novice held Cathy's hand for strength, curious to see so many present in the room, including a stranger with a protruding lip and chin.

Maither, where is my maither? Is she here too? she wondered, her eyes flicking back and forth through the group. There was a very young woman with a shawl around her shoulders sitting in the corner. Her head was bowed and there was something familiar about her. Ostensibly, she had been told, it was for them to say their farewells to her, and Sally had agreed to listen to her Uncle Tommy and Cathy speak about the preacher. Then,

227

alarmed, she turned to run back to Wroe's group because Sebastian came forward to speak. Cathy held on tightly to her hand.

"Nay, nay, Sally, my darling. Please listen to Cathy and me first, eh?" Tommy gently took her other hand in his as he spoke but Seb suddenly broke in, "Sally, I love thee. Please stay for a few minutes and listen to them."

The plea from Sebastian was heartfelt and deep. There was intensity in Seb's expression, in his eyes, that was something new and unsettling. She was curious, afraid, and still she embraced Catherine, her eyes fixed upon Sebastian, who tried to hold Sally's gaze. Was she listening?

"No, Sally, you must not go with this charlatan, this lying man, the so-called prophet, John Wroe! Refuse his prayers, his entreaties to accompany him to other lands. If not for me, then listen to your friends. Do not go aboard that ship or we may lose thee forever – please!"

Cathy squeezed Sally's hand even tighter, with tears in her eyes she pleaded, "Sally, my dearest friend, my childhood playmate, my sister in life forever, please hear my pa and James. They too have been hurt by John Wroe, and now, now they would reject him completely from their lives. They have much to tell you. Please, I beg you, listen – and then, come home with us."

The young woman with the shawl looked up and called to Sally, "Listen to them, Sally, listen… please!" It was Betty.

Sally gasped, stared at Sebastian, then, as though in a trance, her gaze was drawn to something above them all, at somewhere in a space outside the walls that confined them. As Cathy's words filtered through to her misty mind she slowly turned back to Sebastian. The man's arms were raised and he reached out to hold Sally to him. There was unquestionable pain distorting his features, which became an agony of rejection and shock when Sally's defensive palms blocked his further advance. There was no direct contact but her magnetic repulsion rendered a force much greater than her feeble, trembling hands could ever produce.

"Why are you here, Seb? Hast thou not hurt me enough? Broken promises, shame before my friends and family, and now thou would destroy my newfound faith. My last hope of something I may hang on to, something to make my life worth living... I fear my heart may be broken... I've never felt worse emotions before... Can this anguish be worse than losing Pa and Gabriel?"

Sebastian fell to his knees before her, his forceful baritone reduced to a strain against a weeping wail. His hands were clutched as if in prayer.

"Sally, my darling, my dearest... My life! I beg you to forgive me. My ambitions and selfish desires have for a long time now cloaked my feelings for you... It was not until you were no longer a part of my life that I discovered how much I loved you. Not to see your lovely face and hold you every day is something too painful to bear... Please forgive me. I will die without you... Please take me back, Sally... Please, I beg you."

The rest of the company present in the room shuffled uncomfortably towards the door. Perhaps it would be better to leave Sally and Sebastian alone? Suddenly, she realised what was happening and screamed, "No! No! All of you go, but leave Uncle Tommy and Cathy here with me. I want to hear more from them, and them alone."

James looked to Cathy for consent to stay. She shook her head. He went out with Jack, Wesley, Sebastian, Button and his niece following him. The inspector then took it upon himself to leave the inn and wave the Digby and John Wroe away. His determined chin and lip proud as granite. Between gritted teeth he growled, "Goodbye and good riddance!"

After listening to Thomas and Cathy for ten minutes Sally began to berate herself for 'being such a fool'. There were tears of regret and relief from both young women. They had all embraced and Tommy went out holding his daughter's hand. He breathed a big sigh and said, "Sebastian, Sal would like to speak to thee on your own, while we all chat amongst ourselves."

***

Sally's clever brain had begun to tell her heart something that had very slowly seeped into her consciousness. She realised that Sebastian was just another person, like her – just like Wesley and her mother and anyone else in the world. She'd had to remind herself that each person had their own inner wishes, aims and hopes for the future. Sometimes, their intellect got the better of their emotions, and at other times the opposite was the case. Occasionally, we frail human beings had to seek a fragile balance between those two states of mind and heart. Sally knew how much she had always valued her independence in managing the farm with her uncle and brothers since losing their father. Her determination to hang on to that freedom made things so difficult, when she also wanted to share the rest of her life with Sebastian. Had she misjudged things so badly?

When Sally had stopped to think hard about her own reasons for wanting to marry Sebastian, then she admitted that from the beginning, it was for his apparent sophistication, his ambitious outlook on life, and his higher level of education. She enjoyed listening to his esoteric, well informed conversations. In simple terms, she told herself, it was for the marked difference between Seb and all the men she knew, and loved most of all, in her own farming family. And now it was her turn to feel ashamed because in spite of his faults, she had slowly learned to truly love Sebastian over the months they had sought each other's company. It would be impossible to think of her future without him in it. Despite everything it was now obvious to Sally that Sebastian had grown to love her. How could she abandon him for a cause that she did not believe in? Following the hypocrite, John Wroe, and his false faith would never compensate for leaving Sebastian. Sally held him in her arms briefly but resisted his kiss. She stepped back and, out of habit, stared into his eyes checking for more falsehoods – regretting her actions immediately. *This feeling has to stop*, she told herself.

"What is it, Sal? Please, tell me; please, please – give me a chance, and I will try my hardest to put it right."

"And what of all thy past promises to me, Seb? Where are they in the love thou professes to honour me with?"

"My dearest, darling, Sally Sefton, if you can bear to forgive me my stupid and selfish acts; if one day you will love me, as now I know I love thee, then I promise to honour thee as my equal, forever. Thou will always be a better person than I could ever be. If I have to wait until thou loves me, then so be it. I wish to be with you until God chooses to accept me into His Heaven, where I'll wait for you forever."

Sally briefly placed a single finger gently on Sebastian's lips to silence him; then kissed him, just as gently and briefly. Even so, he had to continue speaking:

"Whatever you want, Sal, then I desire that too. There will be no more wild ideas about railway investments; no fancy thoughts of becoming a gentleman farmer. I will be content to live with thee, toiling on the land side by side, forever and ever. And hopefully one day, we'll raise a family of our own, all of them farmers to the core – just like thee! I'll even take the pledge of abstinence like Thomas Priestley."

Perchance, just maybe, Sebastian's wild speculation of weeks ago, about farmers providing food for the growing urban population, was about to come true for them, in their future togetherness. She laughed and kissed him again.

"Perhaps we should rule out the impossible, for now, my darling," she joked. "Love me forever, as I know I love thee, Seb. That's all I really desire and then we can face the future together, whatever it may bring."

They embraced again, kissed once more, and went hand-in-hand, to reveal to the others that they were to marry 'once more'. Cathy had been silently holding James' hand while they waited in the noisy adjacent room. Hearing the announcement made her burst into tears of gladness and she turned to look deep into James' eyes who swept her up into his arms. Without a word they too embraced and kissed, sharing the joy for the happy couple. Suddenly, as they spoke quiet words of love to each other, there was another acceptance of a new proposal of marriage. They whispered it to Thomas and Jack; Cathy's brother, ignoring all sense of subtlety and tact, exclaimed loudly to the whole room, "My sister and James are to marry as well! Let's give three cheers to the two couples!"

The noisy racket of the tap room ceased for a few seconds because everyone was looking back and forth from Cathy and James, then to Sally and Sebastian, as the four stood smiling at everyone else in the room. Then three uproarious cheers and applause replaced the hushed calm and the happy young women's arms encircled each other's waist, sharing the moment. Sally's flowing auburn mane contrasted with Catherine's tidy flaxen bun, in an encore of the time they had watched a magnificent sunset while standing in a field of lambs. James and Sebastian exchanged hearty handshakes with each other and then from three other men in the search party. Meanwhile the drinkers in that Liverpool bar were chanting out, "When? When? When?" over and over again. The mule spinners' daughters, still 'sisters in life' and each now comfortable in their lovers' arms, were quick to agree the place and date for their wedding day – "Saint Andrew's church next May Day!" they joyfully announced.

Chapter 21
Ever After

THE wedding ceremony went ahead on a beautiful day in the following springtime, much to the relief of everyone concerned, and with the fresh blessing of Parson Trunchman. Emma and Charlotte were delighted to act as bridesmaids to Sally when she married Sebastian. Cathy invited Rachel and Betty to be her bridesmaids when she married James. They were both delighted to accept and the whole day was completed without a hitch.

Betty had become an assistant in Gibson's Store until Cathy moved out of the Priestley home to live with her husband in Flixton. Betty proved to be a quick learner of the retail trade and was appointed to be the manageress when Jack gained a job with the railway company. He was also attending the Manchester mechanics institute in Cooper Street and so had no time to assist in the shop. This is not to imply that Jack had lost all interest in his parents' shop. Whenever he was at home, he often found time to chat to the pretty niece of the Manchester detective inspector about business and new gadgets taken into stock. Jack even offered to show Betty the walks in the public parks around the town and their rides out on occasion became a favourite outing.

A year later Ellie Sefton and Martha Brewer became very happy grandmothers to twin baby boys, Joseph and Jonas. Despite his grumpy reluctance to congratulate Sally and Sebastian a second time on their wedding day, Jonas Brewer wept with delight when he met his grandsons for the first time. He was never able to attract Seb back into his funeral business, and yet he immediately arranged a substantial trust fund for the grandchildren. Cathy and James occupied married quarters in the new school for three years and were not blessed with children until then. James had become the assistant headmaster to Mr Macdougal at the end of the previous term and wanted to move out of their school accommodation before the baby was born. Persuaded by the headmaster that it would not be problem if they stayed there to bring up their children Cathy and James stayed. Their little girl, Rebecca, became a favourite with their colleagues and the pupils who were boarders, whenever they took a stroll around the school grounds. The bonny baby, sitting up in her pram, in pretty pink dresses, had a very happy smile and a chuckle for all. She had a cheering effect on both girls and boys who were reminded of their own younger siblings. Often they felt homesick and sad, being away from home for weeks and months, and 'delightful Becky' raised their spirits.

Wesley and Sebastian slowly formed a new and sincere brotherhood, working together with Uncle Daniel restoring the dilapidated old cottage near Cheddleton. Ellie's worries about Seb and Sally sleeping in Sally's room for a year came to nothing. She shared her concerns with Granny Esther after they'd heard more about Wesley hitting Seb outside the church. Without sufficient funds to pay outside craftsmen to do the work meant that Sebastian had to 'roll up his sleeves and get to it' as Daniel had told him. When it turned out that Seb really enjoyed the task and could saw and plane wood, plaster walls and paint as well as the other two men he earned a new respect from his brother-in-law.

Jonas and Joseph were only four years-old when their doting uncle, Wesley, had taken them to sit on his knee in order to hear some more stories from their Great Granny Esther. She had not been well for some time and was confined to her bed with 'rheumatiz' in her back and knees. She was also still feeling drowsy after lunch but everyone tended to 'allow her, her little ways' now she was seventy-something. Each twin clutched a woollen lamb knitted by Great Granny and stared slightly in awe while she was propped up with pillows by Ellie, who departed to prepare the evening meal.

"Wesley, darling, where had I got to before?"

"Thee'd told them about thy husband going to fight Napoleon in the war, afore I was born, Granny and then, how you went to be housekeeper in a big house after suffering in the workhouse for years in London."

"Oh, aye, of course. I remember now... Well, boys, your grandfather, Joseph, who was Wesley's pa, was sent away, while I was in that workhouse, to work in a cotton mill in Cheshire. And, erm..."

"My name's Joseph." It was a mumble from behind a woolly lamb held in front of the face of the mumbler, big brown eyes peeping just above the lamb's fluffy back.

"Yes, it is, my dear. Because that's where thy name comes from... Anyway, Joseph was my son and my other son is Uncle Daniel who is helping Wesley and thy father to build you that new house, down by that bridge, over the river."

At this point Jonas struggled free of Wesley's clutches to climb up on to Great Granny's enormous eiderdown and lie fully out, face down, to ask, "Was he my grandpa as well?"

"Of course, Jonas, and your other grandfather is thy pa's father. And that is how you got your name... Now then, Uncle Daniel did a very bad thing when he was a boy and he got sent to a land far, far away to be punished. And that's why it's so important to be good... Oh, Jonas, darling, do you think thee could move away from my legs. You're a bit heavy on my knees, see."

Wesley scooped him up with one hand with Joseph held under his other arm. His woolly lamb hung from his mouth, clutched there by some of his remaining milk teeth. Jonas immediately copied this and he had two more front teeth, which was the current way of distinguishing between the twins.

"Come on, you little scamps. Thee canno' stay much longer cos you're wearing Great Granny Esther out."

"They'll be alright for a few more minutes, Wesley... Now then, tell me whether you're saying thy prayers every night, when you go to bed."

"I do, Great Granny, but Joe forgets all the time!"

"Oh no I dunner, cos I 'members to tell thee as well!"

"No arguing now; I'm just very happy to hear you both speak to Jesus every night."

"And, and, Great Granny, it's not the cheeses that you eat," said Jonas proudly.

She looked quite puzzled at this statement and caught the eye of Wesley. He looked equally puzzled back at her and shrugged his shoulders, saying, "Could you say that again, Jonas?"

"It's not cheeses."

Joseph assisted his twin. "No, Great Granny, it's not the same cheeses we eat with bread and butter, cos this cheeses is a man who was the Son of God." He had awe and wonder in his voice.

"And he was the baby in a manger when he was born in Beff-lu-hem," added Jonas, respect dripped from his every word.

Wesley and his grandmother made instant eye contact as understanding hit each of them at the same time. They looked down and bit their lower lip, and then they bit their upper lip, and finally they gulped, almost choking on the laugh that insisted upon breaking the deep reverence the twins had brought into Great Granny Esther's bedroom.

She muttered something about being very tired and Wesley cleared his throat, coughing as he said, "Say night, night, lads... Cough! We've got to give Granny

236

Esther… Cough! Cough! a chance to sleep now." Then he carried them out and closed the door very carefully.

Wesley reminded the twins about this occasion a few years later when he was asked, as her youngest grandchild, to speak at Esther's funeral. Luke took care of the funeral arrangements, having become the new owner of the business when his father retired. Sebastian graciously refused to join his brother because he had become fully immersed in Seftons Farm business. He and Sally had sourced a new breed of cattle, known as Lincoln Red, which had greatly increased the farm's income from beef. They'd agreed with Daniel and Wesley to start looking for a different sheep herd.

Thomas and Milly retired after ten more years and Betty took over the running of the store completely, slowly buying them out to provide their future pension. She employed two more members of the Button family as assistants and a new branch opened in Cheadle the year before the Priestley's retirement. Catherine and James were content to stay as teachers at Cheadle Hall Academy for many more years but moved out and into their own house in nearby Cheadle Hulme. They later had another girl, Sophia, and a baby boy they named William. Both these children entered the teaching profession and later became involved in Forster's Education Act of 1870, which proved to be a milestone in educational development.

Glossary of Words and Terms

abart: about
allas: always
anuvver: another
arter: after
baggin: lunch snack
bob (cash): slang for shilling coin
bobbin: cotton reel or spindle
bottle kiln: type of pottery firing oven
breeches: trousers
brimstone: sulphur
buke: book
carbolic: disinfectant
carding: combing to clean cotton, wool
clouts: trousers or clothes
cobbles: small round stones
consumption: tb or tuberculosis
coppice: cleared woodland area
crown (cash): five shillings
doffing: changing mule spindles
dray: cart with no sides
dunner: don't or doesn't
dunnit: doesn't it
drover: driver of livestock
faither: father
farthing: one quarter of an old penny
fust: first
fustian: thick rough cloth
gig: light horse carriage
goodun: good one
ha'penny: half penny coin
half-crown (cash): two shillings & sixpence
hanky-panky: improper behaviour
hisel: himself

indenture: formal contract
jiggered: exhausted
joshing: playfully teasing
lickle: little
luke: look
maither: mother
muvver: mother
mebee: maybe
mun: must
naffin: nothing
nowt: nothing
nowty: grumpy
oop: up
overseer or overlooker: supervisor
physic: medicinal drugs/medical person
piecing: joining broken yarns
pressgang: a group who force others to join army or navy
privy: a toilet/wc
rarnd: round
reet: right
saggar: fire clay box to hold pottery wares in kiln
scavenging: cleaning up of waste cotton
shilling: twelve old pence (five new pence)
shoddy or short silk etc: cheaper quality fabric
shuttle: weaving bobbin carrying weft yarn
silk throwing: winding of yarn onto bobbins
snap: small lunch or snack
spinning mule: Crompton's large spinning machine
stook: bundle of grain sheaves set to dry in a field
tanner (cash): slang for sixpence coin
taters: potatoes
tek: take
tha knowst: you know
thesen or thysell: yourself
throstle spinner: a spinning machine
thrupence or threppence: three (old) pennies

tuppence: two (old) pennies
wotcher!: hi!/howdy!/hello!
worsted: smooth woollen cloth
wunner: wouldn't

Acknowledgements

- Hannah Woman of Iron by Barbara Sowood
- John Wroe and the Christian Israelites by Lynne Gray
- Mr Wroe's Virgins by Jane Rogers
- Prophet John Wroe by Edward Green
- Victorian Investments by Cannon Schmitt, Nancy Henry and Anjali Aronekar
- Cover design Ralph Peacock's The Sisters 1900
- Beta-readers Walter Reid, David Higginson and Graham Bean.

About the author: G J Griffiths is a retired Science teacher who is also a UK baby-boomer. His first novel was **Fallen Hero;** and **So What! Stories or Whatever!** was his first book in the **So What!** series. When he is not writing G J Griffiths enjoys walking in the English or Welsh countryside, always with his binoculars ready for bird-watching. He has always enjoyed reading a wide range of literature, both fiction and nonfiction, and is still writing poetry and short stories occasionally. Later new ventures are the children's science fiction stories – **Ants In Space** and **They're Recycling Aliens;** historical fiction novels: **The Quarry Bank Runaways** and **Mules; Masters & Mud;** and a poetry collection, **Dizzyrambic Imaginings**.

If you enjoyed reading **The Mule Spinners' Daughters** why not share your enjoyment with others and post a Review at:
Amazon USA:
http://www.amazon.com/G-J-Griffiths/e/B009IFXAHS

or Amazon UK:
http://www.amazon.co.uk/G-J-Griffiths/e/B009IFXAHS

More information about G J Griffiths and his books may be discovered at:

https://www.gjgriffithswriter.com

Printed in Great Britain
by Amazon